I0655077

The Judas List

A. G. Hayes

Savant Books
Honolulu, HI, USA
2012

Published in the USA by Savant Books and Publications
2630 Kapiolani Blvd #1601
Honolulu, HI 96826
http://www.savantbooksandpublications.com

Printed in the USA

Edited by Mary Yamin-Garone
Cover by Kristin Arbuckle

Copyright 2012 A. G. Hayes. All rights reserved. No part of this work
may be reproduced without the prior written permission of the author.

13 digit ISBN: 978-0-9852506-7-6
10-digit ISBN: 0985250674

All names, characters, places and incidents are fictitious or used
fictitiously. Any resemblance to actual persons, living or dead, and any
places or events is purely coincidental.

Dedication

To Keith G. Nelson: Over the years, we climbed many a steep hill together.

Acknowledgements

My publisher, Daniel Janik; my editor, Mary Yamin-Garone; my book cover artist, Kristin Arbuckle: Thank you for your combined talents in making this book possible.

The Judas List

Chapter 1

VIENNA, WINTER, 1945

Nikolia Youmatoff didn't know exactly where he was but a sense of impending doom filled the dark, dank vault. He recalled hearing a church bell chime but Vienna was full of churches. His companions had unloaded the army trucks and dragged dozens of sealed crates into the vault and stacked them alongside hundreds of obviously valuable objects.

That night, Youmatoff suspected, they stored away a supply of riches that could have been sufficient to sustain starving Ukrainian farmers for decades.

Youmatoff could clearly see Reichmarshall Herman Goering's white pigskin face by the flickering candlelight as he sat behind a gray steel desk at one end of the musty crypt. Wax from a thick ocher candle rimmed and dripped down onto the ornate candlestick. Goering held a blueprint on which he scribbled the word, *"Uberholt."* Youmatoff's limited German translated it as "obsolete," though he wasn't sure. Goering then refolded the blueprint and slipped it into a leather bound book. He opened a desk drawer, picked up the compact wire recorder sitting next to the candlestick and gently placed the recorder in the drawer.

Several soldiers and an officer were overseeing prisoners of war crouched on the floor at the far end of the vault. The prisoners were replacing flagstones they had moved. The officer reached down and turned a key then indicated they lower the last stone into place. The POWs were part of a group that had delivered the wooden crates and unloaded them into the sepulcher-like space. Youmatoff's assignment was to carry boxes of books for the Reichmarshall.

The officer approached the Reichmarshall, saluted, handed him the key and returned to his men. Goering took the peculiar shaped key and slid it beneath the cover of the volume holding the blueprint. He placed the book atop other books in a box on the desk.

Youmatoff saw him tap the book and Goering said something Youmatoff interpreted as *"Here's the blueprint to the future."* Youmatoff didn't have time to ponder as Goering pushed back his chair, heaved his bulk up and surveyed the area of treasures. A smile twisted his lips and he slapped his thigh with a golden Field Marshal's baton.

"Bring that box of books," Goering told Youmatoff as he strode from the vault.

What Youmatoff did next was done without premeditation. Picking up the book that had held Goering's attention, Youmatoff removed the key and slipped the book into the front of his thin canvas shirt. He tipped the candle and splattered a mushroom edged blob of wax on the desk, placed the key in the wax and pressed a perfect impression.

He moved to the entrance, looked back and saw one of the soldiers reeling out what appeared to be copper wire. A voice from outside cursed at Youmatoff to hurry.

The moon was high. He saw they were in an ancient square that was unfamiliar to him. A German SS officer took the box of books, placed it in the trunk of Goering's staff car, slammed the trunk shut and got into the car. A second later it roared out of the square.

Youmatoff felt the weight of the book inside his shirt. The original key *and* the wax impression were in the pocket. "The secret to the future" was in his care.

He was alone in the empty square. Suddenly pistol shots sounded from within the vault and Youmatoff knew at once the other prisoners had been executed. Terror-stricken, he fled into the darkest shadows and bolted from the square.

The Judas List

Chapter 2

RENO, NEVADA, WINTER 2009

"Believe it, Joe. We still use foot soldiers in the game of espionage, even in today's political correctness and electronic wizardry."

Henry Stevenson was a taciturn silver-haired man in his early sixties with a face that was easily forgotten. He leaned back in his executive chair and rested his chin on the tip of a pyramid made by his long slender fingers. He observed the reaction of the two agents he had summoned to his office.

Special Agent Joseph Falk nodded. He was handsome, chestnut-haired, in his thirties. He'd heard the 'Atta-Boy' speeches plenty of times. They never changed. "We were beginning to think we were the only two left." He indicated the petite blonde female sitting beside him.

"I understand." Stevenson collapsed the pyramid, slid open a drawer, removed a large envelope and laid it on the desktop. "An old investigation is being reopened that has, over the last few weeks, become an extremely troublesome problem for United States' foreign policy." Stevenson paused. Susan Koski's green, tawny-speckled eyes were trained on him as he continued. "Tom Stewart has ordered that you two meet with him right away."

Stewart was director of Cerberus, a covert agency named for the dog of Greek mythology, said to have had three heads and served as keeper of the entrance to the infernal regions where the gods resided. Those who had adopted this name believed that much of the U.S. was in danger of falling into the external regions, the gutters of humanity. Cerberus was clandestinely funded and supported by an anonymous cartel of intelligence personnel known only to the president. Tom Stewart was the head of the agency. Officially, Falk and Koski were FBI special agents assigned to liaise with unique units of the Office of Homeland Security. That had given Tom Stewart the ability to spirit them into Cerberus. Stewart had used their talents in several demanding investigations over the last three years. All were resolved successfully.

Stevenson checked his watch. "You're booked on a Lufthansa flight tonight." He tapped the envelope and pushed it across to Falk. "Airline tickets and a letter Stewart wants you both to study enroute. He'll give further details of the assignment at a briefing when you arrive in Vienna."

Dinner had ended. One or two reading lamps glowed in the cabin of the 747 as Koski and Falk read the letter.

In Canada, Nikolai Youmatoff entered a small clearing and paused, having put six miles of Ontario's majestic forestland between himself and home. That's what he called his now vacated log cabin and the neighboring town. The fact that he would never see home again gave him a rush of exhilaration although he'd been happy there until Ann died.

He looked up at Twyla Point and its narrow cascade of water splashing its solitary way down to Ring-of-Moon Lake. There it would continue on to the snarling Lower Rips River then make a watery curl and finally join other waterways to the Great Lakes region.

Youmatoff lowered himself to a small rock outcropping and dusted off a layer of the last snowfall. Thoughts of the prayer book, the key and the blueprint nagged at him even though he had disowned them. He had mailed them to the man who saved his life at the conclusion of the war.

In the end, the souvenirs of a long ago night in which he had been obliged to assist the Nazi, Hermann Goering, meant nothing to him. His pursuers, he feared, wouldn't believe that. They would think he knew more. He shook off these thoughts and looked around him.

Smell preceded recollection of the day he and Ann had last trapped in this region and rested here. A gentle Chinook wind off the eastern slopes of the mountains had mixed with the stonewashed flax scent of her hair. This fresh, seedy smell now made him quiver for her touch. He reminded himself that Ann was gone and he was adrift, alone.

As Youmatoff rose and headed deeper into the forest, farther from the Canadian Mounties dispatched to detain him, he was prepared to acknowledge that Ann's death and the withholding of children were fate's unquestionable foresight.

The Judas List

Chapter 3

It was 6:30 a.m., December 11th, when Falk and Koski cleared customs at Vienna's Schwechat International Airport.

Koski scanned the rows of faces waiting outside the gate. "Do you see him?" Many were drivers holding handwritten signs with the names of their pick-ups scrawled across them.

"Not yet. If I know Tom Stewart, he'll find us before we see him."

As they walked toward the airport's main entrance, a nondescript young woman suddenly appeared beside Falk. She spoke perfect English. "Follow me. There's a car waiting." When Falk and Koski didn't respond immediately she added, "I'm Mr. Stewart's driver."

The large glass doors automatically slid open and they followed her out into the icy December air of the city dubbed "Paris on the Danube." She quickly led them to a silver gray Mercedes with tinted windows parked at the curb. Inside, a thin, impeccably dressed man in his late fifties with hair the color of the Mercedes greeted them.

"Good morning, Joe. Good to see you again." He shook Falk's hand and turned to Koski. "I'm Tom Stewart."

"Susan Koski." She offered her hand.

Falk watched his partner take quick measure of the man. She would find his grip gentle, two-handed, emanating an inner strength that belied his age. His voice was soft, his vocal pattern deliberate, carefully calculated to reflect thoughts that had sufficiently germinated. She would later confess to Falk that her initial impression was that Tom Stewart was slick. Over time, a deeper understanding of the man would reveal the profound compassion and integrity Falk admired and had come to rely on.

Stewart leaned forward and addressed Falk. "I've booked you both into the Romischer-Kaiser Hotel. I'll be staying there for a few days then move to a different location that I'll pass on to you. We'll have breakfast in my suite at eight and I'll update you on the situation." He gave Koski a final nod. "Your luggage will be along in a moment."

Forty minutes later they entered the hotel through the revolving glass door. Falk was impressed with the old-world atmosphere: potted palms; thick, damask, rose-colored carpets; highly polished burled woodwork; gleaming brass. A birdcage elevator slowly moved aloft through a lacework of black wrought iron.

"Wow," Koski remarked as they followed the porter with their bags to the elevator. The cage gradually made its sedate, well-oiled ascent.

Falk checked his watch. "Just enough time for a shower, shave and a clean shirt." They were shown to adjoining rooms on the third floor. "Give me a ring when you're ready," he said. "We'll go down together."

Koski paused in the doorway. They had traveled without the usual courtesy accorded to law enforcement personnel. Their weapons were broken down and secured in locked carrying cases. Stewart wanted no extraneous paperwork or evidence of their arrival in Vienna.

"Joe, I feel naked without my weapon." She spun away with a smile and entered her room, closing the door behind her.

Falk entered his room. He was mesmerized by the luxury of a

bygone era. A high, ornate ceiling added a sense of vastness to an already large room. Tasteful furniture was arranged to enable easy conversation around the burning coal fire in a marble fireplace. Then the phone rang.

"You have a desk in your room?" Koski's voice was almost a whisper. Falk glanced around.

"No, I don't."

"Check in the other room, should be one."

He moved to the next room and saw it—a small writing desk against one wall. Returning to the phone, he affirmed her hunch.

"Good, check the top right-hand drawer. There should be something there to dispel that naked feeling. See you in a bit." The phone clicked off.

Falk opened the drawer and saw a Beretta 92F in a shoulder holster. Boasting a 15-round magazine, the Beretta weighed in at 2.52 pounds fully loaded. He lovingly slid the weapon from the holster. It had been recently cleaned and lightly oiled. He reached into the drawer, removed a fully loaded magazine and snapped it into place, experiencing a sense of security at the business-like *click*. He cocked the piece, hefted its weight, set the safety and placed it back into the smooth leather holster, wondering why he hadn't checked out the rooms and their contents.

Koski had, heeding one of the most basic rules of Quantico training. He silently swore. Before he met her he'd been a loner, working in the Bureau's elite Rover Division. Then he was paired with Koski on a couple of assignments—operations in which he'd come to rely on her. Now, minutes into their present mission that had the potential to be even more dangerous than the others, she once again demonstrated her skill, discovering the weapon she was obviously meant to find while he took time to admire the furnishings.

Because he no longer worked alone and wasn't required to rely solely on himself, he had become one-half of what he once was. Had he also become lax, dependent? Was he, in his late thirties, in danger of losing his edge?

He sighed and shrugged off the notion. That he had fallen in love with Koski and she with him tended to abrogate all other considerations. He headed for the shower, wondering just what kind of mission Stewart and Cerberus had in mind for them.

Two years ago Falk resisted initiation into Cerberus but ultimately, like Koski, he acknowledged the need for an organization that covertly supported humankind's highest aspirations. Dressed, refreshed and with the Beretta snugly fitted beneath his arm, Falk was ready for breakfast and whatever else Stewart had on the agenda. There was a knock at the door.

Koski patted the left side of her jacket. "Did you have a gift in your drawer, too?"

Falk took in her mischievous grin and the sparkle in her green-eyed gaze. Special Agent Susan Koski, with her tousled haircut, dressed in a black pantsuit over a heather gray turtleneck sweater and wearing black leather boots looked as if, were she slightly taller, she should be strutting down a Paris catwalk.

He put his arm around her shoulder. "Sure did, gorgeous. Let's go."

Falk rapped sharply on the door to Stewart's suite. It opened immediately.

"Come in, take a seat," Stewart said in his soft voice. "I've ordered breakfast, full American, none of that continental coffee and croissants. You'll need a hearty meal to begin this day." He indicated two easy chairs opposite his desk.

"From now until this assignment is completed, you doctors of archaeology are part of a four person team sponsored by the Smithsonian Institute. My cover is director of archaeological activities assigned to liaise with the Viennese city. We'll have the cooperation of the local police and Interpol. Our Embassy won't know anything of our true mission. Because you two aren't known in this part of the world the chance of being recognized is slim."

The short, snappy instructions signaled the urgency of their new assignment to Falk.

"Do we have any idea where in the city Goering might have hidden his plunder?"

Stewart smiled wryly. "Not really. We know where we thought it might be back in 1975. We just never had the opportunity to look for it."

A knock at the door announced room service. Stewart called out, "Come in." A white jacketed waiter entered, pushing a well-appointed food trolley. He quickly arranged the breakfast and left.

Stewart continued the briefing as they sat at the table. "I want you to listen to this while we have breakfast." Stewart removed an iPod from his pocket, inserted it into a speaker cradle and turned it on. A man's educated and well-modulated voice began.

"It was in the sandwich of time between the end of World War II and the winter of 1975 when events took place in Vienna, Austria, that continue to affect world powers today. My father, Dr. David Benson, was in Vienna that year, attending the third reunion of a group of partisans of which he had been a member during the latter part of the war. In 1945, those freedom fighters joined with local insurgents to resist the Nazi invaders.

13

"The night of the reunion my father was killed by an unknown assassin. One of the partisans, Lego Moyzisch, had addressed his fellow reunioners, telling them how he had saved a Russian officer's life, a prisoner of war held in a displaced persons' camp outside of Vienna.

"The Russian knew that if he was sent back to Russia he'd be shot for becoming a German prisoner. Lego, a Czech, was also a DP, working as an interpreter in the American Army orderly room at the camp."

By giving the Russian forged papers stating he was Polish, Lego had saved the man's life. In return, the grateful Russian—Nikolai Youmatoff—told Lego a secret he learned while a prisoner of the Germans: the approximate hiding place of Herman Goering's spoils of war, gold and treasures worth countless millions. The hiding place was there in Vienna. "I traveled to Vienna in 1975 to claim and return my father's body to California. It was during that time I was coerced into using my knowledge as an archaeologist to organize a covert team and search for Goering's loot. I was led to believe I was doing a service of national importance. The assignment was short-lived, however, due to political infighting between the Austrian government and Washington.

"The Austrian Socialist Party was running Kurt Waldheim for president of Austria. Due to his secret capacity as a Nazi officer during the war, Waldheim wanted no spotlight turned on that aspect of his past by attempts to search for loot pillaged by the Germans that might be unearthed in Vienna at that time. There was one other factor.

"Reliable sources reported that if the cache being sought was in fact the fabled Goering plunder, there was the possibility of finding a so-called "Judas List." It's a compendium of individuals and organizations that had secretly helped finance World War II that

Goering reportedly compiled. They intended to increase their manipulating power over world finances for generations to come, control the future United Nations and selected member nations after the war.

"This so-called "Judas List" was planned to undermine America's Armed Forces by manipulating them to undertake a major part in mindless military actions throughout the world and the support of despot dictators." After a soft sigh he continued. "Deliberately orchestrated civil war and unrest also became part of the devilish plan. I, of course, cannot confirm or deny the existence of such a list and it would be beyond the scope of my interest."

Respectively,

Mark Benson

Stewart turned off the iPod. "Here in Vienna is a place called the Dorotheum. Founded in 1707 by Emperor Joseph I, it's a cross between a museum and an auction house. Four times a year experts, dealers and private parties from around the world meet to purchase important works of art or to merely observe the going prices." Stewart paused. "It's believed that the Goering treasures could still be hidden somewhere below the cellars and foundation of the Dorotheum."

"Wouldn't the loot have been discovered long ago?" Falk asked.

Stewart took a bite of food and shook his head. "During the war the vaults beneath the Dorotheum, along with all Vienna's major museums, were emptied of valuables that were then hidden deep in the Bavarian Mountains.

"The Dorotheum remained empty throughout the war. The story goes that Goering saw it as a perfect hiding place and secretly had the loot taken to Vienna and buried beneath the empty building. Allied bombing toward the end of conflict damaged the Dorotheum.

Extensive rebuilding was carried out at the conclusion of hostilities. An attempt to find any so-called loot was made at that time but there was no sign of hidden treasure."

Falk cleared his throat. "What about the "Judas List" Benson mentions? As I see it, Benson's bleak economic ruminations aside, the possibilities that a combination of people and organizations whose names are supposedly on this list, who not only supported Hitler and manipulated the past but also are controlling world events and finances today, is a serious thing to consider."

Stewart watched Falk over the rim of his coffee cup but said nothing. Falk continued.

"The part about the U.S. and our Armed Forces being maneuvered into taking part in mindless actions throughout the world are certainly true. For God's sake, we've watched it happen. There may be something to it, Tom. Such a record may be real. For almost 80 years people have pondered how Adolf Hitler went from a lance corporal in World War I to become dictator of Nazi Germany by 1933. Who backed him? Where did the massive financing and materiel come from that permitted them to create an army, navy and air force in secret that took the allies seven years to bring to final surrender?

"The years between 1914 and Hitler's rise to power were fraught with intrigue that may still be at work today; arranging for another mad man to repeat even worse atrocities on the world."

"If the listing exists, Joe, we must be the ones to find it. The main reason for the sudden urgency to locate that damn list is due to a report we received a matter of hours ago at Cerberus.

"During the Nuremberg War Crimes Trials there had been a report that Goering made a fruitless attempt to make a deal with one of the American trial judges that he be executed by firing squad, not

16

hanged as a common criminal if found guilty.

"Goering rebuffed, tried blackmail, saying when allowed to speak in his own defense in court he would announce the location of the list. He would reveal how Hitler and the National Socialist Party had been supported and by whom and how the same people arranged for a new Fourth Reich to arise within the next 75 years and attain world domination."

Stewart took a deep breath. "Herman Goering never had his chance to speak in court. He was found dead in his cell, a so-called suicide by cyanide."

"Good God," Falk exclaimed. "Are you saying it wasn't suicide?"

"Look at it this way, Joe. Goering was in a maximum security cell and searched daily—inside and outside of his body. Security was provided 24/7 by specially trained military police personnel. One from each of the four powers—American, British, Russian and French.

"A letter written by an 85-year-old veteran just before his death was mailed to the White House by his wife. She discovered it among papers in his desk." Stewart held up his hand as Falk started to speak.

"The man had been a guard at the prison in Nuremberg. He was ordered to give Goering a cyanide pill to make it look like suicide. Evidently, Goering decided it was better than dying like a common criminal because that's how his death went into the history books."

"Did the letter indicate who gave the order?" Falk questioned.

"No. He simply wanted us to know that if what Goering said about a new group of maniacs taking over the world was true the list had to be discovered—fast. The time frame mentioned was about up."

Falk looked grim. "It ties in with what world economists have said for years, that early in the twenty-first century massive takeovers will have narrowed down all power to certain mega corporations. They would run everything, including heads of world governments and the world economy."

Stewart cocked his head and his eyes narrowed. "If such a list does exist, Cerberus has decided it could have been preserved in an unconventional form, not simply written on a piece of paper. Goering would have planned its use as any extortionist would. He'd make it unique and in a virtually indestructible form...perhaps a wire recording..."

"What's a wire recording?" Koski asked.

"The father of the tape recorder," Stewart explained. "Wire recordings were widely used by the German Army prior to tape. Sound was recorded onto a magnetic wire held on spools. The wire could record and play back sound, with marginally good quality. Goering would have used a German machine manufactured during the 1940s, a German microphone, wire, spool—German everything."

Koski shook her head. "I had no idea there ever was such a device."

Falk was intrigued. His mind had raced ahead to a fantastic conclusion. "What if a dirty tricks 101 contingent, like a radical Islamic, Israeli, Russian or Palestinian group, finds out about this?"

Stewart's expression darkened. "We believe they have. Our latest report is Mikhail Brasinov's thugs have wind of the loot."

Falk stared at Stewart before saying, "Brasinov, that psychopathic Bosnian mass murderer? I thought he was on the run from the United Nations' War Crimes Commission."

"Right. And believed to be hiding in the Czech Republic, possibly in Brno," said Stewart. "We also have it from a reliable source that he became aware of the list shortly after we were advised by the letter. Brasinov is well protected and will remain hidden. I don't have to tell you that his men are a brutal group of sinister paramilitary thugs that killed and raped their way across Bosnia. They'll show no mercy."

Stewart rose from his chair and crossed to the desk. He seemed exceptionally relieved that the earlier conversation was behind him, yet there remained an edge of uncharacteristic nervousness in his manner.

"This is going to be a tough assignment and a difficult race to be first to the unknown site," Stewart continued. "You're both anti-terrorist experts and, make no mistake, that's what we're up against. We know Brasinov is working with an Islamic terrorist group. It's doubtful you'll ever personally confront him but his right-hand man, known only as Pasha, will be leading the search."

Stewart pushed back from the desk and went to the window. He stared out at the rooftops of Vienna, his back to his companions. "I've arranged your passports and other necessary documents authenticating the Smithsonian connection. They state that you're traveling with an official American archaeological delegation visiting Vienna to study stolen works of art and peruse the possibility of other undiscovered works around the world.

"One other thing, you'll be working with a newcomer to Cerberus, a man you both know from your participation in the Nevada-California investigation. Cerberus chose him solely because his talents fit our needs. He'll be backup for you in the event Brasinov's men get too close or outnumber our estimate."

Stewart turned and faced them. "I know I can put my full trust in your ability to forget past differences and accept Rod Eiker as a working member of Cerberus. His participation in this venture comports nicely with our desire to succeed."

Falk couldn't believe it. "Eiker! You mean he's on our side now?

That son of a bitch caused us more trouble than any ten men did. He almost killed Koski and me. He'd sell his mother to the highest bidder. Tom, what are you thinking? The man's a vicious killer."

"I understand but he works for us now."

"What exactly will Eiker's role be in all of this?" Koski asked.

"To be there at the end... In case we need him."

Falk's mind flashed back to those bitter winter days when he and Koski had fought their way across the High Sierra—through snowbound forests, matching wits with crooked politicians, Nevada gambling cartels...and Rod Eiker.

Falk turned to Koski and knew by her expression that she shared his disgust.

Stewart noted their reactions. "To quote Emerson, 'As there is a use in medicine for poison so the world cannot move without rouges.' Get some rest, both of you. You have a difficult assignment ahead."

After the agents left, Stewart sat in his chair, leaned back and closed his eyes. "Joseph Falk," he said aloud. "You always manage to give me a few anxious moments."

The assignment he had given Falk and Koski was only part of the big picture. If they succeeded in locating the list, 'The Global Village' and 'International Community' loving politicians worldwide would be looking for new jobs.

Chapter 4

"Fisher's Antiques," Emma Lewis announced, picking up the phone.

"If Pasha arrives before I get there," John Steele said gruffly, "have him wait."

Emma acknowledged his order, hung up the phone and wondered how she had allowed herself to become enmeshed in Steele's latest scheme. Indeed, why had she deluded herself for years into believing that he was her friend? His conduct in the last few days tended to indicate otherwise. She felt used and didn't like it.

She walked back to the small office area of the antique shop that still bore the name of its founder and took a photograph in a silver frame down from a shelf. She studied the familiar picture wistfully. "Oh, Aunt Louise," she whispered, "if only you were here. There's so much I wish I knew."

Emma had inherited the shop and a small upstairs apartment on the Am Numarkt in Vienna from her Aunt Louise, who died two years before. Her aunt had opened the shop after World War II, deciding to remain in Vienna rather than return to England.

Emma had spent time with Louise on many occasions since she finished school in England. There were postcards at Christmas, phone calls—and then the news of Louise's death and that Emma had inherited the shop.

Emma was thirty-four. She'd been working as a teacher for a small, private school in Oxford. Since she had broken up with her fiancé two weeks before being notified of the inheritance, the shop seemed a timely diversion. Being a woman who made up her mind quickly, she had quit her job, flown to Austria and assumed proprietary duties all within a month.

The only child of deceased parents, she had no family in the U.K. and believed that no one would particularly miss her. She studied the five figures in the group photograph.

Her aunt had fought alongside a rugged band of partisans who found their way to Vienna shortly before Russian troops "liberated" the city in 1945. Louise, in the center of the picture, was nineteen then, looking like a Cossack princess, dressed in buckskin trousers, black turtleneck sweater, boots and a bandoleer of bullets slung across her chest.

On her right was a tall, handsome man wearing an American Army cap, his jacket displaying the Medical Corps insignia. His soulful eyes stared at the camera while his chin reflected strong determination. Emma turned the picture over and read the names Louise had neatly printed on the back, corresponding to their positions in the photograph.

The American was David Benson. On Louise's left was John Steele, tall, blond, tanned and leathery, smoking a stub of a cigar, dressed in crumpled and patched Canadian battle dress and wearing a pair of German Army boots. A Sten gun was across his chest.

The remaining two men were older. Far left was Horst Ekel, the oldest. White-haired, with tufted Franz Joseph side whiskers, Ekel was frail and brittle. He also was the owner of the Romischer-Kaiser Hotel where the group had held their reunions in 1955, 1965 and the last in 1975. Horst more resembled an old watchmaker than someone who worked with local insurgents defying the Nazis.

To the far right stood Lego Moyzisch, the tough, barrel-chested Czechoslovakian displaced person who had joined the group and fought his way to the outskirts of Vienna.

Emma placed the photograph back on the shelf. She knew that David Benson had become a noted archaeologist after the war and that, like Louise, was deceased. Horst Ekel was gone, too. She knew nothing, however, of the fate of Lego Moyzisch. It occurred to her that she now regretted never having inquired about Lego's present circumstances.

It was possible that John Steele was the only surviving face from the old photograph.

When Louise died and Emma arrived in Vienna to assume ownership of the shop, Steele met her at the airport. An antique dealer himself, he was a helpful and comforting companion during those early days.

Over time, he had become ever-present, insinuating himself into her otherwise solitary life. Recently she had begun to feel smothered and controlled. Then she learned about Steele's involvement with Pasha and his intention—and apparent need—to involve her.

It started a few days ago when he mentioned millions of dollars lying around, there for the taking. All Emma had to do was follow orders. He would attend to all the details. It was a sure thing, he had said; actually, the belated continuance of a plan put into motion by Lego Moyzisch when he last spoke to Steele, Louise and the others at the 1975 reunion.

Steele was quick to point out he had never asked anything of her.

He had been there for her from the day she arrived in Vienna and introduced her to influential individuals in the antique business. He went so far as to intimate that because he had literally saved Louise Fisher's life on more than one occasion in the 1940s, a certain amount of loyalty was owed.

Emma hadn't been privy to the details Steele was working out with his Arab friend, Pasha, but a cold feather of fear had perched on her shoulder the last few days. One that refused to flutter away.

Chapter 5

Over the years, John Steele had not only dealt in *objet d'art*, he also collected a circle of scurrilous business associates who were involved in everything from antiques to assassinations.

Mikhail Brasinov was now one of those associates. Brasinov needed Steele's skills to recruit the right people to locate Goering's treasure. Brasinov also had discovered a new piece of information that was little known at the end of WWII.

During the ethnic differences between Serbs and Muslims in Bosnia, Brasinov had ordered the torture and death of thousands. One of those was a man who tried to save his life by trading the true account of who stole the Africa Corps' payroll during WWII in return for his freedom. Brasinov agreed and was told the story.

The Africa Corps, under the command of Field Marshal Erwin Rommel, plundered North Africa and Egypt of their art treasures with thoroughness typical of the German Army. They took everything. Millions of dollars worth of art cunningly transferred to German custody via the Luftwaffe at the height of the North African campaign, when it was almost impossible to get enough fuel and ammunition to fight the war.

Rommel had been furious. He was a soldier taking orders. At the same time he knew Goering was responsible for flying the treasures out of the Middle East while his troops were fighting with less than enough supplies.

Rommel complained and Hitler recalled him to Germany. It was while Rommel was there that the Africa Corps' payroll vanished.

Arabs had no use for trusts in paper money so it was decided the Corps be paid in gold. The gold, along with other treasures, went to Goering's lair—Carinhall, a great country mansion. A monument to his first wife and a symbol of his own aggrandizement, it was but a stopover on the way to Vienna.

The man who told Brasinov the story of the heist was shot in the head, hands tied behind his back and tossed into a mass grave.

The doorbell jangled and Emma glanced up to see John Steele standing in the doorway.

"Any word from Pasha?" he asked, striding across to a small table that held a coffeepot.

"No, John." Emma felt her stomach tighten at the mention of the man's name. Steele noticed her agitation.

"Listen, Emma. I've explained this to you before. Sometimes we have to do business with people we don't like. That's the way it is."

"We don't have to do business with mass murderers," she complained. He had told her just enough to ensure she would pass along messages from Pasha, who used her shop as a communications center. She didn't want to know more.

"Look at it this way," he said as if trying to lighten the mood. "Pasha is simply a man trying to start a new life after losing everything in the Bosnian conflict. Remember, Emma, there were some 200,000 people killed in that war. Pasha didn't kill them all and he didn't start the war."

Emma turned away and busied herself with paperwork. She

wished she could ignore the sense of loyalty she felt for Steele. However, it wasn't only a matter of him befriending her when she came to Vienna and supporting her while she was learning the antique business, it was his connection to her past and his prior devotion to Aunt Louise and the others in the group of partisans. She owed Steele on many levels.

Steele poured two cups of coffee, set one on her desk and remained standing as he sipped his. "I told you Pasha can help me arrange for the right men to go after what your aunt and I were informed of back in 1975 and what we're entitled to. I have maps, books, papers and plans, everything they need."

Emma couldn't help herself. "Everything except the muscle and guts to find it yourself, is that it? What do you think Aunt Louise would think of you now, going into business with Islamic terrorists?"

She saw the anger rise from within him like a hot flame, burnishing his cheeks. For a moment, she thought he might even strike her but he needed her, at least for now.

"I won't even bother to answer that, Emma. I've made an agreement with these people and I intend to keep it." He pointed at her with the coffee cup. "If I don't, both you and I will be killed. It's that simple."

Emma remained silent as he banged his cup on the desk. "I'll be at my apartment if Pasha shows up or calls."

He turned and walked out of the shop, the bell jangling furiously as the door slammed shut.

At his apartment on Wahringer Strasser, Steele was slumped in an easy chair, finishing a potent drink still waiting to hear from Pasha. He watched as Rosie Wimmer sorted a pile of papers at a desk next to the window. Rosie was pretty, mid-thirties with long, straight, dark hair.

She wore little makeup and had a nice figure.

"Get me another drink, Rosie," Steele grunted.

She looked up from her work and a slight frown creased her forehead.

"Just make the drink," he barked, reading her disapproving expression. The phone rang and Steele scooped it up. "I'll be here," he said and hung up. "That was Pasha. He's coming over."

"Do you want me to make sandwiches?" She looked over her shoulder as she dutifully mixed his drink.

"No, this isn't going to be a social meeting. Once he gets here you can take those ledgers to the shop." He took the drink from her and sipped thoughtfully.

Rosie Wimmer had worked for Steele for more than three years. She had her own apartment in the city, supplied by Steele, and ran the larger of his two antique shops. She knew her business and was well liked in the trade. Steele knew Rosie silently fantasized that one day he would ask her to marry him. Steele enjoyed the game. He took care to let his intentions be undecipherable. The doorbell chimed.

"That must be him," Rosie said. "I'll get it." She went to the door and Steele heard voices in the hallway. He finished his drink in one swallow and eased from the chair as Rosie led Pasha into the room.

The man Steele knew only as Pasha was a thin-framed, middle-aged Arab with a pale coffee-hued face devoid of animation. He carried a leather briefcase. His heavy-lidded eyes were black as scorched oil and unlit by inner warmth, his voice a rasping whisper as he acknowledged Steele.

"Herr Steele." Pasha spoke good English with only a trace of an accent.

"Can I offer you refreshment?" Steele asked.

"No, thank you. I can only stay a moment."

"Please, take a chair."

Pasha seated himself but remained stiff, his back straight and inches from the backrest. "There is a group of archaeologists—a delegation from America—due here seeking government information on lost, stolen and missing art treasures from World War II. Do you know anything about them?"

"No. Then again, there's always some group or another here in Vienna looking into missing art objects. It's ongoing."

Pasha continued, "We believe the delegation is backed by American Intelligence."

"Then I suggest we move quickly, the sooner the better."

"That's our intention. Brasinov demands we start at once." Pasha snapped open his briefcase and removed a package wrapped in brown paper. He outlined a detailed set of instructions, ending with, "Do I make myself clear?"

Steele assured Pasha he understood fully. Pasha nodded, rose from his chair, went to the door and waited for Steele to open it.

He touched Steele's shoulder but not with assuring camaraderie. "We will prevail in this endeavor." He left before Steele had a chance to say how much he was already beginning to doubt it.

The Judas List

Chapter 6

Falk and Koski's second briefing took place in Tom Stewart's car. He handed a package to Falk sitting in the back seat with Koski. "Here are the passports for you and Dr. Koski and a phone number where you can reach me any time." Stewart eased the car forward.

Falk stuffed the package into his jacket pocket. "Are we certain this guy Steele is working with Brasinov?"

"Yes, Steele has been under our surveillance for years," Stewart replied. "That man has been more useful to us running loose than if he'd been on our payroll. Yes, we're certain."

"How long has Steele been watched?"

Stewart stopped at a red light. "Since before the Bosnian conflict."

Falk's eyebrows arched. Cerberus certainly believed in long-term surveillance.

Stewart continued. "There's someone else we've kept tabs on for a number of years. Nikolai Youmatoff, the Russian officer whose life was saved by the Czech, Lego Moyzisch. We're aware Lego provided the Russian with forged papers." The light changed and they moved forward.

"Army Intelligence checked Youmatoff out through usual procedures, made sure he was not a plant, then, in 1945, they shipped him to Canada where they could keep an eye on him. I understand he's still alive and very spry at over 80 years old."

Falk and Koski swapped glances and Koski remarked. "Hell of a long time."

"You think so?" Stewart replied.

Falk smiled wryly. "This was usual for the Allies, I take it—packing a man off somewhere, fitting him with a new identity and telling him to keep his nose clean until needed or..."

"Of course. In 1975, shortly before the third reunion of Dr. Benson and Louise Fisher's group, Youmatoff surprised us. He sent Lego a package. We thought it somehow was connected to the location of Goering's plunder, some information Youmatoff hadn't divulged. We planned to intercept it but there was a bungle of some sort and the package got through."

Falk winced. "We have no idea what it was?"

"Apparently it had no meaning in terms of the Goering business—could have been a knitted sweater for all we know. Evidently Lego said nothing at the reunion that would attach any significance to the package."

"Were the Communists also watching Lego at that time?" Koski asked.

"Absolutely. He'd been held in a displaced persons camp run by the Allies at the end of the war. That always worried them."

Falk stared out the window as Stewart deftly threaded the car through evening traffic past the Opera House. "Did they attempt to do anything about the package?" Falk questioned. "Could they have intercepted it?"

"I doubt it. They knew there'd be a reunion every ten years. Like us, they figured that in time anything important would turn up. We know they were watching very closely in 1975 but, as you now know, nothing happened except for Dr. Benson's death. Then the Austrian government asked us to leave."

"And this operation has gone into effect now because something *has* turned up?"

"Yes, Joe. A few days ago Youmatoff sent Lego another package. This time we intercepted. It was an old blueprint to the original passageways under the Dorotheum. There was no note from Youmatoff but we figure Lego knew who sent it. Youmatoff had drawn a straight horizontal line crossed by three Xs in the margin. It was the way prisoners of war identified themselves in the camp where Youmatoff and Lego met."

Stewart glanced at Falk through the rearview mirror. "We made the obvious assumption. We copied the blueprint and sent it to Lego. He has no idea we saw it. We also contacted the special branch of the Royal Canadian Mounted Police. We expect they'll have Youmatoff in hand soon at which time we'll find out what, if any, other pieces of the puzzle are needed to find the treasures' exact location."

Koski looked over at Falk. "I'd say, so long as you have the blueprint all that's needed are people with special skills in architecture and subterranean foundations, modern and historic, plus degrees in Gothic design and history."

Stewart smiled. "Your associates from the Smithsonian have all that. They'll be here by morning."

"All the years you were waiting," Falk said, "following Steele, playing cloak-and-dagger with the Russians, you must have had a clever agent close to the action."

"We played cloak-and-dagger with others as well. Our agent was Louise Fisher. She was good, all right; damned good."

"No one ever found out who killed Dr. Benson?"

"No," Stewart replied.

Then his killer is still out there, Falk thought. If they got wind of the present activity involving the rumored treasures they would be burning to get involved.

Chapter 7

One thousand and seventy-six miles from Vienna as British Airways flies, a single light shone from the second-story window of a three-story brick boardinghouse squeezed between two others on a quiet back street.

This was Number Nine Cable Street in the town of Southport, Lancashire, on the northwest coast of England.

Rodney Eiker listened to a Rolling Stones CD and did sit-ups. He was starting his second set of a hundred when the muffled tune on his cell phone emitted from his jacket hanging on the back of a chair. He got to his feet with the grace of a gymnast and plucked the phone from the pocket.

"Yes?" He listened intently, his face registering no emotion. "Very well. I'll find it, no problem." He snapped off the phone and returned it to his jacket, crossed the sparsely furnished room and turned off the Stones mid-song.

The room was quiet except for the ticking of a cheap wind up alarm clock on the table.

Rod Eiker was forty-six. He was born in Manchester, England, an ex-SAS soldier who had seen bloody action from Belfast to Beirut. Now he was a freelance soldier of fortune whose last assignment had been in the U.S. It involved a murderous plot designed by crooked politicians and a Nevada gambling cartel.

His assignment completed, he escaped the country, leaving a trail of death and destruction in his wake. It was to be his last job. He had earned enough to retire and he did, until he received a phone call from Tom Stewart shortly after he returned to England.

Cerberus had been impressed with his skills even if they had been used against the U.S. government. Stewart offered him complete immunity for his crimes in America on the condition he work for Cerberus. If he refused, he would be dead within a few hours.

Eiker had no choice but to agree. Now, a year later, the phone call had directed him to report to Stewart at the Bristol Hotel, Vienna. He was to fly out that evening from Manchester International.

Chapter 8

December's bitter cold had crept deep into the stonework and flagstones of the ancient church, making the air difficult to inhale. A bent figure dressed in black lit a wrought iron rack of candles with a long wax taper at the foot of a marble statue.

Smoke from the taper curled heavenward, its waxen odor sharp to the senses as it contacted the freezing air. The figure turned and the dancing flames of the flickering candles in their red glass containers reflected on his pallid skin like a thousand points of hellish light. Heaven would never shine in an incandescent way on the face of Pasha.

Steele waited until the man in black snuffed the taper and then began his slow walk toward the back of the church.

They met in the apse beside the great wooden door. Pasha spoke first, his voice hushed and harsh. "You have information about the American team?"

Steele checked his watch. "Two hours from now I meet with a man who knows who they are."

"What's his name?"

"Jack Switzer, attaché at the American Embassy here in Vienna."

"Brasinov is anxious. He doesn't like to wait." Pasha pulled open the door. He slipped his repellent self from the house of God just as an icy draft of air entered.

Snow gently sifted down onto the city's steep rooftops as Steele and Switzer left the Dorotheum, walked across a square and stopped beside the ornate stonework of the Donner Fountain.

Switzer was scared. He operated in fear, with fear, through fear and by the use of fear.

Intimidation of those he commanded came naturally as did his own obsequious behavior in the presence of those from whom he took orders. He knew he, his wife and child would live only as long as he followed those orders and was useful.

Steele pointed across the square to the Capuchin Church. "Know much about that place, Switzer?"

"Of course, exterior is Romanesque and Baroque that has effectively superimposed itself upon Gothic in some of the church's interior decoration."

"What we're looking for isn't in any textbook," Steele growled as he glanced around the almost empty square. "When are the Americans expected?"

"Two are due tomorrow morning."

"Shit."

"Two are already here. They arrived early."

"Who are they?"

"Drs. Joseph Falk and Susan Koski," Switzer replied. "They're staying at the Romischer-Kaiser."

"Who else at the Embassy knows of their arrival?"

"No one, not even the Ambassador. I was contacted by our man in Washington because of my role in this endeavor."

Together they walked through falling snow. Steele glanced toward Saint Augustine's, historical burial place of 54 urns in the

Herzgruftelkammer (The Heart Crypt) containing the hearts of the Habsburgs. "We're being watched, Switzer, but keep walking. We're going inside to meet someone."

They continued the rest of the way to Saint Augustine's in silence. As they entered, Switzer felt the penetrating cold mix with a dank odor of age and dampness.

The door swung closed behind them with a dull, resounding thud. They crossed the vestibule and Switzer peered around the interior of the church. Initially, all he saw was a dim gray light sifting through the stained glass windows.

When his eyes grew accustomed to the gloom, he focused on the red votive light at the side of the altar. As they moved forward, his shoe struck the side of one of the pews. The sound was amplified in the silence and echoed up the stone columns, curved with the arch high into the transept then faded away into space, as had a million hymns over ages past.

"Sit down, Mr. Switzer." Pasha's rasping whisper gasped from the darkness of a pew. Steele guided Switzer to a seat.

"How much time do we have?" Pasha asked.

"Two will arrive in the morning, early. Two are already in Vienna at the hotel Romischer-Kaiser."

A low rattle not unlike the growl of a wild animal sounded from Pasha's throat. "Then you will fetch *those two* to me—here, tonight."

Outside an American Express tour bus trundled through the square, evidently late from a city tour. It turned onto Dorotheegasse and past the front entrance of the Dorotheum. A few tired faces peered out at the slush-ridden street, reflecting little interest. No doubt they had seen the city's main attractions at night and an insignificant side street had nothing to offer.

A young boy looked out at Steele and Switzer and grinned. A fat-faced man with a chewed, unlit cigar glanced over his shoulder. The hydraulic brakes hissed as the bus stopped at the corner then merged into the flow of city traffic.

"Good night, Switzer," Steele said as he walked into the darkness. "We'll be in touch." Switzer turned up the collar of his raincoat and walked in the opposite direction, certain of Steele's last statement.

A limo pulled up outside the Hotel Bristol. Rod Eiker tipped the driver and was on the sidewalk before the door attendant reached the vehicle. "I can manage," Eiker said. He hefted his leather carry on and walked through the revolving doors into the warmth and elegance of the foyer.

The Bristol was one of the few great hotels left in the world, a haven from modernity and its accelerated pace. Eiker sensed the heady atmosphere of another time period seeping through his skin as he strode to the desk.

The desk clerk swiveled the register for Eiker to sign. Once the formalities were over, the tall, neat man with a reserved smile slid a key across the polished counter. "Room 312. Enjoy your stay, Herr Eiker."

Eiker nodded, picked up the key, walked to the elevator and jabbed the Up button.

In his room, he tossed his bag on the bed and went to the window. He noted a few people hustling in and out of the subway entrance on the corner near the opera house, which was dark. He closed the drapes, removed a toilet case from his bag and entered the large, tiled bathroom.

A tired face stared back from the mirror. Despite his body's extraordinary physical condition, his facial reflection reminded him that he was getting a bit old for the game. He turned on the cold water tap and cupped icy water over his face, gasping at its sting. He was drying his face when the phone rang.

He picked up. "Good evening, Eiker."

"Who's this?"

"Mifflin, Harold Mifflin. Tom Stewart is unable to meet with you. He asked if I would fill in for him. Do you have time for a drink?"

"Sure, why not?"

"I can be at the Bristol in, say… ten minutes?"

"Okay, the bar then, ten minutes."

After Eiker hung up he went to his field kit, removed a plastic 9mm and placed it beneath his pillow. The Marakov that Stewart's limo driver had supplied was in his shoulder holster and needed a slight adjustment, as did his tie, and he was off.

He walked the deep carpeted hallway to the elevator and contemplated this man Mifflin, remembering a face-to-face with him in Hong Kong. Like Eiker, Mifflin had a reputation for getting things done, not caring how he accomplished them.

Although he was sure Mifflin's determination stopped short of his own. Harold Mifflin had become a legend in the CIA, perhaps more feared than respected. Eiker also recalled hearing that Mifflin had retired several months ago and supposedly was living in Southern California raising roses.

The sound of Gershwin softly playing on a piano in the bar took his mind off Mifflin for a moment as he glanced around for a table. It was still early, plenty of choices. Eiker opted for a table against the wall facing the entrance. As he sat down he wondered where Mifflin's men were. He had no doubt they were already in place.

"I'm expecting someone," Eiker told the waiter. "Heavyset man.

Can't miss him. When he arrives bring him a double Jack Daniel's. I'll take a double scotch, splash of soda, no ice." The waiter nodded and left.

Eiker was halfway through his drink when Mifflin appeared at the entrance, peering into the smoky gray air, a battered felt fedora pulled down over his forehead. He looked only slightly older than the last time Eiker had seen him.

A stubby man a little over five six, he'd planted his stumpy legs apart as if ready to do battle, a jutting jaw reinforcing the demeanor. Winston Churchill look-alike, Eiker thought as he waved. The solid mass of mankind stomped across the room to his table. The waiter with the double JD was there immediately.

Mifflin doffed his hat and nodded at the drink. "Nice touch, Eiker." He tossed the fedora on the floor beside his chair and wrapped a brawny hand around the glass. "Cheers." He took a long, masterly swig then offered his beefy hand across the table and Eiker returned the handshake.

"You haven't changed much, Harold."

Mifflin gave a low, rumbling laugh. "Liar." He finished his drink and signaled the waiter for another round. "I never thought I'd be briefing you. I thought you were a freelancer."

"I was." He gave a sardonic grin. "But I couldn't resist Tom Stewart's invitation."

"Yes, well things change, don't they?"

"CIA drum you out, Harold?"

"No, just the regulation retirement. I'm a consultant now."

"You almost nailed my arse in Hong Kong."

Mifflin nodded. "Only your dramatic leap onto the Star Ferry saved your ass."

They were silent for a moment, remembering when they had been on opposite sides. The waiter delivered two more drinks and left.

"Now here we are, partners, so to speak." Fifteen minutes later Mifflin had given Eiker the rundown on the operation to date and Eiker's exact part in its potential conclusion.

"What you propose will be damned tricky," Eiker said, his cool eyes mirroring the risks his mind calculated, "if even possible."

"You can do it," Mifflin stated flatly. "Probably the only man who can." Nodding immodestly, Eiker downed his drink and called the waiter. "Coffee, strong and black."

The Judas List

Chapter 9

Falk and Koski were enjoying a nightcap in the bar at the Romischer-Kaiser. A waiter approached their table and informed Falk there was a messenger from the American Embassy waiting in the lobby and that the courier said it was important.

Falk and Koski exchanged a glance as Falk pushed his drink aside. "Be right back." He followed the waiter between the tables.

In the lobby, the waiter indicated a man of medium build in a raincoat sitting next to a Chamaedorea palm. Falk nodded and moved in the man's direction.

Switzer got to his feet and flashed his ID. "Jack Switzer, American Embassy. Sorry to bother you so late Dr. Falk but the Ambassador needs to see you at once."

Falk glanced at the ID. "Wouldn't a phone call have done?"

"Afraid not, Doctor. The Ambassador thought it wise not to trust the phone on this one." He gave a weak smile and looked around as if antsy to get on with it.

Falk eyed the man carefully. It was obvious he was nervous and on edge. "You okay?" Switzer glanced back toward the bar then to Falk. "Okay, sir?"

"Yeah, you seem edgy."

Switzer quickly put on what looked like a genuinely tired smile.

"Possibly due to working a sixteen-hour day, Doctor. The Ambassador has had me on the go getting everything in order for your team from the Smithsonian. Won't be any rest for me until we have you all together and ready to go."

Falk knew at once that something was wrong. Stewart had emphasized the Embassy was in the dark as far as their assignment was concerned. "I'll get Dr. Koski." He started back to the bar.

"No need, Doctor. I'm sure she'd rather relax here at the hotel. We won't be long."

Before Falk could answer Koski emerged from the bar and headed toward them.

"What's up? Everything okay?"

"I was just telling Dr. Falk that there's no reason for you to come along." Switzer glanced at his watch. "It's getting late. You have a busy schedule tomorrow."

Koski opened her green orbs wide and beamed them directly at Switzer's elusive eyes. "And you are?"

"Sorry," Falk said. "Kos, Dr. Koski, this is Jack Switzer, American Embassy."

Koski simply nodded then turned to Falk. "I'd rather go along. I'm not tired."

Falk reconsidered his initial impulse. If this was a trick it would be wiser if Koski stayed behind. At least she would be able to inform Stewart of what happened.

"No," Falk exclaimed. "You should turn in. We do have a busy day tomorrow. Besides, you were going to call your Uncle Tom, remember?" Falk checked his watch. "Better do it soon or the time difference will have him fast asleep."

Koski met Falk's gaze, her intelligent eyes registering awareness.

"You're right. I forgot the time difference."

"Shall we go?" Switzer asked as he moved toward the door. "I have a car and driver waiting outside." Falk felt assured. Koski knew where he was headed and with whom. Nonetheless the feel of the automatic in the shoulder holster gave him added assurance.

Koski watched them leave and headed to her room to call Tom Stewart. As she entered the old-fashioned birdcage elevator, a man slipped in beside her just as the concertina door closed.

A black Mercedes waited at the curb outside the Romischer-Kaiser with its engine running. Switzer pulled open the back door and stepped aside for Falk to get in.

As he folded into the interior, the soft *PHUTT* of an air-propelled tranquilizer dart was the last thing Falk heard before slumping into a thick, swirling blackness.

Slowly, through a gradually rising sense of consciousness, Falk realized he was no longer in Switzer's car. He struggled to focus. It was a dimly lit room with a high, beamed ceiling that was as cold as the lump in the pit of his stomach.

A meager, cracker box room with a bare, concrete floor and little furniture, it was reminiscent of a cell. Falk saw Switzer sitting at a small wooden table with his back to him and the room got meaner.

"Where am I?" Falk asked.

Switzer turned. "Ah, you're awake." Then there was the sound of an iron bolt grating and a door swung open. Koski was ushered in, her hands cuffed behind her back, flanked by a man and a woman.

Struggling to get to his feet, Falk discovered he was tied to the chair and didn't have the strength to stand.

The man who just entered came over and crouched in front of Falk. "My name is Steele. I have no doubt you've heard my name mentioned since you arrived in Vienna." He straightened to his full height. "If you really *are* doctors of archaeology all well and good. You'll be an asset. If, on the other hand, you're not, you're going to have to continue to play the part. I know few genuine archaeologists who carry automatics in shoulder holsters."

"In any case, we could use your help. I have all we need to start the search—maps, architectural plans of the Dorotheum—original and those used for rebuilding after the war. No doubt I know more about the area we're going to search than any of your people from the Smithsonian."

Falk cursed silently. "Why do you need us?"

"I'm working with someone who has no patience. He expects me to provide an expert and I said I would. That's you, Doctor. Dr. Koski will remain a hostage until we have achieved our objective. After that you'll both be free to go."

Falk was more alert now. His vision was clearing, enabling him to see across the room to Koski and the attractive, thirtyish female beside her with medium brown hair pulled back in a tight French braid. Her basic black dress was cut high at the neck and just below the knee. It was clear from her pained facial expression that she wished she was anywhere but here.

"You won't get away with this, Steele," Falk said. "You'll be the first one they look for. You're too well-known."

"Being well-known and being found are two different matters and I have no intention of being caught. I've looked forward to what we're about to do for too long."

He started to pace as he continued. "Beneath the *Innere Stadt*, the inner city of Vienna is a labyrinth of passages dating back to Roman times. I have a starting place—a vault beneath the Saint Augustine

Church—and a monk whose knowledge of the subterranean secrets of Vienna is legend."

Switzer seemed compelled to add what Falk thought might be making him so edgy. "There are others besides our friend Brasinov looking for the treasures."

"He's right," Steele said. "Seems some hard asses in the Czech Republic got wind of what we and Brasinov are up to and want in on the deal. So you help us get to it first and you and the lady doctor can go home. No problem."

No one knew where Falk and Koski were and wouldn't for some time…if ever.

Falk replied, "What guarantee do we have you'll let us go after this is over?"

"None. You'll have to trust me." Steele went over to the woman next to Koski. "You two ladies are going to be close for a while. I'd better introduce you. Emma Lewis meet Dr. Susan Koski."

The Judas List

Chapter 10

Steele kept an automatic pressed hard into Falk's ribs as they walked down a side aisle in Saint Augustine's. A stand of flickering red candles cast jagged shadows of their bodies on the wall.

"Hold it," Steele said touching Falk's shoulder.

Out of the gloom a figure came toward them; a man dressed in the dark, flowing robes of a monk, the cowl pulled forward covering much of his face. He made a brusque, beckoning motion and led Falk and Steele down the aisle to a brass gate on one of the side altars. The gate yielded to his touch and they followed him up three shallow steps and around behind the altar. He pulled his cowl aside and looked around. Seemingly satisfied they were alone he turned his attention to the stone altar. Falk heard a soft click then Steele and the monk leaned their weight against a section of the altar that creaked open.

The aperture was barely wide enough for a man to squeeze through. The monk went first then Falk entered into the black, dank cavity. Steele was last in. Falk heard him grunt as he pulled the stone slab shut behind him.

"Okay, now listen." Steele's voice sounded muffled inside the narrow passage. "This leads to a vault. Downward incline all the way. Keep your hands on the walls. Don't worry about your head. There's enough room above us."

There was a sputter and flare of a match followed by a pungent odor of brimstone. Falk glimpsed his own distorted shadow on the rough-hewn stonewall before the match fluttered out. The monk reached beneath his robe and removed a flashlight, switched it on and its beam stabbed through the blackness.

They walked for several minutes during which Falk was aware of the sound of dripping water and the walls were wet beneath his fingertips.

"Hold it."

It was the first time the monk had spoken and Falk noticed there was no trace of an Austrian accent. Steele took the flashlight and held the beam on a studded iron door. The monk rattled keys as he worked on the lock.

The monk grunted. "Got it. Go, slowly."

Steele shoved Falk forward. In doing so he dropped the flashlight, smashing the lens on the stone floor. Cursing, Steele fumbled his way into a small chamber. A second match hissed and Steele touched the flame to a thick stub of candle on a small table.

They were crowded into some kind of crypt but the weak glimmer of candlelight permitted Falk a glimpse into the gloomy corners. He stiffened when he saw a pallid human foot protruding from the shadows.

Steele picked up the candle and crossed the room. The light exposed another foot and legs before casting its flickering disclosure on a man bound, gagged and stripped to his underwear. The captive's eyes were filled with terror. Falk concluded that he was probably looking at the real monk.

"Grab a chair, Falk," Steele said and Falk seated himself at the table. "This guy has the information you'll need." Steele gestured toward the bound monk and ordered his bogus counterpart to return the "bathrobe."

The impostor did so. As he slipped off the heavy vestment, Falk saw he was fully dressed. The shivering cleric, who was shoeless, grabbed the garment and pulled it on watching the trio in terror.

"Okay," Steele said jerking his head toward the hapless cleric. The pretender monk hit the churchman across the mouth with the back of his hand, hauled him to his feet and pushed him into a chair across the table from Falk. The man trembled as a trickle of blood oozed from one corner of his mouth.

Faux Monk, as Falk designated the impostor in his mind, spat out rapid-fire German. The terrified man shook his head and made some reply that *Faux* Monk translated.

"He says he'll die first."

"Fine," Steele rasped. "Tell him he has no idea how slowly and painfully I can make him die. Advise him he'll be responsible for the deaths of two other innocent people who will never see another Christmas and that isn't the Christian way."

Falk watched the monk. Vague instinct told him the man understood what was being said but remained silent as *Faux* Monk went into a guttural onslaught, punctuating his point with a solid smash to the man's head.

"Goddamn it, Steele," Falk roared. "Call the ape off. He'll kill him."

Steele feigned shock. "Why Dr. Falk, such language in a place of worship."

"You mean, crazy, son of a bitch. You enjoy this." Falk itched for the chance to slam his fist into Steele's face.

"Control yourself, Doctor. That guy," he jabbed a finger toward the holy man who lolled back in his chair, "could be your ticket home. He must give us information and assistance."

From what he could see of the poor bastard, Falk figured he was in no shape to give much of anything. The man who had done the punching pulled the monk's head up.

"He's out cold."

"Damn!" Steele's fist came down hard on the table. It was the first time Falk saw Steele overtly agitated, the first time he'd seen a crack in that all-too-smooth exterior. It was good to measure a man's limit. It was the first step in defeating him.

Steele was dammed good and recovered quickly. He reached under the table and picked up a package wrapped in brown paper. Tossing it to the center of the table, he stood back.

"Take a look inside, Doc. Tell me if it's any good."

Falk reached out, pulled the parcel toward him then slowly tore off the wrapping. What he saw surprised him. It was a Carmelite edition of a *Book of Hours* in mint condition. Falk opened the heavy leather cover and studied the first page.

The inscription indicated the prayer book had belonged to the Bohun family in 1390. Each page was illuminated with drawings of angels and cherubs, birds and snakes, blessed icons and words lettered in gold. Falk's knowledge of antiques was limited to auctions and estate sales his now deceased wife used to drag him to but he had seen similar books and guessed this one to be nearly priceless.

Steele leaned close to Falk, his breath hot and sour. "You and this pope hopeful should have a nice chat tonight." He straightened. "It better be the kind that produces information we can use otherwise you're getting a preview of your own tomb."

Steele moved toward the exit and *Faux* Monk followed.

"How the hell am I supposed to talk to him?" Falk shouted. "I can't speak German."

Steele grinned. "Then try Latin."

"What is it I'm supposed to find out?"

"Back when those books were made, hidden messages, clues if you will, were placed in the wording or the pictures. Families used them as a cryptogram for their secrets. You'll find it's written in Latin, Greek and Arabic. It's like a Rosetta Stone in book form."

"Then why leave me in here with this person? Take the book and have someone decode it."

Steele neared the table and pointed at the monk. "His expertise is in ancient books and writings. Your expertise is in archeology. Put your heads together and see what you come up with."

"And where did the book come from?"

"The Czech Republic," Steele replied. "That's all you need to know."

Falk was about to question Steele further but he left the crypt and slammed the iron door shut behind him.

Falk pulled the missal toward him; his own macabre shadow looming against the cold stonewalls as he studied the book. Closer inspection confirmed his initial determination that it was a Gothic missal over seven hundred years old.

The monk moaned, regaining his sensibility. Dizzily, he lifted his head and wiped his bloody mouth with a trembling hand. Falk glanced up. "Do you speak English?"

The monk's voice was low, traces of fear still evident in his eyes as he answered, "Very little."

Falk sighed. "Good. We must find a way out of this hole."

The man shook his head and remained hunched over the table.

"There's only one way." He nodded in the direction of the small iron door.

Falk took the candle, crossed to the wall and scrutinized the door inch by inch. He found no way to open it. Returning to the table, he tapped the missal.

"Where did this come from?"

"I don't know," the monk replied.

Falk slid the book across the table and held the candle close, enabling the man to see the detailed workmanship of the rare and valuable object. He watched his eyes, expecting a reverent reaction to the tome's significance and beauty. There was none. Was he still dazed from the pounding he had taken?

Another possibility crossed Falk's mind. Was he a genuine monk? Would a monastic that knew the ancient books and details of the passageways beneath the city not recognize the value of a fourteenth century prayer book? He was formulating his question when they both heard it: the sound of the iron door rasping open. One perfectly placed shot struck the monk squarely between the eyes and Falk was grabbed and dragged twisting and kicking from his chair. At some point he dropped the book. The last thing he remembered before everything went black was the monk's blood splattering across the tabletop.

Chapter 11

Koski, desolate and silent, sat in the same small empty room that Steele and Falk had left earlier. Emma was seated beside her with a quavering .45 aimed in Koski's general direction. It was evident to Koski that Emma was an unwilling accomplice in this affair. Trained to read faces and body language, Koski had witnessed the woman's resolve waiver several times, the anguish of indecision visible in her silent expressions.

Nevertheless, Koski had concluded it was time to neutralize Emma and get out of there when Steele burst through the door.

"Where's Joe?" Koski demanded when she saw Steele was alone.

"Don't worry. He's safe." Steele poured a cup of coffee from a thermos on the table and cradled the mug with both hands.

Koski watched Emma, who closely eyed Steele as he sipped the brew.

"Something's wrong, isn't it?" Emma asked. "Where is he, John?"

"He's tucked away in Saint Augustine's Church working on our project."

Emma's eyes widened. "You most likely were followed."

Steele smiled sardonically. "We were *not* followed. Falk is safe in a vault with a monk deciphering a Gothic missal."

Emma was on her feet more nervous than ever. "God, Steele,

you've fallen into a trap. We're all as good as dead!"

"What the hell are you talking about?"

"Whoever's in that vault with Falk is no monk." Emma's high voice cut the air in the room. "I'll bet my life on it."

Steele laughed. "Then you'd lose, my dear. One of my men captured him in the church earlier, took his robes, hid him in the vault, dressed himself as the monk and stayed at the church until I arrived."

"When was this original monk put into the vault?"

"Couple of hours ago, why?"

Koski noticed that Emma's nervousness was waning, her voice gaining confidence.

"John," Emma asked, "Did you ever mention the loot to Rosie Wimmer?"

Steele hesitated a moment, sipping his coffee. "Yes, what of it?"

Emma gave a bitter laugh. "You tipped off the Israelis via Interpol. The "monk" you left with Falk no doubt was an Interpol plant. Someone else already has the real cleric."

Steele was dumbfounded. "You must be nuts. Why the hell would she go to Interpol for Christ's sake?"

"John," Emma replied sarcastically, "Rosie Wimmer has been an informer for Interpol for the last five years."

"I don't believe that."

"Just because I've been accommodating to you over the years doesn't mean I've been dumb or blind. I've learned a few things. The head man at Interpol-Vienna is Franz Kutna. He and Rosie Wimmer are members of the *Urgun-Zvilumi,* a group dedicated to searching out every last living Nazi of any consequence and finding any remaining Nazi caches hidden during the war."

Steele's face blanched as Emma continued. "Kutna was planted in

Interpol, the perfect job for his life's mission."

"How do you know this?"

"Did you think Rosie and I never talked? If you continue with your plans you'll have tough competition. Get Falk back here. Maybe we can work together as a team but I doubt you'll find him. I think you've botched your first move and if I'm right we're sitting ducks. My guess is either the Israelis or the Czechs have him."

Steele's jaws clamped tight. He had to be sure. "Stay here. Shoot her if she tries to leave." He left the room, slamming the door behind him.

Koski and Emma faced each other in silence.

The Judas List

Chapter 12

It was shortly before dawn and a frosty mist hung over Vienna as the man driving the snowplow squinted in the glare of his headlights. The plow knifed its way through the snow, pushing it aside like a curvilinear wave in a sea of foam. He was thinking of a warm breakfast when suddenly his plow jarred.

He jammed on the brakes when he saw a body slide up with the pile of snow, twisted in a praying position on the mound the plow just created. The driver's hand shook as he switched off the chugging engine.

When the police arrived, he talked to the officer while the revolving blue light atop the patrol car split the darkness with hypnotic intensity. An ambulance pulled up, its siren growling to a halt. The medics removed the body from the snow bank and placed it on a gurney.

As the emergency vehicle drove off, the plow driver crossed himself and said a silent prayer for the poor monk who died with no shoes on.

The Judas List

Chapter 13

When John Steele re-entered the room where Emma and Koski waited, his face was gray. Koski could tell at once that Emma had been right. *Oh my God! Joe...*

Steele didn't look directly at them as he spoke. "Someone has been watching the church," he mumbled. "The vault's empty."

"What's happened to Joe?" Koski demanded.

In her first outward gesture of compassion, Emma gently touched Koski's shoulder. "We'll find him," she said. Then she turned to Steele, her deep blue eyes clear and determined. "I think you'll agree we'd better leave here immediately—separately, a few minutes apart."

When Steele didn't reply but stood frozen in indecision, she went on. "Don't you see, John? If we stay together we're all in danger. Pasha's men will easily hunt us down."

Koski paused, wanting to sprint into action yet needing to see how this conversation played out. At the mention of Pasha, Steele's peevish eyes took on a furtive, feral look but he didn't move.

"If we split up," Emma continued, "we may have a chance to stay alive. If not..." Her voice was pleading. "It's our only hope, John. You know Pasha's people will kill us if they find us." Her last words were finally persuasive. "You failed them."

"Okay!" Steele thundered. He rushed to the door and turned

briefly. "But I'm not giving up on finding the loot, Emma, remember that. I'll find it if it kills me." He flung the door open and fled the room.

Emma slumped into a chair, the automatic slipping from her hand to the floor. "Thank God he didn't insist we go with him," she murmured. Her entire body began to shake. Koski walked toward her, her own knees feeling slightly weak with momentary relief. She picked up the gun, unafraid now of any threatening response from Emma.

"Oh, God, I'm so sorry...I don't know why I ever listened to John or thought he was my friend...It's just that I..." Her voice cracked. "I felt indebted to him and I thought..."

"Emma," Koski said, stopping her. "It's okay. You'll be okay now. If I were you I'd get out of town.

Chapter 14

Falk tried to open his eyes but the pain in his head said to forget it. He was dimly aware that he was upright in the back seat of a moving vehicle and his wrists hurt badly. He opened his eyes slowly. He was in handcuffs and Jack Switzer sat beside him.

Falk groaned and turned to the window. A snow-covered landscape flashed by in a reel of almost endless monotony, broken now and then by bare trees and stonewalls. Soon it would be daylight. He had no idea where he was or where Switzer and the driver were taking him.

The car, a black Peugeot, slowed to let a horse-drawn cart loaded with empty potato sacks plod through a crossroad. The driver of the cart barely noticed them from under his woolen cap and continued his slow pace. The car dropped into low gear and went around the cart with a snarl of exhaust causing the horse to rear, almost jerking the driver from his perch. Falk closed his eyes as the car fishtailed on the slick, icy road, regained traction and howled off down the bleak curving road.

In her small apartment above the antique shop, Emma Lewis concluded a phone call and grabbed the coffee pot in the same moment the car containing Falk was racing out of town.

Emma placed the pot on the table, saying, "All Rosie could tell me was that her people put a watch on my place." She poured steaming coffee into two antique mugs. "We're safe for the moment. Rosie said Dr. Falk was last seen in a car with Czech diplomatic plates. They were heading northeast out of the city."

Koski set down her mug. "Northeast—you mean the Czech Republic?" Her first thought was to contact the American Embassy but Stewart had warned them against talking to the Embassy or anyone else.

"Rosie and Kutna have alerted Interpol," Emma began but Koski interrupted, not listening. "I'm going after him."

Emma gave her an incredulous look. "If he's being abducted into the Czech Republic...forget it, Susan."

"What do you mean?"

Emma was almost apologetic. "For one thing, if you're caught you may spend the rest of your life in an East European prison. There's also no guarantee you'll find him and..."

"You operate an antique shop, Emma," Koski said. "How many guarantees are there in your business?"

Emma shrugged.

Koski downed her coffee. "The business Joe and I are in offers none but that doesn't stop us from doing it." From the quizzical expression on Emma's face, Koski figured the woman was trying to juxtapose no guarantees with the field of archaeology. "No matter," Koski said and got up.

Emma put on her coat. "C'mon, we'll take my car."

The first sign of daylight was breaking as they drove across the awakening city. "We'll catch the morning train to Bratislava," Emma said, "transfer to a local to Kuty, a small town at the fork of the river across from Hohenau. I know someone there who will help us."

They fell silent. Koski slumped back and stared ahead. In five days, it would be Christmas. She thought of candles, trees with many colored lights, warm wax and bayberry, the message of peace struggling to preserve itself. She pulled her coat tighter around her as Emma turned into the parking lot of the Nordbahnhof railway station.

Walking into the old, cavernous station, Koski saw the grime and gloom of an age long past mixed with modern. There were the usual harried early morning travelers one saw on every railway platform, their faces a combination of happiness and harassment. Koski herself was bewildered at the last few hours. Normally she would have easily adjusted to foreign surroundings, been able to cope with any situation. This time she found herself in a limbo of uncertainty.

Was it that she was in a strange country and unable to speak the language or turn to any friendly agency due to the secrecy of her mission? Or was it simply that she was lost without her partner, without his encouragement and optimistic outlook…without his touch?

Emma tapped her elbow. "Wait here. I'll get the tickets."

"I'll come with you."

"No, stay. It's too easy to remember a couple of women buying tickets." Emma crossed the station platform and entered the ticket line.

Koski watched, marveling that Emma, a small antique shop owner, had such unusual shrewdness about things like two women being noticed. She went over to a bookstall and browsed through magazines. She could look at the pictures if she couldn't understand the words.

Emma appeared with the tickets. "Let's get some breakfast. We have time."

Koski nodded and wondered what paperwork, if any, they might need to cross into the Czech Republic. They entered a busy café and found a table.

"You hold the table," Emma said. "I'll get the food."

Koski waited, visa and passports on her mind. Had Emma, in her rush to get out of the city, overlooked this important consideration?

Emma returned and planted bread rolls and small packages of butter and jam on the table then got the coffee. She laughed and sat down. "Phew. I'd hate to see this place during rush hour."

"Emma..." Koski broke her roll and buttered it slowly. "I don't think Americans can cross into the Czech Republic without papers of some sort and I don't have any."

Emma nodded. "I know. Pass the jam, please."

Koski's surprise was evident. Here she was, certain she was going to dash Emma's plans and she calmly asked for the jam.

"On the train," Emma said, "later in the journey, after we cross the border, there will be the routine ID check. Rosie has the word out ahead of us. Don't worry. You'll get through."

Koski decided it was time to talk to Emma about her connection to this Rosie character. "What did you say the name of Rosie's organization was?"

Emma shushed her. "Forget I ever mentioned it." Checking her watch, she announced it was time to go.

Emma led the way out of the café. As they passed through the ticket gate, a large man in a leather trench coat, whose demeanor conjured up images of secret passwords and invisible ink, oozed his way into a nearby phone booth although they never saw him.

"They're boarding the train to Kuty now," he reported then hung up and wheezed out between the wood and glass concertina doors.

Once on the Vienna-Bratislava-Prague-Bahnoffenlocalstutz, the two women found a compartment and sat down. Emma checked her watch. "Nice timing. The train leaves in eight minutes."

Koski grew increasingly uneasy having to rely on Emma, a woman she had only just met yet whose instincts and knowledge she sorely needed.

The Judas List

Chapter 15

The clock on the dash of the Peugeot indicated they'd been driving nearly two and a half hours. The pain in Falk's wrists from the unusually tight handcuffs was agonizing.

They had turned off the main highway at a small town called Wilfersdorf. Now he saw a sign at the fork in the road: Hohenau 35 Km. The driver swung the car in the direction of Hohenau and they flashed through the village of Angern.

Through a row of leafless trees, Falk glimpsed a roadside shrine with a peaked slate roof and a statue of the Virgin. Off to his right was a fair sized river, its fast-flowing center edged with ice. The road followed the river for miles and he grew weary of watching the slate gray water. His mind filled with the possible logistics of escape. If the chance came, he was ready.

Switzer spoke to the driver. "I'll make my contact call when we get to Hohenau. Give us a chance to get a hot drink." The driver nodded.

"Christ, Switzer, these cuffs are digging into my flesh!" Falk said. "When do I get them off?"

"Maybe never. Sit back and enjoy the view."

Falk's arms also felt as if they were coming out of their sockets. "What the hell do you think I'm going to do, jump from the fucking

71

car?" Falk wanted to escape not splatter himself across the pavement. He would wait until the odds were in his favor.

His wrists twisted painfully in the restraints. "If I wind up in the hospital with an infection I'll be of no use to you bastards." He saw a flicker of concern in Switzer's cold eyes. "Look." He lifted his arms "I'm not kidding."

What Switzer saw seemed to make an impression. "Okay, while we're in the car." He reached over and slipped the key into the steel manacles and Falk eased out of them. The blood started to circulate as he rubbed his chafed wrists until they retained a bluish color.

"Any damned tricks and you'll be dead, no matter how much we need you. Understand?" Switzer reached across and checked that the doors were firmly locked.

The car stopped and Falk saw the red and white pole indicating a railway crossing projecting across the road. There was a dull, off-key clang of the crossing bell and a train hurtled past, windows blurred, wheels clattering. Then it was gone, followed by silence until the creak and groan of the crossing pole went skyward in a series of jerks and came to rest in a present arms position.

"We're making good time," the driver called back to Switzer. "That was the Vienna-Bratislava-Prague Bahnoffenlocalstutz."

Falk leaned back in the Peugeot as it bumped over the railroad crossing and down a second-class road. He thought about what the driver just said—Bratislava-Prague.

Christ! He was in the Czech Republic!

When did they cross the border? He must have been out cold when they did. He saw a sign: Hohenau 5Km. He was getting closer and deeper…but into what? He had no idea. All at once he knew he didn't want to find out.

The narrow road ahead wound up a steep hill. There were thick groves of trees on his side of the car—woods that came almost to the edge of the highway. The car would have to slow considerably to navigate the curves and make the ascent. It was a chance.

Switzer must have read his mind. "Make a move to get out of the car and you'll be dead before you hit the ground."

"You think I'm dumb enough to try? I don't have a clue as to where the hell I am."

Falk's reply must have satisfied him because when Falk slammed the heel of his hand into Switzer's nose he took it full on. Falk felt the bones crunch.

The driver of the car half turned and pulled his gun but the road was slick, the bends tight. He couldn't handle both. The vehicle swerved erratically. Falk lunged, grasped the gun, unlocked and opened the door in one synchronized motion that surprised even him.

Lunging from the automobile, he landed in a clump of snow-covered bushes. The driver lost control, swerved and crashed. Falk heard the smash of metal as he leaped to his feet and bolted into the woods.

He ran until the air in his lungs felt like fire. Afraid he would pass out and be found, he stopped and slumped against a tree, his chest heaving. He listened for sounds of pursuit but all he heard was the pounding of his own heart. He had to keep on the move, force himself to go deeper into the woods.

He realized he still gripped the Walther P38 automatic he'd taken from the driver. He stuck the weapon in his pocket, the reassuring weight tugging at his jacket. Ahead, past the woods, he saw flat country and a wide, metallic-hued sky.

He thought of Koski in Vienna. Was she able to escape and get word to someone? He realized she didn't have anyone to contact. Stewart had checked out of the hotel Romischer-Kaiser, telling them he'd be in touch from a new location. Koski was resourceful but…

He felt a stab of pain in his left leg from the hard landing. Still he had to go on. Leaving the safety of the woods, he crossed a field and came to a narrow dirt road. The snow was soiled and sparse. Puddles encrusted with thin gray ice and frozen earth showed through in spots. Falk limped passed a fork in the road where little more than a cow path intersected. He glanced back over his shoulder repeatedly but saw no one. That was when he spotted the tire prints frozen into the earth.

At first he thought they were car tracks but then realized they belonged to a motorcycle. He scanned the area: silence and the ever-present, bone-chilling cold.

Cautiously he approached the next bend in the rutted track. On the right was a long stretch of pines, their twisted trunks curved southward from years of prevailing north winds. Even now, with no breeze to stir the icy air, the trees looked tormented, clinging to the frozen earth by the tips of their roots that strained upward in a shapeless tangle.

Glancing to his right he spotted a farmhouse set back from the lane, almost hidden by undergrowth and scrub. Bleak as it was, Falk was tempted to go to the door and seek aid. Instead he continued until he saw weather-scarred outbuildings with some rotting in sections. One structure that once was a barn caught his attention. A solid thick wall on one side and the tile roof seemed intact over most of the frame. Ancient clay tiles patched in spots and clumps of grass sprouted from the roof at random intervals.

He had to rest, needed a place to hide for the night. Clambering over a rock wall, he dropped to the other side and crawled toward the barn.

The bulky wooden door was unlocked but had warped over the years. He had to strain to make it give. Inside he smelled the odor of rotting vegetation as he warily limped to a dark corner, gathered scraps of hay, piled them into a heap and squirmed inside, the Walther next to his cheek.

It was dark when he awoke. His watch had stopped, the luminous hands showing twelve twenty-five. It probably broke when he jumped from the car. His stomach growled. He crawled to a broken window and peered out at a bare, frosty meadow illumined by the moon riding midway overhead. He figured it was around two or three in the morning.

Again his stomach protested. He reached out and plucked old wheat straws stuck to the sill and chewed the stems. In the distance, Falk heard the sound of a train whistle tugging at the cold night air and thought of its warm compartments and fresh brewed coffee.

The whistle faded. He leaned his forehead against the grimy windowpane and thought of the dirt road and motorcycle tracks. If it was a police patrol it would search this area, these buildings. Cold fingers of uncertainty walked down his spine. He decided to move on.

The Judas List

Chapter 16

Koski stood in line at the ticket gate at Kuty. She watched her traveling companion hold out both tickets to a uniformed collector who took them without a second glance. Together they walked across the platform and out of the building.

Emma scanned the busy city center and pointed. "Good. Here comes a number seven bus. It'll take us right to their front door."

"Whose front door?"

"C'mon, let's go," Emma said. They ran across the street and were among the last to board, swaying down the aisle as the bus pulled away. They found two empty seats and sank into them, each with a sigh.

They didn't notice a black Skoda sedan make a U-turn in the city square and tail their bus, staying about three car lengths behind.

Koski was tired. "Okay, Emma. Where exactly are we going?"

"A place on the Rijnove Revoluce," she whispered. "There's a small grocery shop with an apartment above it. We'll be safe there."

"What about Joe?"

Emma shook her head as if to discourage conversation. Koski obliged, allowing Emma to concentrate on the stops to be certain they didn't miss theirs.

Two men boarded the bus at the next stop and took seats behind them. Koski felt an inexplicable chill as they slowly walked past but she didn't want to distract Emma, who concentrated on the street signs and didn't dare say anything in English.

The bus lurched to a stop. As it pulled away one of the men tapped Emma on the shoulder. He spoke English with a thick Slavic accent.

"You both will get off at the next stop."

Koski felt ominously lightheaded. Her heart pounded. She wasn't in her element and that pissed her off. She turned and glared at the two burly men.

"Do as I say." The man who spoke smiled in Koski's direction but his eyes had as much warmth as an asp.

Emma turned to Koski. "Don't worry. It'll be all right."

Don't worry!

The men followed them off at the next stop. Immediately the black Skoda pulled up at the curb and Koski and Emma were ordered in.

The man who had been silent sat in back with them and asp-eyes slipped in next to the driver. Their back seat companion removed a Magnum .357 from his jacket and rested it on his knees.

Koski's green eyes flashed. "How dare you think you can hold us? I demand we be taken to the American Embassy at once." She knew she wasn't supposed to involve any embassy but under the circumstances she had to try something.

The man nodded. "You'll be taken to Brno and interviewed by internal security. Don't worry. If all goes well you should be flown back to Vienna tonight."

He muttered something in Czech and the car picked up speed. Reaching into his pocket, he removed a slim, silver cigarette case and snapped it open. He reached back and offered it to Koski then Emma but both ignored the gesture. He smiled, extracted a cigarette and lit it. "Enjoy the ride to Spilberg."

Koski thought the name Spilberg rang a bell. They were now on the outskirts of Kuty headed for Brno. Within hours they would be under the control of Czech Internal Security at Spilberg Castle, a residence with a history going back for centuries. It was a notorious history not improved by the present covert occupants.

Koski wondered about Falk. Where was he? Was he safe? She gazed out the window and her mind tried to devise a way to extricate Emma and herself from the mess.

Was it possible that Rosie Wimmer and her people knew of their capture? Her stomach began to tighten and for the first time she considered the possibility of not getting out of this situation alive.

The Judas List

Chapter 17

Switzer, his nose bloody and sore, made his contact at Hohenau, reporting the loss of his prisoner. He was enraged, afraid of the consequences of failure, aware that the bartender, polishing glasses behind the bar, surreptitiously glanced at him. Then, probably reminding himself that glasses and drinks were his job, not trying to second-guess what obviously was internal security business, the man turned away.

Switzer slammed the phone back on the hook and left the building cursing that his cell phone had no coverage in the mountains. He crunched through the snow to his car where the driver was attempting to pull the twisted metal fender away from the tire.

Falk moved cautiously through the freezing dawn. Any minute he expected to hear the sounds of an early morning patrol. Instead, the only sounds were squawks of quarreling blackbirds that seemed to consider him a threat to their scavenging.

Two purple finches planed toward the ground, their wings skimming the snow. As they banked skyward, their calls faded as they gained altitude and sped across the pearl gray sky.

Falk suddenly crouched when he heard the threatening growl of a motor in the distance. He ducked instinctively into the brush and pulled the Walther from his pocket.

He had an excellent command of the road from his position behind the hedgerow. When he saw the stubby green-gray armored car and its ugly 75mm jutting like an accusing finger from the turret, he knew that if those in the vehicle spotted him his P38 would be of little use.

The menace slowly ground its way through the mud and ice. Falk remained stock-still until it rounded a bend and passed from sight, the sound of its motor fading. Falk bolted in the opposite direction. He had covered about twenty yards and was running full tilt when he ran straight into a kneeling figure—Switzer!

With his eyes unblinking, Switzer's face was a wolfish grin. "Good morning, Dr. Falk." A long barreled, blue-black automatic pointed at Falk's face. Behind him, two uniformed soldiers threatened him with automatic carbines.

Falk sank to the ground and tossed his gun to one side. In that moment he almost didn't give a damn if they fired.

Switzer rasped, "Very wise, Doctor. I had hoped to shoot you for resisting arrest." Switzer's tone was nasally from the plaster cast across the bridge of his nose and both eyes were black and blue. He gestured to the soldiers to pull Falk to his feet and recuff his hands behind his back. "This time they stay on until we get to Brno."

The armored car that apparently hadn't gone far returned and pulled up beside them. A young officer poked his head out of the turret hatch and saluted Switzer. They exchanged a few words.

"Okay, Falk," Switzer said. "We're going for a ride."

The soldiers tossed Falk up on the vehicle's rear engine deck as if he was a sack of potatoes. Switzer climbed up beside him. The soldiers walked behind as the armored car got into gear and slowly moved down the rutted track. They covered about two miles and halted at a railway stop near a loading platform with a small hut and water tower.

Switzer snapped. "We get off here."

A soldier reached up and pulled Falk from the deck. He fell in a heap to the snow-covered ground. The commander snapped a salute to Switzer and ordered his vehicle on its way.

"A train is due in half an hour and has orders to pick us up," Switzer explained as Falk tried vainly to struggle to his feet. "You'll be in an interrogation room in Brno in two hours."

Three soldiers came from the hut dragging a tarpaulin. They tossed it over Falk and rolled him against the side of the wooden shack.

The Judas List

Chapter 18

Rosie Wimmer was worried. She had returned to her apartment from the antique shop nearly an hour ago and still no sign of Steele. He should have returned by now. She poured herself a drink, crossed to the window and gazed out at the city aglow with Christmas lights. She sipped her brandy, aware of nagging concerns.

At the sound of the door opening she whirled around then froze. A dark, handsome man in a long leather overcoat and a green Tyrolean hat stood there with a gleaming Voroshilov revolver held rock steady and aimed at her heart.

"Please," he said, "remain calm. I'm here to help you."

Rosie looked from his Omar Sharif brown eyes to the gun, neither of which shifted an inch. She leaned against the wall. Rosie Wimmer was not easily scared. She had dealt with all kinds of killers.

Two men came in after Omar and closed the door behind them. Now, she thought, I could get nervous. "What's this about?" she insisted.

"Follow them." He flicked his revolver and the men headed for the bedroom.

She noted a professional detachment in the men's eyes. In the bedroom, one of them approached the bed, slid the mattress to one side with great care and stood back. He pointed to a compact, well-designed bomb strapped to the bed frame. A timing device set to activate in three hours was visible.

"That's for openers," Omar said.

Rosie's thoughts raced toward an explanation but there was none.

He swung open a clothes closet door and with the tip of his revolver moved aside the lapel of the leopard-skin coat that Steele had given her for her birthday.

"Had you removed your coat from the hanger..." He made a gesture denoting a puff of smoke.

Rosie stared at the hideous booby-trap for a long moment before she began to tremble. Realization robbed her of control and she sank to a chair, shaking feverishly.

The man took a cloth coat from a hanger and placed it around her shoulders. "Sorry, there was no other way." He gently urged her toward the door. "We have to get you out of here."

They left the apartment and took the elevator to the garage. They walked to her Mercedes in silence. The tall, handsome man held Rosie's arm as one of the others opened the door and released the hood latch. Another raised the hood and stood back.

"Let's say you left the apartment," the man beside Rosie hypothesized, "never sat on the bed, never disturbed the leopard coat. You would have died on this spot when you started your car." He pointed to a neatly wrapped package snuggled against the engine manifold. "Nothing new, but damned effective."

Rosie attempted to save her sanity. "How do I know you didn't set all this up?"

He smiled and shrugged. "You don't. But why would we?"

A silver four-door BMW drove up and slid to a halt with a soft squeal of tires. The back door opened and Omar gestured politely for

Rosie to enter. She did so, staring blankly ahead as they followed and the car moved swiftly out of the underground parking structure. They had topped the ramp and were about to turn into the flow of traffic when a vivid flash of brilliant orange exploded from the garage. Rosie saw this reflected in the rearview mirror. Her mouth dropped open as her mind dizzied off into space.

Omar settled back in the seat. "We decided not to defuse it," he explained. "This will give Steele something to ponder."

A light snow began falling over Vienna as the BMW worked its way through the late afternoon traffic.

Falk was in agony. Wrists handcuffed and ankles bound with rough hemp, he lay on the ground beneath the tarp outside the shed at the railway stop. Switzer and the soldiers huddled inside. Wind slashed across the countryside, driving swirling snow before it.

Finally a train whistle in the distance prompted those in the hut to appear. A soldier released Falk's ankles and hauled him to his feet, leaving his wrists enveloped in the freezing, twin circles of steel.

"I'll be damned glad to be rid of you," Switzer snarled and gave him a shove. The whistle screamed louder, closer. A steam engine, like a huge black monster, clanked and hissed to a stop with a screech of metal-on-metal beside them. It was a passenger train of six carriages. Faces peered out of frosted windows at the unexpected stop. A fat man in a blue serge uniform and a peaked cap with red braid stood at the top of a set of three wooden steps.

He nodded and smiled when Switzer called up to him, showing large, yellow teeth.

Switzer propelled Falk up the steep steps. The fat man laughed and Falk smelt an onrush of garlic and sausage breath as he pushed past the man's barrel shape. "Left, through the door," Switzer ordered.

They entered a postal car where men stood at long tables sorting mail. The workers glanced up but quickly returned their gaze to the sorting table.

"Sit on the floor, back to the wall." Switzer carefully rechecked the cuffs. "Don't try anything. There's no way out of here until we get to Brno."

Falk sank to the floor and eased his head back against the splintered wood. A jolt and the car began to move. At least it was warm in the train, Falk thought, and closed his eyes.

Chapter 19

Steele stood outside his cordoned off apartment building and played the part of the distraught tenant. He was concerned about Rosie who, someone said, had been seen walking to her car earlier.

"Hey!" he shouted in German to a nearby police officer. "I live here. What the hell is going on?"

"Explosion in the garage," he clipped. "No one can enter until cleared by the authorities."

Steele heard someone call his name. It was a neighbor.

"Steele," the man said excitedly, his face troubled. "They say it was Rosie's car that exploded."

"Oh my God." Steele slumped slightly against him.

"Get the man in charge," the neighbor called to another officer. "This man was living with the woman who..." He looked sympathetically at Steele and left his remark unfinished.

Steele admired his own performance. He was coming home like an innocent. Johnny Depp himself could not have given such a stellar performance.

A young soldier led Steele to the building's entrance. "Wait here."

Steele stood, looking desolate and alone, as emergency crews passed, pulling hoses and barking orders.

Captain Gunther Vlad of Austrian Military Intelligence greeted

Steele with a curt nod. "You are a fortunate man, Herr Steele; fortunate to be alive." He removed a thin, black cigar from between his lips. "My condolences."

He extracted a crumpled note from his pocket and glanced at it. "On the death of Rosie Wimmer. We understand she was in the car. The vehicle has been totally demolished." He returned the note to his pocket. "A close friend I take it?"

Steele replied solemnly. "We were to be married. What exactly happened, Inspector?"

"Captain," Vlad corrected. "When explosives are used in a crime the Army takes over." Vlad screwed up his eyes and moved the cigar to the other side of his mouth.

"Herr Steele, explosives were found in your apartment. Perhaps you could answer some questions for me."

"I'll do anything to help find the devils that killed Rosie..." Steele let his voice trail off and it cracked with what he hoped simulated emotion.

"Expert work, Herr Steele," Vlad said.

Steele stiffened, thinking for a moment that Vlad knew. "You know...you know who did this?"

Vlad shook his head. "Not yet but we will." He blew a stream of smoke skyward. "Do you have any enemies?"

"Not that I know of. Should I?"

"You *are* a businessman."

"To the best of my knowledge I have no enemies—business or personal."

"The car in the garage, was it yours?"

Steele cleared his throat. "Yes, a company car for my fiancée."

"I see." Vlad stared at the floor. "Does the name Emma Lewis mean anything?"

Steele felt his stomach twist. "Emma? Sure I know her, know her well. In fact, we're in the same line of business. She has a place here in Vienna."

"Place?"

"Yes, an antique shop on the Am Numarkt."

"Do you see her socially or just to do business?"

"Mainly business. Why do you ask?"

"Routine. So you are both in antiques." Vlad smoothed his uniform jacket. "Do you have friends in the Jewish Liberation Movement?"

Steele shook his head. "I've never heard of such a group."

"I see. Political groups are of no interest to you?"

"I have no feelings one way or another. My business is selling other people's dreams so to speak. Living somewhat in the past renders me unaware of contemporary politics."

Vlad contemplated the stub of his cigar. "I see. Perhaps it's also possible, is it not, for one to become immune to feelings, become like antiques, simply awaiting the best offer?" He didn't wait for an answer. "Your apartment is safe now. Thank you for your cooperation. I'll be in touch with you soon."

Steele headed to the elevator and his apartment. He didn't like the questions. What did the son of a bitch mean he would be in touch soon?

The Judas List

Chapter 20

It was late afternoon when the train Falk was on arrived in Brno. Slowly it clanked into the gloomy, old railway station, past rows of stone and brick houses, grimy warehouses and buildings looking more drab and dull than ever in the early dusk of an equally dreary winter day.

"On your feet, Falk."

Falk struggled to get up. Two men in raincoats entered the railroad car and, at Switzer's nod, led Falk off the train and along a dank, poorly lit platform to the entrance beside the ticket master's office. A black car waited at the curb. Switzer hurried Falk into the back seat, flanked by two men. Switzer sat beside the driver.

As they weaved through traffic, Falk caught brief glimpses of the city. Stopped at a traffic signal, he saw a large, ornate fountain surrounded by fruit and vegetable stands lit by the flickering yellow glow of paraffin lanterns. Peasant women hooded in dark shawls bent over their produce.

When the light changed and they left the tranquil scene behind, its memory, contrasted with the prospect of his destination, deepened Falk's gloom at the thought of Spilberg Castle.

Switzer had filled him in on its history dating back to 1278— grim tales of torture chambers and hideous instruments of physical torment. At each turn of the zigzag climb up the hill toward the ominous castle, he glimpsed the fortress from various angles. None was inviting.

It was dark when they swung into the spacious, gravel courtyard and drove past the front entrance to a small entry virtually hidden at the far left of the massive stone structure. Falk, Switzer and two of the men entered an undersized anteroom containing two soldiers and an officer. Switzer finally removed the handcuffs.

"You won't need these in here." He grinned maliciously. "No place to go." He nudged Falk with his elbow. "Perhaps I'll see you again, Doctor. I have to await orders." His eyes blazed with acrimonious fire. "Whatever is decided, I look forward to the pleasure of killing you first chance I get."

Falk took a step toward him but the two soldiers gripped his arms. Switzer laughed and left the room. The officer barked orders and the soldiers opened an inner door and shoved Falk through the opening.

"Where are you taking me?" Falk demanded.

"To Commissar Victor Horidecki, Minister of the Interior," the officer said in perfect English. "He will interview you."

Anger fueled Falk's irritation, overpowering weariness that itself was bone deep. "And if I don't *want* to be interviewed?"

The soldier to his right lashed out with his gloved hand. Falk reeled from the sharp blow to the side of his head and the two renewed their grip on him. They walked for what seemed like miles along bone-chilling passageways until they finally stopped outside an oak door recessed into the thick stonewall. The officer knocked and a muffled voice bid them enter.

It was a large, warm, well-furnished room. Floor to ceiling

tapestries hung on one wall beside a huge open fireplace where a log fire burned. A wood-paneled wall held ornately framed oils, dimly illumined by concealed lighting.

Behind a decorative desk, an old man was busy writing by the light of a brass reading lamp with a lime green shade. He glanced up and waved the soldiers and the officer back against the door.

"Please sit down, Doctor," Horidecki said in a soft almost amiable voice. "You must be tired." They exchanged appraising glances.

"You're damn right I'm tired. I want to know what the hell I'm doing here. I want to talk with someone from the American Embassy. Now!"

Horidecki smiled. "Self-righteous indignation when all else fails. Well done, Doctor."

Horidecki was pink-faced, had closely cropped gray hair and deep, lightless brown eyes. He leaned back in his chair and studied Falk from beneath shaggy gray brows.

Falk was becoming angrier by the second. "I was brought into this country against my will. I have certain rights and you're damn well aware of that."

Horidecki unhooked a pair of steel-rimmed glasses and laid them carefully on his desk. "My dear Doctor. I'm afraid you're now a missing person."

"Why was I taken from Vienna?"

"We decided it was an advantage from our standpoint. It gives us a certain benefit to be on home ground, less chance of interruption. At any rate, Brno isn't that far from Vienna." He leaned back. "Had you not decided to play the hero and run off into the woods we could have had this little talk yesterday and you'd be back in Vienna at this moment."

"What do you want?" Falk slumped in the chair, the warmth of the fire sabotaging his crisp demeanor.

Horidecki opened a box of cigars, bit the end off one and spat it into his wastebasket. He snapped a gold plated lighter to flame and sucked the cigar to life in a thick swirl of smoke. "Did you ever do any fishing in the United States?"

"What are you getting at?"

"I suppose when you fish in America, as anywhere, you use bait. Well, Doctor, you are our bait." The end of the cigar glowed. Tapping away the ash, he continued. "We in the Czech Republic know about the secret hiding place—not the exact location but the approximate site of Herman Goering's last act of mystery. We desire to be the first to locate it at all cost."

"Why?"

Horidecki showed obvious surprise at the question. "Surely you know that aside from its financial value such a discovery would, in itself, be a reward."

"Give me a break," Falk snapped. "I've been through hell the last couple of days and I damn well know it's not been for the benefit of mankind or crowds who visit the museums."

Horidecki blew a smoke ring toward the ceiling and smiled. "You're right."

Chapter 21

On the floor of a freezing cold cell in Spilberg Castle, Koski and Emma slept fitfully, huddled together for warmth against the whitewashed stonework. They shared a threadbare blanket hardly adequate for one.

Koski snapped her eyes open at a slight sound and remained motionless as the door slowly creaked open on dry, rusted hinges and stopped. A bulky guard lumbered in.

"Wake her," he told Koski. "I'll take you to the director now."

Koski shook Emma, who came awake gradually, stiffly. She was tired and disheveled.

At the door, Koski turned to a soldier outside and said flatly, "I'm an American and she's British. We want to see our consulates."

He stared at her, not understanding, then moved his carbine, directing her forward. Exchanging futile glances, the women obeyed and were led to Horidecki's office.

Falk looked up as the door opened and his jaw went slack. He pushed from his chair and toward Koski but a guard intervened with his rifle, training it on Falk.

Falk spun to one side, grabbed the rifle and gave a fast twist, dropping to one knee at the same time. The guard lost his grip on the weapon and Falk jammed the butt into the hapless guard's throat. He went down without a sound. Falk turned just as the second guard swung the butt of his weapon at him. The swing stopped midway by a command from Horidecki.

Falk shoved the guard aside and swept Koski into his arms. "You okay?" He stroked her hair.

"Yes, yes, I'm all right."

They kissed and as he pulled away she said, "Joe, Emma and I were trying to find you. What happened?"

Falk placed a finger on her lips. "Later." He turned to Horidecki. "Both of them stay with me. You want me...they're part of the deal."

Horidecki smiled. "Such devotion. As much as I would like to concur with your demand, it cannot be. Let me explain..."

"No explanations. The three of us or no deal."

"Joe," Koski said softly.

"We're together and we're going to stay together."

Horidecki sighed. "Doctor, allow me to make myself clear. My objective is to persuade you to locate whatever artifacts were stolen from Egypt. In turn, my government will hand them back to Egypt in the name of the Czech Republic. If I fail the three of you will die."

"If you fail your government mister, all four of us will die," Falk spat.

Horidecki said nothing. He was aware of the price he would have to pay.

Falk continued. "You need me, Horidecki. Get the women back to Vienna. Let them check in with their consulates and I'll be your man." Horidecki shook his head.

"Let me try," Emma said. She quickly spoke to Horidecki in Czech, gesturing emphatically. It soon was clear that an argument in his own language did little to move the hardened official.

Horidecki crossed the room and pulled a silken cord beside the marble fireplace. There was an immediate knock at the door.

"Come," Horidecki said. A soldier entered carrying a large manila envelope that he handed to his superior. Horidecki removed a letter opener from a desk drawer and slit the seal.

Without removing the contents, he looked at the trio and spoke. "A man named Lego Moyzisch hasn't been seen at his residence for several days. His wife would appreciate hearing from him. You see, she's in protective custody until he returns."

He tapped the envelope. "We have something that once belonged to him. We do all we can to locate any of our missing citizens who might need our help."

Falk remembered that Lego was one of the partisans mentioned in Mark Benson's letter. He saved Nikolai Youmatoff's life.

Falk scoffed. "That's how you help? Throwing their wives in prison?"

Horidecki said something to the officer, who immediately ordered the soldiers to escort Koski and Emma from the room.

In a flash of movement that Falk barely followed, Koski twisted away from the man and chopped the side of her right hand into his clavicle. Seizing the moment, Falk lunged at the second soldier, who spun instinctively and brought his gun butt down, grazing Falk's head. He slumped to the floor.

"Joe!" Koski cried and fell to her knees at his side. Falk shook his head and slowly climbed to his feet. Koski gently ran her hand along his cheek. "We'll make the bastards pay."

Horidecki rose from his chair. "Enough! Doctor, perhaps now you won't make the mistake of underestimating my determination." He lowered back into his chair. "Handcuff these reckless women and take them back to their cell."

Another armed guard had entered and Falk was forced to watch helplessly as Koski and Emma were handcuffed and dragged from the room.

"We don't have time to waste," Horidecki continued. "There are too many others interested in our fishing expedition. I'd advise you to listen carefully."

He paused and studied Falk. Deciding the effects of the blow had subsided, he went on. "We need Middle East trade, Doctor. It is imperative to our growth, our existence. Our country produces the finest weapons in the world. Our Skoda Works can meet every military requirement of the Middle East and its neighbors. They need our industrial output. We need hard currency."

He drummed his fingers on the desktop before picking up the envelope. "You're being given the chance to be instrumental in a project that will enrich the lives of millions." He removed a folded sheet of paper from the manila envelope. "Look at this."

Falk took the sheet. It was a blueprint. He recognized the word *Dorotheum* among other German words on the plan. The blueprint was of the foundations of the Dorotheum, a detailed plan of the original structure. His eyes caught a penciled marginal note scribbled in Latin. It was a reference to the *Book of Hours*. The same one he had been studying when hauled from the crypt and the monk was shot to death. How did this scribbled note connect to the actual prayer book? He was becoming more curious. He handed it back. "What do you want me to do?"

"The physical prowess you and Doctor Koski demonstrated here tonight makes it clear to me that you're not archaeologists as represented. Nonetheless, I'm sure you were chosen for good reason."

He slipped the blueprint back into the envelope. "This will be waiting for you in Vienna along with instructions."

Falk figured things couldn't get much worse, but then Horidecki said, "Switzer will drive you back tonight."

The Judas List

Chapter 22

A tide of dusk rose in the mountains and across the sky on the second day of Nikolai Youmatoff's trek. He walked diagonally through Canada's wilderness and continued determinedly along an old trap line.

Despite his more than eighty years, Youmatoff's genes were pooled from stout peasant stock and living a woodsman's life had kept him hardy. He broke over the crest of a beech-covered ridge carpeted with week-old virgin snow and wound his way down into an alee depression beneath a cliff where he halted.

He relieved himself near a tree, his stream leaving scattered yellow-rimmed cavities in the snow where his aim, as it seemed destined to do in his waning years, wandered. Hunger gnawed at his innards. Under the overhang, he swung the pack and bedroll from his shoulders. He dug into the rabbit skin interior of the hide pack, extracting utensils, a rusty grate and an old tin pannikin.

Soon fire crackled to life under the grate he had suspended between two rocks and he fed the flame with a handful of dry spruce. A portion of the white fish he had angled earlier boiled in butter and water in a pan. A cloud of odorous steam filtered up and was lost in the blackness above his small pool of firelight.

After the meal, Youmatoff eased back against an old birch and stared into the fire. His dark blue wool cap pushed up above his ears and the red bandana knotted at his throat hung loosely.

With a boot toe, he nudged some birch bark into the faltering flame and it flared anew.

Youmatoff wondered what happened to the others in the vault that night. Of course Goering was dead, but what of the rest?

He sat in companionable silence with the woods for several minutes then spread his bedroll in the sheltered "V" between two bulky boulders beneath the cliff. He wasn't wholly concerned about the Mounties. This was his milieu and he knew how to cover his tracks. Still inexplicable sounds persisted in the woods.

Before closing his eyes Youmatoff spit tobacco into his palms then rubbed the juice liberally over his face to ward off black flies and other pests while he slept.

Tomorrow he would be moving into areas of the forest of which he knew nothing. He looked up at the black mass of unfamiliar Caribou Peak silhouetted against the slightly lighter sky. If he didn't become hopelessly lost, he would be out of the woods and in Ottawa in less than forty-eight hours.

Chapter 23

After Koski and Emma were escorted from Horidecki's office, they were ushered to another cell in Spilberg Castle. It was small and freezing with a narrow window set high in the wall overlooking the courtyard. Two rickety cots, filthy straw-filled mattresses and twin lumpy pillows were the accommodations. A dim low wattage light bulb shed a weak glow over the disheartening scene.

When the iron door slammed behind the exiting guard, Koski bent and tested the mattress. It was hard and dank. "No frills," she groaned. She shook out a thin, moth-eaten, gray wool blanket. "I'm so beyond tired." Stifling a yawn, she sank to the edge of the cot. "Don't worry, Emma. It's too damn cold for bugs. Get some rest."

Eventually they fell into a fitful sleep. Koski moved restlessly at the sound of a car starting in the gravel courtyard. She pulled the musty blanket to her chin. In a few hours it would be dawn.

Falk, his wrists again in handcuffs, sat between Switzer and a formidable guard in the back seat of a black, four-door Skoda that drove out of the castle courtyard and headed down the winding hill toward the inner city of Brno.

He watched tall, dark stone buildings pass in a monotonous array. Thin moonlight from a gauzy crescent moon glimmered like silver water on the frost covered slate rooftops. There was nothing to prepare him for what happened next.

A tearing crash of metal conjoined with shattering glass and a shuddering jolt and one side of the car was instantly gone, sliced away. The driver, who moments before had been a living, breathing human being, was now a mass of bloody pulp. Switzer had half-turned, his features frozen in shock before vanishing in a red smear of his own blood, jagged steel edges of the car retaining fragments of his flesh and clothing.

When the jarring, shattering, insane moment passed, Falk saw the road beside him where the other half of the car had been. He gulped and fell sideways onto the asphalt.

He was alive amid a tangle of metal, blood and snow. Then he saw the gleaming, knifelike edge of the snowplow that had severed the Skoda and three men appeared out of the darkness.

"Hurry," one said, shining a flashlight beam on Falk, unlocking the handcuffs and pulling him to his feet. "There's little time."

Falk dazedly looked back as the man led him to the fountain in the square. He saw the guard who had been sitting next to him in the car groggily trying to get to his feet. One of the men beside Falk ran back to the wreck and shot the guard twice in the back of the head.

Falk leaned back against the curved stone rim surrounding the fountain, his heart thumping wildly in his chest. Water cascaded from the fountain, the wind catching and sending it in a fine spray of sparkling mist that turned to frost in mid-air. A distant clock chimed 5 a.m.

"Who are you?" Falk asked weakly.

"We're here to help you get back to Vienna."

Falk shook his head to clear his thoughts. Was he hearing right? "You mean...you arranged that crash?"

The man nodded.

"Help me? I *was* on my way back to Vienna! How the hell did you know I wouldn't be in a different seat? I could have been the one smeared all over the pavement."

"Seating arrangements never change when prisoners are transported by car. This is a disciplined country." He steered Falk to a car standing in the shadows. "There's no time to waste." He and Falk scrambled into the back seat and the man with the ready pistol drove. A light, icy mist began to fall.

"My name is Horst," the man beside him said. "We had to eliminate Switzer. He'd have killed you five miles out of town."

Falk rubbed his red, swollen wrists. "Half an inch either way I'd have been eliminated with him."

"Sometimes we have no choice."

"Horidecki won't be pleased."

"No. Switzer was one of his best men."

"And you, Horst, in what intriguing international scheme of yours do I figure?"

"I work for Colonel Zhilin." He tossed a .45 onto Falk's lap. "Know how to use that?"

Falk looked at the automatic. What he wanted were answers. "Who's Colonel Zhilin?"

"It matters nothing to you, Doctor. You didn't answer me about the gun." Horst took the gun back and began a discourse that sounded like the Colt .45's manual.

"Why do you want me to have the weapon?"

Horst shrugged. "It's your choice."

Falk thought he'd play the game. "Okay, say I take this. If I try to use it, it backfires and blows my head off, right?"

Horst remained stoic. His ears moved back and forth a centimeter, nothing else. "Doctor, you have a devious mind."

"Look, pal, after what I've been through I'm lucky to still have a mind. I don't trust a soul, so take your gun and shove it."

"I was offering it as protection. There's a possibility we could be intercepted before we cross back into Austria." He flipped the weapon back onto Falk's lap.

The car turned left and Falk saw a street sign that read, Ulice 9Kvetna. He wondered what it meant.

As if reading his mind, Horst said, "It means the Ninth of May Street in English."

Some things, Falk thought, gained in translation.

"By the way, Doctor, the gun wasn't loaded." Horst tossed the ammunition clip to Falk, who knew all along that it wasn't loaded. He said nothing as he slipped the clip into the handle, chambered a round and set the safety.

The car suddenly started to slide on the slick, icy pavement, and the driver made the mistake of slamming his foot on the brakes. The rear end slid to the left, the front to the right, and the vehicle slid off the road. Falk felt the front wheels go down off the deep shoulder with a shuddering thump and the car came to a stop.

"Damn!" Horst said.

The driver got out, surveyed the situation and reported the bottom of the car was marooned on the frozen shoulder, leaving the rear wheels without traction. They could dig the axle free but it looked as if the engine block was cracked. He recommended phoning someone to pick them up.

"Use your cell phone dumbkopff. Wait here till they arrive then meet us in the church," Horst ordered. As he opened the door and they climbed out into the cold morning air, Falk slipped the .45 into his jacket pocket.

Horst pointed across to the Church of Saint James and its three-hundred-foot steeple. Turning to Falk he said, "There's an early mass. No one will bother us."

The Judas List

Chapter 24

Inside the Church of Saint James it smelled of incense, dampness and old age mixed with chilling cold. The early hour congregation was small. Two lit candles on the altar indicated a low mass being said by a tall, thin priest and a sleepy-eyed altar boy.

Horst nudged Falk and indicated a scared and timeworn pew.

Falk had an uneasy feeling. It was as if he was a hostage inside the church. He knew he had to get away, free himself from his so-called rescuers. His gut feeling told him this Colonel Zhilin probably represented another faction bent on finding the treasures and they needed the expertise they believed Falk had.

Once they figured out he couldn't or wouldn't help them...he had to make a run for it as soon as the chance presented itself.

The altar bell rang, indicating communion. Falk watched the mostly elderly congregation get stiffly to their feet and step into the aisle for the walk to the altar rails. This was his chance and he took it.

Slowly he rose and pushed into the aisle, joining the line of communicants. His move took Horst and the other man by surprise. Glancing back, Falk saw them talking as they, too, stepped into the aisle and were separated from him by more than a dozen people.

A side entrance caught Falk's eye. Moving into an empty pew, he quickly crossed to the side aisle and headed for the door. It was large and old with a huge, wrought iron doorknob…and locked tight.

Horst and the other man followed to the side aisle. Realizing Falk was trapped they took their time. Falk knew he had to escape out the front door. As he turned, he saw the man with Horst reach into his shoulder holster and the hole in a dark round barrel looked directly in Falk's direction. His gut feeling had been right!

A parishioner bumped the man, gracing Falk with a few seconds in which to act. Removing the .45 from his jacket, he released the safety and aimed, steadying his right wrist with his left hand in the classic weaver stance and squeezed the trigger—all in one quick movement. His next realization was that his head remained on his shoulders meaning the gun hadn't been rigged. It didn't make sense. Why had one man given Falk a perfectly usable gun and his companion try to kill him?

The sound of the discharge boomed like a cannon inside the church. Falk's aim was true and the man with the gun never got off a round. He stood for a second with an astonished look on his face, a small hole in his cheek beneath his left eye. Then he turned in a jagged, twisting movement that allowed Falk to see where the back of the man's head once was. Horst, splattered with gore as his companion hit the back of the pew, slid down and crumpled across the kneeler.

Falk bolted for the main door, out and down the steps before the churchgoers' horrified cries rose to full effect.

He ran with the fear of God in his soul. He had killed a man in a holy place. Otherwise, he would be lying back there. He continued to run, not knowing in what direction, his heart pounding in unison with his footsteps. A clanging bell sounded. He jumped back as a three-section streetcar rocked noisily past. He had nearly stepped in front of it. For a moment he was tempted to run after the tram but it was too late.

A narrow side street presented itself. Knowing he had to get off the main road Falk went down it like a sprinter. He ducked into a doorway as a car pulled across the end of the street, blocking his path. A second car sealed off his only other escape just as he was about to turn back. Two men got out and crouched behind the car, leaving the doors open. Falk's mouth was dry, his chest heaved uncontrollably.

He could shoot it out. The shots might bring help. Yeah, right. Who would help him? He glanced up at the tall, stone structure five stories high, one of a block of buildings running about five hundred yards to the end of the street.

The roofs were steep with dormer windows and brick chimney pots. Smoke curled from a stack of chimneys to his right. If he could get into the building and up to the roof... perhaps there was a chance of escape over the rooftops. He tried the door behind him...Locked!

Then he heard Horst's harsh and metallic voice over a bullhorn. "Come out into the center of the street with your hands up, Doctor. You're surrounded."

The Judas List

Chapter 25

Falk remained squeezed back in the doorway. "No way," he yelled. "Come near me and I'll shoot the first bastard I see." He scanned the windows of the barracks-like building opposite.

"Throw out your weapon," Horst shouted. "You haven't gotta chance."

Falk grimaced. Horst might be right but Falk was tired of being ordered and used. He wouldn't be subjugated by the likes of Horst again. "Forget it, Horst. You wanted me to have a gun. I intend to keep it."

All at once Falk saw what might be a chance. Across the street, a metal door in a long brick wall opened and he caught sight of an inner courtyard. Two women with scarves over their heads and wicker baskets on their arms came out. Their heads were bent together, collars up against the cold and completely unaware of the drama in the street. As they stepped clear of the door Falk made his move.

He bolted, no more than a blur to the men at the end of the street. Shots rang out and both women screamed. A bullet splattered against the wall and a piece of plaster clipped Falk's chin as he went headlong into the courtyard. Falk headed for the nearest door and darted up an interior flight of stone steps. The sound of gunfire caused windows to open and heads to appear. Falk reached the first floor and from a small balcony saw one of the two cars come screeching through the gate.

He faced a second flight not visible from below and double-timed them. His legs trembled with exertion. Ahead were the last few steps to the rooftop. Suddenly a door opened and a woman looked out. Their eyes met and locked. She opened her mouth to scream but fell silent when Falk pointed the .45 at her face.

Pushing her back into the apartment, he followed and closed the door. He didn't try to speak, simply signaled for her to sit at the table. She was about fifty, small and thin with bright blue eyes wide with fright. After checking to be certain they were alone, he eased back a lace curtain a few inches and peered down into the courtyard.

There were the two cars and a third was coming through the gate. Men were scattered in all directions, several with cell phones to their ears. One heavyset man scanned the buildings through binoculars. As Falk watched, the binoculars moved in the direction of his window. It seemed as if the bastard was about to look directly at him. He quickly let the curtain swing back into place. Horst would no doubt start a door-to-door search that would leave little chance for escape.

He tucked the .45 into his jacket pocket and held out his hands to show the woman he meant no harm. For the first time he realized how he must look to her: stubble of beard, blood on his chin, red-eyed and gaunt from the experiences of the last few days. He tried to smile as he backed out through the door into the passage, knowing that if she opened a window, stuck her head out and yelled it would all be over. Before he could decide if he should gag and tie her up, the woman spoke in a thin, hesitant voice.

"You are American?" Falk nodded emphatically. She went to the door and looked up and down the passage. "Don't go to the roof. What you call?" She whirled her hand over her head.

"Helicopter?"

"Ja! So—it soon be here…you never get free."

Falk knew she was right. Once on the roof, a helicopter hovering overhead… he would be a sitting duck.

In broken English she whispered, "Do not tell of me…go to stairs, down. Then to the basement go…" Her words trailed off.

Falk smiled broadly. "Thanks…*danke*."

Her door closed behind him without a sound and he headed for the inside stairs. He was halfway down the second flight when he heard it. Someone was coming up. He pressed back against the wall, the .45 at his side. Whoever it was was in a hell of a hurry.

Falk raised the automatic and aimed at the open stairwell as a man came around the corner. He stopped in his tracks. It was a young man in his early twenties, big and muscular, his biceps straining his shirt-sleeves. They stared at each other for a second then the sudden clatter of a low flying helicopter broke their mental connection.

Falk made the mistake of shifting his eyes for a split second and the man was on him like a lunging animal. Falk saw a blur, felt his head snap back as the man rammed into his gut with a terrible force, slamming him back against the concrete wall like a rag doll. The .45 wrenched from his hand.

For a moment the attacker seemed undecided whether or not to shoot but the helicopter came closer, the blades echoing and making a slapping sound outside the building. The man turned and ran up the stairs. Whomever he was running from must be a bigger threat than taking a chance on the rooftop.

Falk decided the man's pursuer could be close behind. He cursed and listened. The stairwell below was silent. The sound of the chopper above indicated a turn for another pass across the building.

117

Down at the end of the street Horst was thinking, *Good, Doctor. No matter where you run, no matter where you try to hide, the electronic homing device planted in that .45 will send me a loud and clear signal as to your whereabouts. You may as well wave a flag or send up a flare.* He smiled at his own cunning.

Chapter 26

The signal Horst received from the transmitter in the gun indicated that Falk had started down the stairs, changed his mind, turned and made for the roof.

In fact, Falk was slowly easing down the stairs, ears tuned for the slightest sound. He made it to the basement and, through smudged, eye level windows, viewed the courtyard. The men stood in groups, all staring at the roof as the helicopter edged in, hovering like a hawk poised to kill. It swung in close to the rain gutter, moving with deadly efficiency—an instrument of colossal, shattering power.

The young man darted from behind one of the chimney stacks. He twisted and turned, slithering on the slates then rolled behind another chimney. The chopper made an adjustment and edged closer, its Perspex nose dipping as it maneuvered into position.

The target suddenly stood up from behind a red brick chimneystack, both hands grasping the automatic. Falk saw the gun jolt and knew the man was firing. What kind of man was this? He fought as if defiance alone was the measure of courage.

Then a figure leaned from the helicopter and the barrel of a machine gun caught a glint of light. Falk's stomach twisted as the powerful weapon let loose a furious fusillade jerking the man back against the brickwork. He slumped, rolled onto his face and slid down the steep roof. For a few seconds the rain gutter slowed his descent then it gave way and they fell together. The body hit first, a shower of debris falling on and around him in the courtyard.

The man had fought and died alone, a fate to which Falk now seemed condemned. Though Falk didn't even know him, he was aware of a sense of bereavement.

The helicopter moved over the building and out of sight. On the ground, Horst's men ran toward the crumpled remains like a pack of hounds at a foxhunt.

Falk pushed the window open, crawled out and fled the scene while Horst and his men's attention were still on the victim in the courtyard.

Chapter 27

Koski opened her eyes and turned toward the faint tinge of daylight filtering through the cell window. In the distance a cathedral clock chimed 6 a.m. as Emma stirred awake.

Sitting motionless in a nearby chair was the guard who had been with them since their return from Horidecki's office. She was a gaunt woman with a sharp-featured face, dressed in dark leather knee high boots and a black denim uniform.

Koski swung her legs over the edge of the narrow cot. "I've got to find a way out of this place, Emma."

Emma shivered and sat upright on her cot. "But we'd be shot if we tried to escape." Her voice quavered with an inner chill.

"We may be shot if we don't. I'm not betting on these people returning us to Vienna. Once they get what they need from Joe, who knows? We'd better find a way home on our own, no matter what we have to..." She was stopped in mid-sentence by the guard's sudden interjection.

"I speak your language. I can understand what you say." She adjusted the holstered pistol at her hip.

"Fine. May we go to the bathroom?" Koski asked politely.

"You will only leave the cell with me. One of you will remain at all times. You cannot leave together."

Koski rose slowly and approached the woman. "Soon it will be Christmas." It was a soft, controlled voice designed to elicit sympathy. "Our families...our little children will be worried about us. Is there any way we can be allowed to communicate with them?"

The woman was silent, staring ahead. Koski threw her hands up in a futile gesture and returned to the cot.

Emma jumped up and began pacing and wringing her hands. Until then, Koski hadn't been aware of the extent of her panic. "We're going to die here in this rat hole, Koski. I just know it."

She had been a rock since they separated from Steele: *We're going to my place. Pass the jam. It's too easy to remember a couple of women buying tickets.* She had seemed possessed of extraordinary skills and courage. Now she was coming apart at the seams. Koski reminded herself that Emma, after all, was not trained at Quantico. She sighed. "Emma, how do you happen to know Rosie Wimmer?"

Emma nodded as if there was no longer any reason for secrecy. "I met her through John. She's basically the only female friend I've made in Vienna." She hugged the blanket around her as she continued to pace. "She lives with John. It was inevitable that we would become friends, I guess."

"But it's more than a social relationship isn't it?"

Emma stopped walking and sank to the cot, lowering her voice to a whisper. "She has asked for my help on occasion... to pass along a message...let a friend sleep on a blanket on the floor of my shop, the next morning the person is gone, that sort of thing.

"It seemed harmless. Nevertheless, I swore to tell no one, not even...especially...not John. Now I see why she asked that. Rosie, despite the fact that she's in love with him, must have known he couldn't be trusted." She jumped up again. "In the end *I* gave away

Rosie's secret...to John. Oh, God, we're going to die here!" Koski glanced at the guard, who was gauging Emma's behavior. "What does it all mean? What are we dying for?"

The guard unsnapped her holster and rested her right hand on the butt of the pistol. "I warn you. If you attempt anything I will kill you."

"It's okay." Koski jumped up and waved her palms between the two women. "It's okay," she told the guard. She led Emma back to the cot. "Don't worry," she whispered. "I'll think of something." Loudly, she said, "We don't want the nice woman to do anything we'd all be sorry for." Her own words brought a light to her eyes and she turned back to the guard. "We should all get along...learn to coexist. No sense making it more difficult than it is."

Emma threw Koski an uneasy glance at this turnabout. The guard flicked her eyes in their direction but said nothing.

Koski walked closer to the sentinel. "Today, even in your country, the walls have ears. I'm sure there are those who know of our capture, perhaps will let it be known to the West if we were killed..." She paused before the woman. "Am I right?"

The blow landed with vicious force, crushing into Koski's chest and driving the air from her lungs. Pain, as if a red hot rod was plunged into her breasts, made her sway. Her vision was blurred. Gasping for air, she slumped to her knees and rolled onto her side.

The guard was on her feet, knees bent, hands rigid, fingers slightly curved in classic karate stance. She aimed a kick at Koski's head but her target turned in time to deflect the blow with her shoulder. It was a reaction beyond primordial instinct, one learned from years of extraordinary training honed by the practiced teachings of experience.

Koski's hand grabbed the woman's ankle, gave a fast twist and a short jerk and the guard was down beside her. She yanked the woman's head back with all her strength, made a swift half roll and, slamming her arm across her opponent's windpipe, gave two quick jerks. There was a soft splintering sound, a slight arching of the guard's back and she was still.

"Dear God!" Emma exclaimed as she knelt beside Koski and stared at the face, the bright mouse eyes bulging from their sockets.

Koski pulled herself close to the door, placing an ear against it. "Thick doors...no one heard." She looked at Emma silent and staring. "We've got to move fast." Emma nodded numbly but made no reply. "You dress as the guard. You're about the same size and can speak the language. There's a chance we can make it."

Koski pulled at the boots, the body inching across the floor with each tug. "Grab beneath her arms and hold her still." Koski tugged until the boot slid off. "Now the other," she hissed. Emma wasted no time and was soon dressed in the uniform. She tucked her hair beneath the peaked cap, pulled on the still-warm boots.

"Let's get her on the cot," Koski whispered. Together they lifted the body to the mattress and covered it.

Koski placed her hands gently on Emma's shoulders. "You okay?" Emma nodded. Not really, Koski thought, but under present conditions she dare not take time to distinguish between killing and *killing.* "Listen, you tell the guard outside that you're escorting me to the bathroom."

Emma banged on the door. "Guard!" It opened immediately. A man stuck his head in and snapped to attention with a smart salute.

"Allow no one in until we return," Emma said in her most authoritative Czech, miming the dead woman's deep, guttural tone. She pointed toward the mound of humanity on the cot. "I want her to stay right here." The door clanged shut behind them. Ahead was a dimly lit passageway with low wattage bulbs hung at long intervals. Hopefully, muted light and dark shadows would work in their favor and lead them to freedom.

"We'll make it," Koski whispered.

The Judas List

Chapter 28

John Steele switched on the lights in his apartment following his encounter with Captain Vlad. No doubt the authorities had searched but he had to be certain. He went to a small desk and sat. Pushing in on the center drawer until it would go no farther, he eased it back slightly then gave it a hard shove forward. He was rewarded with a soft click.

He looked into the space where his knees had been. To the right, almost at floor level, the edge of a shallow drawer projected an inch from his right shoe. Quickly reaching down he removed a small key. Next he took a magnifying glass from a cubbyhole in the desk and scrutinized the key.

It was still there, a hair-like filament across the grooves. He grunted in satisfaction. If Military Intelligence had found the key and made an impression the filament would be gone. It was an old trick but one that still worked. He tossed the key in the air and caught it. He needed a drink. He was recapping the decanter when he saw it—a quick flash, a reflection from the crystal stopper in the lens of a concealed camera.

He knew better than to react. Play dumb, he thought. He sipped his drink. The crafty bastards…a camera flush mounted in the wainscoting and he had showed them everything! Damn.

He returned to the desk with the key in his pocket and shuffled through some papers. When his drink was finished he went to the bedroom and closed the door. This room also could be under surveillance. He removed a pair of slacks from the closet. As he laid them on the bed, he slid the key beneath the mattress and changed his clothes.

Why would Vlad go to the trouble of hiding a camera in his apartment? Perhaps it wasn't Vlad. He opened the apartment door, set the lock and left.

As he walked toward the elevators two men approached from opposite directions. They followed him into the elevator and the door slid shut with a soft hiss. The hair on the back of his neck rose.

Chapter 29

It was 7 a.m. when Rod Eiker phoned a woman named Lisa Winkler. Lisa was the type who fit into the lectures Eiker had drilled into him many times while serving with British SAS:

Aside from its professional practitioners, Intelligence draws its personnel from a vast reservoir of people. Traditionally, journalists play an exceptional role if only because they are professional collectors of information. This is recognized by most espionage agencies around the world.

Lisa was perfect; a freelance journalist on the international beat who guiltlessly worked both sides of the street. She grumbled and turned onto her back, exposing her full, nearly naked bosom. Her hand reached from beneath satin sheets and located the phone. "Who is it?" she growled. Her demeanor softened when she recognized the voice. She fluffed self-consciously at an improbable mass of orange red hair. "Well," she cooed, "this is a nice surprise."

"Lisa, my dear, sorry to bother you so early..."

"Rod Eiker," she interrupted and fell into a husky, seductive drawl. "You can bother me in bed anytime. Where are you?"

"Here in Vienna. Lisa, I need some information," he said more abruptly than he intended.

Her lower lip slid out. "Only for you would I make conversation so early in the morning. What is it you want to know…and the answer is probably yes."

Eiker smiled inwardly. "Are you familiar with a man named John Steele?"

Lisa crinkled her brow. "Yes, I know of him. A Canadian living here for many years. He owns a couple of nice antique stores. Looking for a trinket? He's very expensive."

"More than a trinket. My business with him has to do with quite a collection."

"I had no idea you were interested in antiques."

"There are a few things you don't know about me."

"Yes, well, that can be corrected. When will I see you again?"

"That was my next question. Are you free for dinner say around the twenty-sixth?"

"If I'm not, I will be."

"Shall we say seven-thirty? I'll pick you up at your place."

"Wonderful. I look forward to it." She paused and added, "Eiker, you're not the first person this week to ask about Steele."

"Who else?"

"Interpol. What's he done?"

"I have no idea. I've heard he has a lead on some interesting pieces of Middle Eastern art."

"Hmmm…I guess that answer will have to do. See you on the twenty-sixth."

As soon as Lisa broke the connection she placed a call to Franz Kutna, Interpol Vienna, and immediately connected

"Good morning, Lisa. What can I do for you?"

"It's about Rod Eiker. He's after all he can get on John Steele."

"What does that renegade want with Steele? I'll check it out right away. Thanks." He replaced the phone and flicked ash from the end of his cigarette. He took a long drag then dropped the butt into the dregs of his coffee cup and rose.

"Magda," he called to his secretary as he shrugged into his overcoat and passed through the outer office. "Take messages. Be back in an hour. If anything comes up you can get me at the Kartendome."

Magda smiled. It was the first time in days he had taken time to get a meal.

Kutna walked two blocks to the Kartendome. Little by little things were falling into place. He entered the building through the back door into a large steamy kitchen.

Fritz saw him and waved. "About time, Franz," he called in a booming voice. "Wait there."

Fritz Lubbe, owner, chef, host to some of Vienna's most famous personages, pushed his well-rounded bulk between worktables, dodging cutting blocks, steaming vats and bubbling cauldrons of aromatic food until he was facing his dear friend.

"You look terrible; far too thin and tired." He shoved aside a pile of dishes on a nearby table and waved to one of the cooks. "You also smoke too much and don't eat enough." He pulled two chairs forward. "Sit down."

Kutna sat and leaned forward across the table. "Fritz, get word to our people in Brno. We must find an American by the name of Joseph Falk and bring him back to Vienna."

A deep bowl of goulash, a large mug of thick, black coffee, half a loaf of dark bread and a dish of butter came to the table and slid in front of Kutna.

"Eat," Fritz urged, "for me."

Kutna smiled and glanced around the kitchen, satisfied that the clamor made it impossible for the place to be bugged—a safe place to talk business, Mossad business. Kutna continued.

"This is vital, Fritz. We've been sitting on top of a Nazi treasure trove since the end of the Second World War…right here in the city." Kutna tore off a piece of bread. "Now there are many after it, including that war criminal, Brasinov. Rod Eiker also is sniffing around town… God knows who else."

He dipped the bread into his goulash. "We want Dr. Falk. We need him. The Czech's have grabbed him, taken him to Brno, to Spilberg. It's not going to be easy."

Fritz nodded. "It never is, my friend."

In her apartment, Lisa Winkler poured a second cup of milky coffee. She knew she was onto something good if she could just piece it all together. There was Eiker asking questions and Czechs sniffing the air of international intrigue. What did Eiker mean about Middle Eastern art? She intended to find out…fast.

Chapter 30

Falk stood at the fringe of a crowd of pedestrians waiting to cross a busy street in Brno. He felt like a lost tourist who had missed the bus. The light turned green and the early morning commuters surged ahead. He followed until he was on the opposite side of the square, near the railway station.

They had taken his money and ID while he was a prisoner in the castle. He knew that without money he couldn't take a train. He had to think of something.

Then he saw the car. A new low-slung, bright red Maserati was weaving through traffic, its perfectly tuned engine growling. His eyes followed as it turned a corner, the driver scaling down through the gearbox like a musician, engine notes reverberating, causing heads to turn and eyes to glaze with envy.

The Italian auto eased to a stop half a block from Falk. A final rev and the engine died. The driver stepped from the machine, crossed the sidewalk and entered a three-story building.

Eyeing the car, Falk sauntered toward the building, an old residence converted into offices. Two of three polished brass plates fixed into the stonework beside the door were in Czech, the other in English. Jan Michalavitch Travel, Ltd., Falk read. Was the man in the car Michalavitch? The brass seemed old, the man young.

A small crowd of admirers who had gathered around the Maserati dispersed slowly as Falk moved in for a closer look.

"Like it?" a voice behind him asked.

Falk spun around, surprised to see the driver. "Yes. How did you know I speak English?"

"You're American, right?" Before Falk could answer the man added, "Perhaps I can be of assistance."

"Are you the police?"

"No. I'm Jan Michalavitch. My office is upstairs. I saw you reading my plate. I thought I'd talk to you since I can always use the business of an American."

Falk liked his approach and decided to be blunt. "I was thinking of stealing your car."

"I see." Michalavitch's gray green eyes were alive with curiosity. "This is a new Ferrari-designed 4.2-liter V8. It makes 390 horsepower and 332 pound-feet of torque. You have picked a very expensive Maserati to steal. Perhaps I was right. You could use the services of a good travel agent."

Falk ran a finger gently along the curve of the hood. "It looks like business is pretty good."

"Oh, it's not mine. I'm driving it to Trieste for a client. I came by my office to pick up some papers. Actually business is rather slow."

Falk got the message. Jan was open for a deal in cold cash, especially American dollars. "What would it cost to drive me to Vienna?"

Jan gestured toward a nearby coffee shop. "Let's get a coffee. Maybe we can arrange something."

They were sipping coffee when Jan leaned close to Falk and in a hushed tone said, "I could arrange for you to steal the car. That way I'd be protected by my client's insurance company."

Falk looked up from his cup. "How much?"

"One thousand American paid to my bank in Munich."

"Sorry, I don't have a cent. No credit cards, checks, nothing."

"What do you mean?"

"I have no passport, no identification. Everything was taken from me."

"You were robbed?"

"You could say that. The police took everything when I was arrested."

"Oh." Jan's interest faded. He shifted uneasily in his chair obviously regretting the encounter altogether.

Falk decided it was time for more desperate measures. "Sorry, Jan. I'm on the run." He lowered his voice to a confidential tone. "I'm going to ask you not to make any sudden moves."

Jan regarded him, questioning, then his gaze followed Falk's arm down to his hand in his pocket. "I have a gun here," Falk said. "It has a full clip except for one round I used when I killed the cop as I made my escape."

Jan was unnerved but reacted coolly. "What are you saying?"

"I must insist you take me to Vienna."

Jan gave a sideways glance. "How do I know you have a gun?"

It was a "B" movie tactic that Falk didn't believe in a million years would work but he did it regardless. With a point of his finger in his jacket pocket he motioned toward the door. "Trust me."

Jan didn't move for a full five seconds then he scraped back his chair and stood, all signs of the friendly wheeler-dealer gone. He tossed a few coins on the table.

"Good," Falk said. "I've always wanted to ride in a Maserati." As

The Judas List

they walked out, he nervously fingered the innocuous air in his pocket.

Chapter 31

Koski and Emma hurried through the dark corridors and came upon a small door with a cracked window. Koski twisted the knob and the door opened to a walled courtyard. On the far side a soldier huddled against a door, his head sunk into his upturned coat collar, a rifle slung over his shoulder.

"Keep walking," Koski whispered. "See that guy? He's half asleep. You're an officer. Tell him to open the door."

Emma never missed a beat. She walked up to the unsuspecting guard and tapped his shoulder. He jumped. Seeing her insignias, he came to attention as Emma let loose with a stream of Czech, dressing him down for being less than alert. "Open the door," she ordered.

The soldier fumbled with his keys, unable to open the door fast enough for her. He snapped a salute as they walked through. Emma knew the Czechoslovakian Army had left Spilberg castle back in 1959, marking a definite end to its military era.

In 1960, Spilberg became the seat of the Brno City Museum. It was evident that the Czech Republic secret police also had kept part of its infamous infrastructure for covert needs.

Once inside Koski knew they'd have to move fast. They entered a long, brightly lit corridor with highly polished floors and doors on either side. "Check the doors on that side, Emma. I'll check these."

"Empty office," Emma said after opening the first. When she opened the next, she whispered over her shoulder, "A janitor's room full of cleaning supplies."

Koski was at her side at once. She pushed Emma in and closed the door behind them. "Lock the door," she said and did a quick appraisal. Coveralls and assorted clothing hung on wall hangers. Rubber boots, buckets and mops filled one corner. The room smelled of soap and floor polish.

"Grab one of the coveralls and a pair of boots," Koski said. Emma nodded and started pulling off the guard's uniform. She wrapped it and the boots into a tight bundle and pushed them out of sight behind some buckets.

"These smell like fish," Emma said, sitting on the floor and pulling on what looked like painter's boots.

Koski wiggled into coveralls. "Grab those two cloth caps... should go well with these."

Emma reached up and flipped the caps off the hook. "Mop or broom?" she asked, handing Koski a bucket.

"Mop, let's go." Koski opened the door cautiously and peered into the hallway, "All clear."

They started down the corridor, boots squeaking and slapping. Ahead were the front entrance and freedom. An elderly white-haired man sat in a ticket booth inside the hallway, staring out at the mesmerizing winter landscape. They passed him without a second glance. His job was to sell tickets to tourists coming in, not detain two shoddy janitors going out.

Both women breathed a sigh of relief when they reached the outside.

"Can you ride a bike?" Koski asked, nodding toward a group of bicycles leaning against a wall. Emma nodded. "It's possible," Koski said with an ironic smile, "we're about to become the first ever to escape from Spilberg Castle on bicycles."

Koski cautioned as they approached the bikes. "Act like it belongs to you. Put the bucket on the handlebars, lay the mop across them, get on and follow me. Don't look back."

"This thing doesn't have any gears!" Emma complained as they started pedaling. "I'm used to a ten-speed."

"It's downhill into the city. You can coast."

Koski was right. Within a few hundred yards the road turned into a steep downgrade. They stuck their legs out, turned up their toes and with buckets swinging raced like kids through the cold morning air.

Once at the bottom, however, they had to crank hard to keep the heavy bikes moving.

Emma gasped. "Where to now?"

"Vienna."

"On these?"

"No, but we can't go near bus or railway stations. Soon as they find out we're gone, the city will be crawling with secret police. Our only chance is to steal a car. Do you know the way back to Vienna?"

"Yes. I've driven it several times but stealing a car...."

"Pull up here, ahead, near that shop. And no more talking. I doubt there are many English-speaking cleaning ladies around here." They wobbled to a halt. Koski lifted her bike onto the sidewalk and set it against the side of the building. Emma followed.

"Leave the bikes here," Koski whispered and faced the shop window. "Keep your eyes on the merchandise."

Emma suddenly rattled off a sentence in Czech and pointed to some object as an elderly couple paused to stare into the second-hand shop window. Koski feigned interest in stacks of old dishes covered in dust, cans without labels, a velvet jacket with moth-eaten sleeves and tarnished brass buttons at the cuffs.

Soon the couple moved on. When they were out of earshot Koski said, "Okay, I'm going to get us transportation if I can find an unlocked car."

Emma's heart beat wildly in her chest as she affected interest in a wooden wine rack full of empty beer bottles and a stuffed weasel with one glass eye peeping out from a stack of old felt hats. She passed her tongue over suddenly dry lips. It seemed an eternity before a car reflected in the glass as it pulled up at the curb behind her. She turned quickly and hopped in and Koski hit the gas pedal.

Koski knew it was coming. "Where did you learn how to steal a car?"

"Same place I learned to kill with my bare hands."

Emma shook her head. "Must have been *some* neighborhood you grew up in."

Koski smiled. "Which way to Vienna?"

"Make a left turn onto Jakubska Avenue, three blocks straight ahead then right and head west across the city."

Five minutes later they passed within half a mile of the barracks-like apartment from which Falk had made his escape earlier and the young man with a stolen gun lost his life.

Koski swore softly as she stopped behind an old truck stalled in the center of the road. The driver waved his arm in a passing motion but she couldn't squeeze past.

"Hold on. We're going to do a U-turn." She pulled hard on the wheel and the tires spun as the car began a 180-degree turn but halfway through a police car came cruising down the street.

Koski waved to the male officers, smiled her sweetest, completed her turn and kept going. It worked. The police officers waved back, one shaking his finger as if admonishing a child.

"Who said chivalry is dead," Koski muttered and headed out of town.

The Judas List

Chapter 32

Colonel Zasztol Zhilin, seated at his desk at Czech Military Intelligence headquarters in Brno, scribbled his signature on some correspondence and placed it in his out-basket. The intercom buzzed. "Yakov is here, sir."

"Send him in." He signed two more letters before glancing up at the short, over fifty, rumpled looking man who approached his desk.

Yakov stared down at his superior's bald, egg-shaped head. Zhilin's piggy eyes were magnified by the lens of his heavy horn-rimmed glasses perched on the end of his large nose.

"Tell me, Yakov," Zhilin raised his pale blonde eyebrows, "the man killed on the roof when you were after the American, who was he?"

Yakov moved uneasily and rubbed a hand over his patchy gray hair. "He had no ID, sir."

Zhilin glared. "He was armed with an automatic fitted with a transmitter. One of our latest?"

"Yes, sir."

"No one knows who he was or how he happened to be carrying the transmitter?"

"No, sir."

"Stay on it, Yakov. I want some answers." He lowered his head in dismissal.

"Yes, sir." Yakov started from the room.

"Tell them to send in Horidecki," Zhilin called as Yakov reached the door. "I believe he's been waiting to see me."

Yakov nodded and left as Horidecki pushed by him.

Zhilin's eyes flashed to Horidecki. "Sorry you had to wait. Police business...you understand."

Horidecki recognized the slap. He had been kept waiting because Zhilin considered it a psychological advantage, another indication of the constant power struggle between them.

He conceded Zhilin's skills in certain diplomatic areas but he wasn't the sort of man Horidecki considered a useful member of the country's united front. Zhilin's credos were action and force. The Colonel, however, outranked him—a powerful weapon in the Czech Republic.

"Please sit down," Zhilin said. "Now about the American doctor, Falk, and the two women. I understand you had them at Spilberg."

Horidecki felt a flush creep up his face but he made no response.

"My information is that you interrogated the prisoners then allowed them to escape from an armed escort." His eyebrows pulled together in an almost pained expression as he continued, "And the two women...on bicycles!"

"They were out of my jurisdiction, Colonel."

Zhilin waved contemptuously. "You'll be held responsible until it can be determined who was at fault."

A muscle in Horidecki's jaw twitched visibly. "You're free to go about your business." He got to his feet slowly. "Colonel, one of my best agents was killed in a car crash...an important link, a well-placed double agent."

Zhilin peered over the top of his glasses. "Who was that?"

"Switzer," replied Horidecki.

Zhilin grunted. "Too bad. Do you have someone to replace him?" He reached across his desk, fiddled with some papers and continued. "Preferably someone in Vienna?"

"Yes, Colonel, of course."

"Who would that be?"

"I'm not at liberty to give you that information, Colonel."

Switzer's death hadn't fazed Zhilin but now he looked up and the flickering light in his eyes betrayed a sudden lack of composure. "What do you mean? You must tell me who the new agent will be."

Horidecki took a deep breath. "It's not my choice, Colonel. I have no recourse. My orders come from a higher power."

Zhilin leaned forward, his face crimson. "Unless you want to be placed under arrest right now, you'll tell me."

"It's out of my hands, Colonel." Horidecki said almost apologetically. "Certainly I would tell you if I could. We've known each other too long to have secrets between us. You see, Vasilkinik swore me to silence."

Zhilin eased back in his chair. "Vasilkinik spoke to you?"

"Yes, sir, before I left Spilberg to come here."

Zhilin was silent for a moment. Rudolf Vasilkinik was a highly placed politico. A well-known, likable man, he could well be the next president of the republic.

During the destalinization movement in Prague in the spring of 1968, a young Vasilkinik had stood beside Alexander Dubcek, comrades in arms. Vasilkinik was capable of uniting the country in the twenty-first century through a combination of socialism and western style democracy—state medicine and pensions, free education, inexpensive consumer goods and automobiles. Zhilin, for whom the old order of fear was the only way of life, detested Vasilkinik. He was desolate at the thought of Horidecki being on speaking terms with the man.

Zhilin picked up a pen and returned his gaze to the stack of papers on his desk. "Very well, I'll leave it to you to inform me when the time is right...when you and *Rudolph* feel it's safe for me to know."

"Thank you, Colonel." It wasn't enough for Horidecki. He had to push it. "I hope I can still call on your office if I need assistance."

Zhilin put down the pen and spread his hands on the top of the desk as if assessing his fingers then raised his disquieting gaze to Horidecki.

"Call me any time, old friend." He let his teeth show a little. "I'd be hurt if you didn't."

Horidecki nodded politely, turned and walked to the door. He had won this little battle with Zhilin and savored the taste of it. Nonetheless, he knew the war was still on. Zhilin said he was free but Horidecki felt about as free as the three prisoners he had allowed to elude him.

Chapter 33

Koski and Emma had made good time getting out of Brno. They were on the E7 heading for Vienna.

"I'm going to pull over and get out of these coveralls," Koski said. Emma had shed hers miles back. "After that we find a place to dump the car."

"Dump it! But…"

"At the next café stop," Koski said as she pulled to the side of the road and stepped out of the coveralls. "Twenty-four hour café stops have large parking lots, plenty of cars, trucks…be an age before an abandoned car is noticed."

"What do we do then?"

"I don't know yet." Koski started the car and pulled back onto the E7. "I just have this feeling it's time to make a change." They had driven a few more miles when she pointed. "There."

Ahead was the standard European road stop. Cars and trucks were parked around a huge modern complex of buildings that catered to the weary traveler.

"Excellent place to hide a stolen car," Emma said as she noted the number of vehicles.

"How much farther to Vienna?" Koski asked.

"About a hundred kilometers."

They entered the restaurant, found a table and ordered sandwiches and hot chocolate. Halfway through her meal Emma leaned across the table. "Don't look now but there are two men over there who've been eyeing us since we came in."

Koski stiffened. "The police?"

"No. Don't turn around."

"What makes you so sure they're not cops?"

Emma feigned a look of indignation. "I can read male body language. Trust me. These guys are looking for action not an arrest. I'm going to give them one of my most irresistible smiles. When they come over I'll ask if they're heading for Vienna."

Koski smiled inwardly at Emma's immodesty. "Okay but what if they're not?"

Emma shrugged. "We'll give them the brush-off."

Chapter 34

Falk drove through the center of Brno, keeping with the flow of traffic. The Maserati was a dream to drive and heads turned as they passed. Falk was hiding in full view and there was something extremely exhilarating about it.

"Jan, point me in the direction of Vienna. If we're stopped tell them I've lost my voice—laryngitis."

Jan gave him a disgusted look. "Even if I do the talking, they'll want your driver's license. Better I drive."

Falk shook his head. "No way. I'll take the chance on being stopped, making a run for it if I have to, just the directions, please."

"Follow this road to the E7 Highway."

"How far is that?"

"About five kilometers," Jan muttered. "You're a fool if you think you can get away with this."

"Maybe it's because I am a fool that I'm still alive."

The traffic was thinning as they drove out of the city.

"Who are you?" Jan asked.

"I'm a guy who fell into the middle of an international mess—and is trying to get out of it."

Jan didn't ask for further explanations. They were now in open country cresting the top of a long hill and had an expansive view of the surrounding landscape. It looked like a scene from a Christmas card.

"Give me an overview from here." Falk eased the car to the side of the road. "I want to have it in my head."

Jan looked across the rugged hills. "Down into the valley..." He pointed to the right. "...the highway runs parallel to the river all the way to Austria."

"Any other roads when we get to the E7?"

Jan shook his head. "There's an old road that runs closer to the river but it takes longer. Very few people use it anymore. The E7 is best."

Falk gazed in the direction Jan had indicated. In the distance, at the bottom of the hill, he saw the old road running to the left. If roadblocks were to be set up, the E7 would be the most likely. He eased back onto the highway and started down the hill.

When they reached the intersection, Jan's attention was focused in the distance. Falk turned left. The car responded beautifully, not a sound from the tires as they made the sudden, hard turn. Jan jerked forward in surprise.

"No! Stop! Turn back."

Falk stared ahead to a clear expanse of roadway. "Relax we're taking the scenic route."

Falk would later learn the reason for the warning. He had turned onto an old escape road leading to the ten-and-a-half-mile track of the Grand Prix of the Czech Republic. Ten-and one-half miles of twisting, hairpin turns beside the River Svratka.

The first twist came up fast. Jan stifled a yell and Falk pulled the car through the bend. This time the tires screeched but held the road. His arms nearly wrenched from their sockets but somehow he controlled the wheel. He said a silent prayer of thanks that the automobile was a masterpiece of engineering, responding like a thoroughbred.

Jan found his voice. "You'll kill us! This is a racetrack!"

Falk knew he couldn't just jam on the brakes. He backed off the gas as the road suddenly dipped in front of him. The car was airborne for several feet, trees and hedges flashing past in a blur. As they landed, Falk cranked the steering wheel and slid into the next curve. He tromped hard on the accelerator to save the rear end from spinning out. The engine howled in mechanical ecstasy and took the bend without a shudder. More luck than good driving.

Falk remembered the Grand Prix ran each August when the roads were in perfect condition. He was driving on snow and ice. He slowed some, alert for any sudden changes in the road.

Jan saw it first. He groaned and pointed a shaking finger. A yellow helicopter with black markings on its fuselage flew low across the fields and was heading straight for them.

"Stop the car at once!" Jan screamed, "Or we'll be gunned down like dogs."

Falk eyed the chopper and decided they could be gunned down no matter what they did. The track ran through deep woods, the trees converging overhead. Falk's hurried conjecture was that the chopper couldn't fly through them. He jammed his foot on the gas. The tunnel of trees grew closer by the second. He had wondered how fast the car could go. He was about to find out.

He hit another dip in the road flat out as if indifferent to the disaster rushing up at them at a speed of 150 KPH and climbing.

Jan gripped the dashboard, teeth clenched and eyes closed, probably wondering how long it would take to retrieve his body.

A few seconds later the slash of the aircraft's blades hissed above them. Next they were in the tunnel of trees, the chopper out of sight. Falk spied the other end of the cathedral of trees about a kilometer away. That's when he realized the chopper didn't need to fly through the trees. The damn thing was waiting for them at the other end, dancing a few feet from the road like a colossal winged insect.

Falk's hands remained steady, his foot solidly on the gas pedal. The chopper pilot kept his craft pointed directly at them, tail swishing from side to side. Beside Falk, Jan moaned and sank to the floor, covering his ears with his hands.

Through the bubble nose of the chopper, Falk saw the blurred faces of men. The one next to the pilot was turning, poking a machine gun through the port window and taking aim. The pilot lifted the machine just as the car's left fender sliced under the landing skids. There was a shudder of attempted correction from the helicopter but it was too late.

The sound of the helicopter engine changed pitch, going from a roar to a shriek as the stress of the violent maneuver caused the machine to stand on its tail. Falk saw the rotors working like a runaway windmill. Then, as if in slow motion, the chopper gave itself to a maelstrom of invisible force and dropped to earth like a stricken, dying falcon. There was a blinding flash of orange as the gas tanks blew and a greasy, black tower of curling smoke rose from the spot. Jan put his head between his knees and threw up.

Chapter 35

Falk kept his foot firmly on the gas. He tried to be rational. No doubt, the helicopter had radioed for backup and it was only a matter of minutes before another picked up the chase. It wouldn't be tough to find a bright red Maserati in the snow. He had to keep going…and fast.

Jan wiped a hand across his mouth. He was no longer the free, flippant travel agent of an hour ago but a man fearing for his life. "I… I know this racetrack." Jan nodded forward. "There's an escape road that runs into the woods. Up there. About 300 meters."

Falk knew about escape roads. He had seen a film of a driver named Ken Miles, who saved his own life many years ago at Tory Pines in California. After a spinout, he'd driven his MG onto just such a forest clearing. Falk pressured the gas. "Right or left?"

"Over there on the left," Jan shouted. "See it?" He pointed and Falk picked out the narrow strip of earthen track, a mere slash in the trees. It was studded with errant saplings and shrubs that had sprung up since last August's race.

Falk's thoughts merged. He wasn't sure whether he was driving the car or the car and the rough frozen road were driving him. A young pine came at him like a fastball whistling down the grove toward the center of home plate. He swerved sharply to the left and it passed inches from his side. Finally he threaded into the ever-narrowing tract of land, braked hard and stopped.

Jan stared at him with open admiration. "Jesus, Mary and Joseph!" he said. Falk felt a strange camaraderie stir between them.

Jan climbed from the car. "Our best bet is to find the river and get to the other side. It's going to be cold. There's a spare jacket on the back seat."

Falk nodded, reached over, retrieved the leather jacket and shrugged into it as he climbed from the car.

They both sank up to their knees in snow as soon as they stepped from the rutted, frozen track. With Jan leading, they trudged slowly toward the river. Falk cursed. They were leaving tracks a blind man could follow.

"Down," Jan suddenly hissed, falling flat. A split second later Falk also went face down. Hearing nothing, he lifted his head slightly and peered at Jan a few feet ahead on the side of a slight rise. Jan motioned him over. "Down there," he whispered. "See them?"

Falk squinted against the white glare of the snow. Two men stood beside a small wooden boat loading fishing gear.

"Yeah."

Jan never took his eyes off the men. "They could be our ticket to freedom." He got to his feet and dusted the snow from his clothes. "Follow me. Don't say a word."

Soon they stood on a ridge looking down at the fishermen a few meters away.

"Police," Jan called out in a loud voice. "Stay where you are."

The two men looked up and turned frightened faces in the direction of the voice. As Falk and Jan walked toward them, Jan whispered, "Say nothing. Just keep looking them in the eye with authority."

"We need to commandeer your boat...police business."

Jan was cool, official. "We'll take you across the river. Give me your names and addresses and the boat will be returned to you."

One of them hesitated for a second, exchanging glances with his companion. They were elderly, rural men living in a country that trained its citizens well to obey police orders.

Jan wrote their names on a piece of paper and the four got in the boat and crossed the fast-flowing water. The small outboard strained with unaccustomed weight.

Falk saw Jan look back, no doubt wondering if he would ever return to life as it was, aware that if caught, he'd be found guilty of abetting Falk.

The boat nosed into the riverbank and the fishermen stepped out. When Jan passed the fishing tackle to them, they shouldered their poles and walked into the woods without so much as a backward glance.

"Can we trust them not to talk?" Falk asked as Jan pushed off, steering with a single oar over the stern.

"They'll go home, say nothing. Police business is serious in this country."

Falk hunched forward with the cold. It was obvious Jan knew how to handle a boat. Maybe they'd make it after all.

Jan pressed hard with the oar, avoiding a suddenly looming coal black rock ringed with foam. "I used to fish this river as a kid, know every rock for miles. Downstream, however, will be different."

"Why not use the outboard?"

"We might need it later. Right now the current will do the job."

As they rounded a bend in the river, Falk saw something that caused a ripple of icy fear to pass through him. An armored car sat beneath a clump of pines, its 75mm gun pointing skyward.

It reminded Falk of the vehicle that had hauled him to the railway siding. Like an attentive cat at a mouse hole, it was silent, unmoving.

"They're all along the river, part of a regular patrol between here and the Austrian border."

"What happened to European unity? I thought borders were out. Do you think they saw us?"

"We must still be in the clear. No one has picked up our trail... yet."

As Jan deftly navigated through the cold, dark water, Falk fell silent, the word "yet" lingering in his ears.

Chapter 36

Kutna was still at lunch when Rosie Wimmer entered the office and nodded to the receptionist, who smiled in recognition.

"He should be back any minute."

"Thanks. I'll wait." Rosie seated herself and started to thumb through a magazine. Kutna entered on page three.

"Rosie!" He brushed her cheek with a kiss. "Been waiting long? I wish you'd called. We could have lunched together."

"I came in just ahead of you...no time to call."

Kutna detected something wrong as he led her into his office. "Sit down, Rosie. You're trembling."

"I'm okay." She sat on the edge of the chair. "Steele tried to kill me."

"What! When?" He fell silent, brooding as Rosie related the story of the bombs in the apartment and her car. "The men who came into the apartment, who were they?"

"I don't know."

"You don't know? Rosie, they could have been lying. They could have set all that up."

"It crossed my mind but I don't think so."

"Why does Steele want to kill you?"

"He wants me out of the way. Remember he told me about the

loot he was after."

Kutna nodded. "Do you think he knows you're Mossad?"

"It's possible but there's no way to find out now. Whatever his reason, I would have been blown away if I'd made a wrong move in the apartment."

"And these men just showed up and whisked you to safety? Were they from Captain Vlad's office at Military Intelligence? They're always involved in anything to do with bombs."

Rosie nodded. "Whoever they were, they drove me away from the apartment and I'm still alive. That counts for something."

"Yes, of course, but..." Kutna paced his office. "Did they say anything that might give us a clue?"

"No."

"Rosie, think hard."

"The leader looked like an Arab."

Kutna thrust his arms skyward. "That's it? He looked like an Arab —that's all?"

Rosie drooped in her chair. "Sorry."

Kutna sighed. "You've had a harrowing experience. Get some rest. We'll talk later. Stay here and stretch out on the couch if you like."

"I will take the rest. I feel safe here."

"Good. I'll be right back. I'm going to check the latest input."

Kutna entered Vienna Interpol's communications room. Beside a wall covered with state-of-the-art computer code analyzers, a gray-haired woman stood in front of a printer as it smoothly delivered a page. She glanced up and beckoned to Kutna. Together they read the message:

TEL AVIV INTEL CONFIRMS SERB SEPARATISTS INVOLVED.

Kutna swore, lit a cigarette from a crumpled pack and left the room.

Back in his office, he sat at his desk. Rosie was already asleep on the couch. He stared at the terse message that was in answer to his call to Israeli Intelligence. The prospect of those bastards getting into the search wasn't good news.

His phone rang. "Kutna," he growled. "Yes, I understand." He replaced the phone as Rosie sat up, awakened by the ring.

"That was about Dr. Falk. He's still on the run in the Czech Republic." He shook his head. "Colonel Zhilin of Czech security is breathing down his neck." Kutna leaned back, stretched his arms over his head, fingers entwined and pulled to release the tension across his shoulders.

Was he getting too old for this game? He turned to Rosie. "Sometimes, Rosie, I wonder why we spend our lives this way."

She didn't answer. She knew why. They were avengers, coiled springs of anger with the need for retribution. They always were ready to dispense biblical justice for the sins against their fathers and even worse sins by those who planned Israel's removal from the face of the earth.

Rod Eiker walked through the revolving door of the Bristol Hotel into the clear, frosty morning. The door attendant touched his cap and swung open the door of the limo at the curb as Eiker crossed the sidewalk. He folded into the warm, spacious interior. The door thudded shut, automatic locks meshing with perfect synchronization.

"Morning, Eiker."

Eiker acknowledged Harold Mifflin with a nod. He leaned back into the deep leather, his voice harsh with early morning throatiness. "What's today's drill?"

Mifflin replied, "To see Tom Stewart. Have a few things to go over."

"Suppose you heard about Horidecki."

"Yeah, I understand he was dead before his body hit the sidewalk on Sady Osvobozeni Boulevard outside Czech Military Headquarters."

"Apparently it happened so fast that no one could identify the vehicle."

The limo turned onto the Karnter-Ring and continued toward the Stadt Park. Eiker glimpsed the statue of Strauss through the trees.

Mifflin grunted. "I wonder where Falk is at this moment."

Chapter 37

The penetrating chill from the river oozed into the marrow of Falk's bones despite the leather jacket he had taken from the Maserati. He told himself that with luck they would pass beneath the bridge at the border in darkness. It was already dusk. A thick mist slid over the countryside like gray smoke, blotting out patches of the riverbank. The trees were distant skeletons, pointing in indistinguishable directions. At the helm, Jan memorized details of the river's path before the rolling mist overtook them.

"It will get even colder when the fog settles," Jan whispered. "That will be to our benefit. It will help deaden any sounds when we pass under the bridge." He dipped an oar, shifted his weight and the boat moved a degree to the left. "Most of the guards will want to stay inside for warmth. It's the eager guard trying to make grade that might see us... the one who stays outside."

Falk knew they were three hours from Austria yet being on the run in an alien country made each hour seem like a week. All at once, the sun, not seen for days, broke through a rift in the clouds and a hazy shaft of light touched the tips of the winter firs. A reddish glow reflected on the low-lying clouds. This lasted less than a minute and then was gone. Gray clouds swirled in, the sky and fog darkening for the night. The brief glimpse of sunlight lifted Falk's spirit. He was more determined than ever to escape.

In his reverie he didn't see Jan slip off his coat. In a flash the man was in the water. He piked beneath the surface and stayed underwater for some time. He surfaced a hundred yards away and swam with strong strokes toward shore. He would take his chances in the woods.

Chapter 38

In the café off the E7 Koski feigned surprise as she looked up at the large man who was suddenly beside her chair, encouraged by Emma's earlier smile. He was dressed in a tweed jacket and pants and a Tyrolean hat with tufts of white crinkly hair protruding above his ears. He removed his hat with a beefy hand, coughed and attempted to introduce himself in Czech then switched to fractured French. Finally he looked back at his friend, who simply smiled and held up his martini glass in a salute.

Emma sighed. In flawless German she asked if there was anything she could do for him. His eyes turned wide and interested at the sound of his own language.

"I was wondering if *we* might be of service to *you*." He pulled his heels together and bowed slightly. Since the heels didn't click the effort at gallantry was wasted.

"Do you speak English?" Emma asked.

"Of course."

Emma nodded toward Koski. "My friend doesn't speak German. It would be easier…"

"Certainly." He bowed to Koski as the man with the martini glass joined them.

"Allow me, ladies. I am Marny Fries and this is my associate,

Herman Lansfeldt. We are computer reps for a large firm."

"Pleased to meet you," Koski said. "This is Mary Jones." She shot a fast glance at Emma, who went along with the introduction as if it were authentic. "I'm Daphne Hailey." She gave Herman the most profoundly interested look she could muster.

"We're trying to decide whether to take the bus or rent a car. You see, our car broke down and it'll be a couple of days before it's ready. We have to be back in Vienna by tomorrow."

Emma nodded and lowered her eyes. Her long, dark, straight lashes cast lacy shadows on her face. Marny and Herman looked from Koski to Emma then to each other. Herman spoke first.

"As Marny said, we're in computers. We're headed to Budapest. I suppose we could go via Vienna…" He glanced at Marny who nodded agreeably.

"Ach," Marny said. "We travel all the time. We're known by all the security personnel at the borders and can make up the time later."

"I thought borders were a thing of the past," Koski exclaimed.

"They are. Nonetheless, the EU has started taking certain precautions since the terrorist actions in Madrid and London. It won't be a problem for us."

They pulled up chairs. "So," Marny continued, "you see, we can be of service."

Koski and Emma exchanged glances. Bingo! By the time Marny was on his third drink, he had cozied up to Emma and was leaning close, one hand lightly tapping her knee at intervals.

Herman promised to drive them right to their front door. His Mercedes had plenty of room. They would travel in style.

"It's very kind of you," Koski said seductively. "We don't know what to say."

"Our pleasure, my dear," Herman whispered. He tipped his glass to consume the last drop then led the way to a silver Mercedes that happened to be parked alongside the car Koski and Emma had abandoned.

Emma sat beside Marny in the back seat. Next to Herman in front, Koski was uncharacteristically chatty. Less than ten miles down the highway, Marny fell asleep, his head on Emma's shoulder. Koski looked back and saw Emma push him away.

The Judas List

Chapter 39

Colonel Zhilin was in a rotten mood. He still didn't have Falk. He glared as Yakov entered his office and stopped in front of his desk.

Zhilin screwed a cigarette into a long ivory holder and held it between his left thumb and forefinger. "Yes, Yakov?"

Yakov reached into the pocket of his crumpled raincoat, extracted a mangled book of matches, scratched a match to flame and offered it. Zhilin squinted as he leaned forward and placed the tip of his cigarette in the flame.

Yakov blew out the match. "I have information that will please you, Colonel."

Zhilin leaned back slowly and blew a thin blue halo toward the ceiling. "If you have good news, Yakov, it will be the first today."

Yakov had worked with the Colonel a long time and had learned to be direct. "The car in the woods belonged to a person in Trieste. It was being transported by a travel agent named Jan Michalavitch. The owner in Trieste is..." He removed a piece of paper from his pocket. "Antonio Valencia."

Zhilin waved away the smoke from his cigarette. "You have this man, Michalavitch?"

"No, but we have the car, sir. It seems the travel agent has eluded us."

Zhilin snorted and crushed out his cigarette. "That is what you call good news?" Yakov was silent and Zhilin continued. "I suppose he vanished into thin air like that?" He snapped his fingers.

"There were two sets of footprints," Yakov replied, "leading from the car to the river."

"Was the American, Falk, with Michalavitch?"

"Yes, sir."

At last Zhilin was interested. "How do you know that? What did you find at the river?"

"Footprints in the mud, sir."

Zhilin began to breathe heavily, his face pinched with annoyance. "I suppose you're going to say they were American footprints."

"Yes, sir, and those of Jan Michalavitch."

Zhilin virtually trembled. "Tell me, Yakov, how could you tell the others were *American* footprints?"

"Our deductions indicate he may have been in the car. We interviewed people who saw the vehicle leave Brno with two men in it. One of the descriptions fits Falk."

Zhilin leaned back in his chair and glowered.

The room was warm. The thick air drooped over Yakov like a damp cloth. "We checked to see how many people had been at the river's edge," he continued, "but it was impossible to say. The snow was trampled. We obtained a boat, crossed the river and examined the landscape on the other side. Again many footprints led off into the woods. It had snowed recently and the prints were almost obliterated...."

"Did you follow the prints into the woods?"

"Yes. They led to a road and then ended."

"Did you find the boat the two crossed in?"

Yakov hesitated. Suddenly he knew what the Colonel was going to say next! Why hadn't he thought of it?

Zhilin pounded his thick palm on the desk. "You dolt. There is no boat because our two suspects are on their way out of the country in it!" He grabbed the phone and shouted a stream of commands.

"Concentrate on the river between the place of entry and the bridge at Drasenhofen. I want searchlights, six boats with two men in each with battery powered lights and automatic weapons. These fugitives must be found!" He slammed the phone down and fixed an icy gaze on his shivering subordinate.

"Yakov, do you have any idea what it would be like to go through life without testicles?"

Yakov swallowed hard and backed toward the door. "I'll get Falk, sir. I will."

When he was gone Zhilin took out another cigarette and eased back in his chair. Once he had Dr. Falk it would be easy to capture the two females, or vice versa.

The headlights drilled into the inky blackness of the night as Herman's Mercedes jostled over ridges of ice on the highway.

Koski concentrated on the odometer as if her intensity could cause the miles to slip away more quickly. Herman, cigar clenched between his teeth, focused on the road. His fleshy face was etched in shadow by the orange glow from the dashboard. In the rearview mirror Koski saw Marny's head lolling back, mouth agape, snoring.

Koski suddenly stiffened. Behind, a flashing blue light careered up the highway. She glanced at Herman. He hadn't seen it. With as much control as she could manage, she alerted him. He slowly eased the car to the roadside.

With just the blue lights blinking, an armored car swept past them in a spray of snow, mud and ice. Thick treaded tires humming, engine growling, in seconds the vehicle became red taillights that vanished into the darkness as quickly as they appeared.

Herman steered back onto the highway. "You looked scared, my leibschen. Did you think they were after us?" He chuckled and nudged his elbow into her side.

She responded with what she hoped was a look of mystification. "I thought they were after you, Herman."

He shook with laughter. "You thought perhaps I was different than I have represented myself to be?"

She smiled coyly and thought, *No, Herman. You are exactly as you represented yourself to be. Moreover, I am feeling guilty, using you this way.*

Herman switched on the radio and a Brahms composition filled the interior. Koski settled back with a deep sigh. Where was the military going in such a hurry? If it was an all-out alert they would be checked at some point.

As if he had been thinking it, too, Herman rolled his cigar to the other side of his mouth. "We'll be in Austria soon. I'll find out what's going on."

Koski decided the less they asked the better. She knew he wanted to appear important, show her what a clever man he was. Poor bastard had no idea he was transporting two escaped prisoners.

"You know, Herman," her voice was a low, seductive growl. "I'm glad today's borders are not like the old days. The longer we're there, the less time we'll have at my place." She cringed inwardly at her own shameless innuendo.

The cigar went quickly from one side of Herman's mouth to the other as if on a string and Koski felt the car accelerate. There would be little time wasted in idle chatter with security. She glanced over her shoulder at Emma, who raised one eyebrow a fraction and gave an almost imperceptible shake of her head. Herman, intent on getting to Vienna, didn't notice.

The Judas List

Chapter 40

The limo with Eiker and Mifflin wound through a narrow road on the outskirts of Vienna in an area known as Grinzing, a popular tourist wine tasting destination.

"Here we are," Mifflin said as he heaved forward when the car came to a halt. "Grinzinger Weinbeisser."

"Straight out of *Hansel and Gretel,*" Eiker replied.

He stepped from the car. A picturesque lantern swung on a black wrought iron support above the scrolled entrance. Fanciful braids of ivy clung to the ochre plaster walls of the fairy tale structure. He surveyed the landscape.

Eiker nodded. "Actually, I'm impressed. An excellent strategic location. Difficult for any possible interloper to approach without being detected, yet advantageous to a speedy departure if one should be required."

Mifflin agreed. "That's probably why Stewart chose it for his temporary quarters."

"Thanks for getting here so promptly," Stewart said as they entered his office. He indicated chairs and jumped right into the briefing. "All we have on Falk as of this moment is that he's somewhere in the Czech Republic."

In less than five minutes Stewart had updated them on what he knew of Falk's passage from Austria to Spilberg Castle and subsequent escape.

"At last report," Stewart concluded, "he was driving a Maserati that we believe was stolen from a travel agent in Brno."

"Christ!" Mifflin exclaimed. "He's a dead man if he's trying to get out of the Czech Republic in a stolen car."

"How old is the report?" Eiker asked.

"Less than two hours," replied Stewart.

Eiker rubbed his chin. "Could you arrange a meeting for us with Kutna at Interpol?"

Stewart pulled his laptop closer and tapped a few keys. "No problem."

Kutna was asleep, slumped across his desk. He startled and reached for the phone, "Yes," he said. "I understand. Send them along…glad to talk to them." He recradled the phone. What did American Intelligence want now? He ran his fingers through his hair, adjusted his tie. He thought of the computer printout he had read a short time ago. He needed all the help he could get.

Kutna ordered cappuccino. Less than fifteen minutes later Magda was serving it to Mifflin and Eiker, who were too antsy to enjoy it.

"Recalling some of your escapades around the world over the last fifteen years, Eiker," Kutna said, "I must admit I'm surprised to see you working with Mifflin."

Mifflin handled the response. "Our involvement in this matter is as private investigators, working for a large international insurance company whose name we're not at liberty to reveal."

Kutna opened a fresh pack of cigarettes, removed one and placed it between his lips. "Really?" he murmured, lighting up.

Mifflin leaned his rotund body forward and set down his cup.

"Enough of this happy horseshit. Let's get down to business."

Kutna reminded himself that it was Mifflin's style to dispense with the niceties and roll on with all the tact of a Sherman tank.

"What do your people in the Czech Republic know about Doctor Joseph Falk's whereabouts?" Mifflin demanded.

"Joseph Falk?" Kutna bunched his brows.

"Let's not play games here, Kutna," Mifflin growled "We…"

"Look," Eiker cut in. "We could work with Interpol…or the Mossad or the IZL. We're all after the same thing."

"Interpol," Kutna said stubbornly and evasively, "will be happy to do whatever it can. What is your most recent information?"

"That he's in Brno," Eiker said, "driving a stolen car."

Kutna nodded. "I have someone working on the Falk matter. I should have word soon."

Eiker stood and eased his neck and shoulders. "By the way, do you have any idea where we can find John Steele?"

Kutna smiled wryly. "When I last spoke to Rosie Wimmer she wished he was in hell."

Eiker didn't take the time to question Rosie's emotional mindset. "If not there," he said coolly, "where else would you suggest?"

"You might try Military Police Headquarters. He attempted to kill Rosie."

Steele hadn't been detained. He'd been allowed to return to his apartment. Then, like a babe in arms, he had walked in and performed for a hidden, very candid camera.

Now the two men who joined him in the elevator tightened against him and he was hardly aware of the quick nip as the hypodermic needle sank into his carotid artery. He walked between them through the lobby to the street. When his body sagged, they supported him, lowered him into the back seat of a waiting Audi and closed the doors without missing a beat. One man sat in the back seat with Steele, the other with the driver as they flowed into the Viennese traffic.

As he slumped with glassy, blank eyes, a prisoner of Brasinov's thugs, Steele tried to remember how he got into this mess. His mind reeled back, taking him to the last time he saw David Benson.

It was a little after 3 a.m. the night of the last reunion in 1975. Steele had gone to David's hotel room and rapped on the door.

"Sorry, David," he said as he was allowed in, "but I have to talk to you."

"It's okay." David nodded wearily toward a chair.

"About tonight, the information Lego gave us on the location of the loot. I think we should go after it."

David shook his head. "Could be what Lego said is true but you know as well as I do how many legends there are about hidden war treasures." He stretched. "Besides, I have to take care of my work back in California."

"You mean you can afford not to." Steele's voice turned harsh and David was surprised.

"That's not the reason. I have patients who depend on me. I don't have time to spend searching for something that may not exist."

"But it *does* exist! I *know* it. You owe it to the rest of us to at least try…"

"Look, John, I'm tired. If you're worried about me knowing, don't be. I don't plan on telling a soul. We can talk more about it in the morning if you like, but I won't change my mind." He crossed to the door and grasped the knob. "I'm going to bed."

"Too bad you're so short on time." Steele was beside him. "Wish I could have counted on you. Since I can't, I don't think I can trust you to keep your mouth shut."

Steele remembered David's eyes, widened in shock. The good doctor started to say something before the lethal burst from the aerosol can atomized his face, but no sound came. He sagged into Steele's arms. Steele carried him to the bed then went to the door, being careful to use his handkerchief on the knob as he softly closed it behind him.

Steele's mind swam slowly back to the present as the drug spread insidiously through his system. Through a haze, he saw a group of Christmas carolers step into the street in front of the Audi.

They walked slowly, waving as they sang. Steele heard voices but the fog in his head disallowed his eyes to focus. When they did, he was able to isolate the lanterns the singers carried on long poles that cast a pale yellow light on the snow. He thought he heard, "Let nothing you dismay…" before the sound faded. He closed his eyes, fell into a deep blackness and was dismayed.

The Judas List

Chapter 41

Falk couldn't believe it. He was alone on the boat with no idea how he was going to escape. A freezing wintriness swept across the dark brocade of water as the Svratka River continued to swirl past the boat. Falk felt the dampness reach out and clutch him. A vaporous, sickle moon glimmered for a moment through heavy clouds.

He concentrated on what he had to do. If only he could make it under the bridge at the border that was close now. He no longer had the expertise of Jan, who had maneuvered the boat as if he was a Colorado River rapids guide.

Suddenly a brilliant lance of light from the riverbank stabbed through the darkness across the water. Falk was conscious of a gasp escaping his lips before he realized the beam had fallen short of the boat.

"Military!" he hissed, struggling to keep the boat beyond reach of the light as it scavenged the black surface.

Falk slowly inched his way back to the boat's stern. He could beach her on the other side and take his chances on foot. He knew he had to stay on the river as long as possible. In the forest, guard dogs would pick up his trail and his sense of direction could go haywire. He could cover more miles on the river than stumbling through dark woods in deep snow.

Falk was jolted from his thoughts by another stream of light, almost white in its intensity, that shot out of the woods and illuminated the water not fifty yards ahead of him. It seemed wide and solid enough to drive a Mack truck across and lit everything in its path. He was moving fast, heading right into it....

Falk leaned on the oar. The craft resisted, refused to answer at first and then slued across the flow of the river. The maneuver wasn't enough to stop him. He still headed toward the slab of light but broadside. The sandbank came up fast just short of the beam. Falk jammed the oar deep into a ridge of foam and bent his full strength into edging her aground.

He jumped, landed in the sand and mud and clawed forward, pulling the bowline with him. Struggling against the weight of the boat, he felt the rope slide through his hands, burning skin as he battled with the craft. The rush of the river sucked the boat in a slow arc toward the light. Twisting the rough line around his hand, Falk dragged himself to a gnarled tree stump.

A quick hitch and the line caught on the roots. It strummed as it tightened, grew taut, quivered and held. He pulled the boat to the sandbank hand over hand until the nose nudged the sand. He pulled the boat until it was secure.

The brilliant beams of light didn't move but poured forth steadily across the width of the river—sentinels at a line of demarcation nothing could pass without suffering the scrutiny of their deadly gaze.

Falk heard the sounds of dogs baying in the distance, muffled by the thick fog covering the countryside. What had Sandburg meant? Fog didn't come on little cat's feet. It came on the mournful wail of the hounds from hell. When the fog lifted his pursuers would see him.

"I don't intend to stick around until daylight," Falk mumbled. He fell flat just as the wide beam of light slowly started moving toward him. It crept closer, lighting every swirling wave, every curvilinear secret of the river's course.

Falk, his face pressed into the freezing mud, could almost feel the light through the hair on the crown of his head. Any second now...

A man's voice called out. Someone had ordered the light extinguished. Falk didn't move.

Two shots crackled through the frost laden air. There was a flurry of voices. Falk kept his face buried in the wet earth as the shouts faded, absorbed in the fog. Next there was a single shot then a lengthening, uneasy silence. It was pitch black.

"What happened?" Falk whispered to himself. Before he could formulate an answer, there was an eruption of machine gun fire in the woods nearby. Again he dug his face into the mud. A second burst ripped through the night, beating a tattoo of fear in Falk's head. Soon the sounds faded deep into the woods.

Falk lifted his head a fraction then buried it fast as the eerie light of a flare ascended above him, sputtering like a skyrocket. It reached its zenith, burst into a pale, shimmering, penetrating glare as it floated over the fog shrouded countryside, trapping him in the periphery of its ghastly glow.

The *brrrrup-brrrrup* of a machine gun rattled in the distance as the flare faded, hissed into oblivion and blackness and silence returned.

Quick, Falk thought, get the boat loose. He fumbled furiously with the ice covered knots. There was another distant burst of gunfire and an outbreak of barking from the dogs he and Jan heard earlier. The bursts were all ahead of him, which meant that Jan might be safe after all. The shooters must think they're still after two men.

Crazy, Falk thought, but it's almost as if someone was creating a diversion. The rope came loose and Falk leapt into the boat and pushed off. He only had a moment of comparative calm before he realized the boat was taking on water.

Looking down, Falk saw water sloshing around his feet. "Must have been damaged when I dragged it onto the sand bank," he muttered. He cupped his hands and tried to bale but it was no use. The water was coming in too fast. Despite his struggles to make the opposite shore, the boat became sluggish and settled deeper into the river with each passing second.

Falk peered into the darkness and wondered if he would make it to the opposite side before the boat sank. Suddenly the searchlight jabbed through the inky blackness. Falk raised his arms to cover his eyes. This time the light was full in his face.

The first shot came. Falk spun sideways too fast and went over the side, tipping the boat and plunging into what seemed like fathomless leagues of ice water. As his descent continued, he heard three muffled shots. It seemed as if Falk's lungs would burst as he swam for his life deep under the surface. He wasn't the swimmer Jan was. He knew he must climb for air.

Chapter 42

Three more strokes and Falk's head broke the surface. He was almost to the opposite riverbank, surfacing outside the range of light.

The searchlight played on the partially submerged boat as the wreckage swirled into a clump of overhanging branches and came to a rest on its side, water breaking across the remains. They'll be on it like a pack of wolves, Falk thought.

His feet touched the stony bottom of the river as its depth lessened. Grasping for tufts of grass, he clawed his way up the frozen riverbank, tree branches scraping his face. His clothes didn't freeze as the air hit them so he knew it wasn't as cold as it felt. He had to put miles between himself and the military...fast.

He rolled onto the flat ground and slithered like a snake into the underbrush. What had Jan said—easy to get lost in the woods, lose your sense of direction? He decided to follow the downstream flow of the river as long as possible.

Stiffly he got to his feet and stumbled along a narrow dirt path, using the thick brush and trees for concealment. He had to keep moving to keep his circulation intact. He knew hypothermia could kill him as surely as a bullet in the back.

He heard faint shouts from the opposite bank. They had been searching for two men. Soon they'd know that both had eluded them.

He thought of Jan swimming for his life and the young man on the rooftop gunned down by the helicopter. He hoped fervently that Jan had made it to safety. He'd probably never know.

In his flight to freedom that was still far from won, Falk was responsible for the fates of these two and others whose fates happened to cross his own. There also was the possibility that Koski and Emma were still suffering captivity in Spilberg.

He clamped his teeth down hard on his lip and stumbled into the blackness. Like a hunted animal his ears strained at every sound. His eyes tried to penetrate the darkness.

Less than a mile from where he crawled out of the river, a flashlight beam looked him squarely in the face. He had heard nothing, had no warning. His heart pounded and his mouth went dry. Motionless, he waited for the bullet he was certain would tear into him. A strong masculine arm went around his neck, cutting off his air and a pistol barrel pressed into his ear.

"Don't move, Dr. Falk." The voice behind the flashlight was a woman's, soft, husky and authoritative. The arm eased just enough for him to breathe. The beam dipped, ran down his body and went out, leaving two amorphous red disks floating before his eyes.

When the limb around his neck loosened, he could breathe easier but was unable to speak for several seconds. His mind raced with questions. How did they know his name?

"Who are you?"

The woman moved closer and he saw her face. Pressing a finger to her lips, she whispered, "Follow me."

She turned and walked ahead, carefully picking her way between the trees. Falk followed, rubbing his neck, the man close at his side. After what seemed an eternity the man gripped his arm and pulled him close against a tree. The woman, silent as a cat, continued toward a small cabin. Falk and the man remained in the deep shadows and waited. When they heard two high-pitched whistles like the sound of a nightingale, the man pushed Falk forward toward a stone and log structure with two small windows and a chimney.

In the distance Falk heard water rushing and deduced that, in daylight, the cabin commanded a view of the river.

The door opened and the woman waved them forward. Inside smelled damp and musty. The woman covered the windows with heavy canvas before scratching a match. The acrid smell was sharp as she touched the flame to the wick of an old-style oil lamp. It flared to light and suffused through the room, affording Falk his first full look at his captors.

The woman was young. Falk guessed mid-thirties and of medium height. Errant strands of blonde hair straggled down under the edge of her black woolen cap. She offered her hand and although her wrist and hand were slender, her grip was firm.

"My name is Maria," she said in English. "He is Heinz."

Heinz nodded. He appeared to be a contradiction, resembling rough, peasant stock with the build and ability to kill but with eyes and a manner that reflected a polished modernity.

Falk started to ask more questions but Maria shook her head. "That's all you need to know about us for now." She left the room and returned almost immediately with a large towel and clothes that looked exactly Falk's size.

"Change those wet clothes. We can't light a fire. Smoke would give away our location." She handed him the towel. "Dry with this." As she left the room she added, "Hurry."

Falk removed his shirt and quickly rubbed his body with the

185

rough towel. Heinz passed him a flannel shirt and in a few minutes he was dressed in a thick woolen turtleneck over the flannel shirt, ski pants and boots and a hooded windbreaker jacket.

Maria returned. "Our information was that you can ski. I hope that's correct."

"Yes." He turned to Heinz then back to Maria. "How did you know about me...clothing size, boots... everything?"

Maria was carrying a tin tray with two mugs that she held up to him. "It's our business to know. Drink this. It'll warm you." She handed the other mug to Heinz.

Holding the mug in both hands, Falk took a deep swig. It was like taking in liquid fire. The brew flowed down his throat and hit his stomach like hot mercury, raw country brandy. The warmth it generated thawed Falk's frozen body.

Heinz laughed and drank his in one long gulp.

Falk finished his and handed the mug to Maria. "Thanks. Now will you tell me who you are?"

Maria and Heinz exchanged a quick glance. "We're smugglers," she said.

"What do you smuggle?"

"People," Maria replied softly.

"You're going to smuggle me across the border?"

"No," Maria replied. "We're going to show you how to get yourself across. You're too hot. We can't risk ruining a network that has taken years to build." She nodded toward two wooden chairs and she and Falk sat down.

"You're going back to Austria with help from the Irgun," Heinz said, standing beside Maria. "Does the name Rosie Wimmer mean anything to you?"

"I met her once, briefly. As a matter of fact..." He started to say that Rosie was with that son of a bitch, Steele, but Maria interrupted him.

"She is one of our contacts in Vienna. That's all we can tell you. We wouldn't have been called in had you not decided to make a run for it at the church."

"What do you mean?" Falk asked.

"You ruined plan 'A' to get you back to Vienna when you escaped from Saint James. One of our men was planted in Colonel Zhilin's group. You would have been freed once you entered Austria."

"Who was your man?"

"His name is Horst."

Falk was dumbfounded. "That bastard tried to kill me...was responsible for the death of a young man..."

"Doctor," Heinz said gruffly, "every day there are operatives out there who die for the sake of this 'Underground Railroad' of ours. Horst couldn't do anything that would reveal himself to Zhilin's men. Let's not waste time debating moral issues."

Maria spoke softly. "You're very lucky we found you at the river. Our subterfuge threw them off, caused them to look in other directions."

"The shots... I sensed they were a diversion."

"A distraction by a well-trained guerrilla force."

She became very solemn and pointed admonishingly at Falk. "Listen very carefully to what we tell you. This time, if you decide to improvise, your life will be cut short."

The Judas List

Chapter 43

When Maria finished detailing plan "B," Falk wished he hadn't made a run for it in Brno. What he had to undertake seemed almost impossible.

"You're certain there's no other way?" he asked.

Maria shook her head. "Repeat what I told you. We must be sure you don't forget anything."

Falk inhaled deeply. "I'm to be taken from here and pointed in the direction of Austria. I'll be given a pair of skis and a wish for good luck in finding a rather vague contact who, hopefully, will be waiting for me among some equally nebulous trees just inside Austria. The only known obstacles I must avoid are mines, booby-traps, guard dogs and Czech military personnel."

He shrugged. "Other than that it's a piece of cake."

Heinz gave him a contemptuous look and Maria said coolly, "We didn't say it would be easy."

Falk reddened at the small sound of her voice. He regretted his flippancy. These people were risking their lives for him. Except for his brief stint with Jan, this was the first time since being in this godforsaken country that he felt genuine warmth from other human beings.

"Sorry," he said sincerely.

"You forgot to mention the package," Heinz told him dogmatically.

"Oh, yes, the package…to be given to my contact the minute we meet."

"Our man will be watching for you as you near the border." Maria's voice was gentle. "We must go."

Heinz turned down the lamp until its flame died. Falk watched the smoke curl to the ceiling. The smell of the extinguished wick triggered a memory of his childhood camping trips.

Maria removed the canvas from the windows and the gray winter dawn filtered in. She left the room and returned with a pair of skis. "If you couldn't ski, you would have no chance at all." She pushed them toward him. "They are waxed and ready to go."

Heinz eased the front door open and cold air rushed in, filling the cabin. Falk zipped up his jacket and looked at Maria.

"The package?"

"I'll give it to you when we get into the hills."

Together the trio moved slowly through the thick snow, Maria leading, alert as a doe. They traveled in silence for close to a mile. Then the sound of the river faded as they climbed higher toward the crest where the snow sprayed back in a mare's tail, tossed by the wind against the first light of the morning sky.

They halted at the top of a steep incline.

"Doctor," Heinz said, "be careful when you get down the mountain near the border. That is where the guard dogs will be— Hungarian Komondors that can tear a man apart in seconds."

Falk shuddered and slid his boots into the bindings.

"Open your jacket," Maria ordered. She slipped an oilskin pouch inside. "Remember, give that to your contact the *second* you meet him." She turned to Heinz and held out her hand to receive an automatic fitted with a suppressor.

"Take this." Falk tucked it into a side pocket of his jacket and pulled the zipper.

"Thanks," Falk muttered. He knew they wouldn't meet again.

Heinz patted his shoulder. "Hurry. There's no time to lose."

"Goodbye," Maria said and turned and went back down the slope.

Heinz pointed across the mountains. "It's a hard run. Don't stop if you can help it. See the small woods, there to the right..." Falk made out a small green patch in the distance. He nodded. "That's about five kilometers. Beyond is a meadow, deep in snow. Take care. There's a steep drop once you pass over it. Down the slope, past the bottom of the black scar that points like an arrow in the direction you must go."

"I see it."

"When you've passed the scar, you'll be very close to a military fortification and you'll enter a small forest. Go slowly, keep moving left. Do not enter the deep woods, understand?"

Falk nodded, trying to take in everything. Heinz continued. "It should take you eight to ten minutes to edge the woods then you'll come to a narrow stream. You can cross on foot. It should be knee deep this time of year.

"Bury the skis before you cross. The longer it takes them to learn how you got away, the better for all of us. Our man will see you long before you see him." Heinz paused and stuck out his hard, callused hand. Falk grasped it.

Without another word, Heinz was gone. Falk felt totally and utterly alone. He gripped the poles and slid his skis back and forth. He was going to get back no matter what it took. He would find Koski and Emma, too. Nobody was going to fuck with his life again.

He jammed the poles deep into the snow and leaned forward. The ground fell away beneath his skis and soon he was moving at top speed in a hiss of snow, the soft moan of the wind singing past his ears.

Shifting his weight, he made a *Stem Christiana* turn across the slope as a wintry sun edged over the tips of the jagged mountains. He viewed this as the beginning of the last leg of his journey home.

Chapter 44

A limo turned onto Dorotheegasse Street and stopped in front of the Dorotheum. Rod Eiker got out and looked up at the tall, imposing building housing the famous auction rooms.

Over the years, priceless objects had passed through these rooms. How was it possible, he wondered, for Goering to hide the fruits of his pillage of Europe in or under the huge stone structure without them being discovered? Perhaps the next few days would tell.

"Wait for us," Harold Mifflin said and handed the driver a piece of paper. "Contact this number if we're not back in half an hour."

Glancing back along the street, Eiker saw a dark sedan in the shadows near the Capuchin Church and figured it was back up, if needed. He also noticed a small bistro in the same block with the name "Miljoo." The lights were on and faint sounds of music drifted toward them.

Mifflin caught his eye. "I have two men in there, too."

Together they walked to a side entrance of the Dorotheum that led through an arch into a small courtyard. A cold wind whirled in the corners, scuttling bits of paper over the cobblestones. Across the yard, a dim light shone over a doorway partially hidden behind a stack of packing cases. The door opened as they approached. Before entering, they were searched and their weapons taken.

"Hell," Mifflin protested, "this is like flying El Al!"

Dr. Yigael Herschel, a tall, gaunt man with a heavy gray beard and a slight paunch, stood at a wooden table, flipping pages of a large city map of Vienna. His expression was straight forward as if somewhere in his youth he had seen a profound truth and had worked all his life to illuminate it for others. He looked up as they entered and walked toward them.

"Sorry for the formalities. Routine. You understand. Your weapons will be returned to you when you leave." He stared at Eiker for a long moment then adjusted his glasses. "Mr. Eiker! This is a surprise. I never expected to see you again."

"Good to see you, General." They shook hands as Mifflin stood aside. "General Herschel, allow me to introduce Harold Mifflin."

Mifflin offered his hand but was silent.

"As you know, Harold," Eiker continued, "General Herschel's background includes being the former chief of the Israeli Defense Forces."

"Indeed I do. The general designed his plan of attack on years of research of the *Old Testament* campaigns and firsthand archaeological knowledge during the Arab-Israeli Six-Day War. He led his troops down long-forgotten routes to the east bank of the Suez Canal and victory."

"I'm flattered, Mr. Mifflin." Herschel turned to Eiker. "And this soldier of fortune has done freelance work for Israel on several occasions. Mr. Eiker contributed some very useful tactics to our military." Herschel waved them to chairs. "Now gentlemen, down to business." He seated himself.

"What began as a secret attempt to locate hidden war loot has turned out to be more than a treasure hunt between numerous hunters."

He tugged thoughtfully at his beard before continuing. "Due to my many years as an archaeologist, my government has asked me to participate. We're bringing in Dr. Falk from the Czech Republic. He'll be here shortly. I also have been informed that Brasinov still believes Falk is the man who will get them to the loot first."

"Brasinov knows the Czechs kidnapped him," Mifflin said. "How do we explain his escape and return to Vienna? After all, mild-mannered archaeologists aren't the sort of people who can escape single-handedly from Czech Military Intelligence. And what did you mean when you said the war loot had turned out to be more than a treasure hunt?"

Herschel smiled thinly. "For now let me say there may be more information to be found other than Goering's gold. Brasinov will learn that the Czech Republic has taken an interest in the search, faked Falk's escape and that the American team from the Smithsonian has returned to Washington."

Mifflin grunted. "Disinformation."

"Perhaps," Herschel said. "I think you'll agree it is to our mutual advantage to pool our resources."

Mifflin was thoughtful for a moment as if to disagree but changed his mind. "You're suggesting a combined operation, Doctor?"

"Yes. We will do far better working together."

Eiker shifted in his chair. "Especially since so many others are getting into the game."

"Thank you, Eiker. I'd hoped you'd feel that way."

Mifflin squirmed and eased his bulk from his chair. "I'll go along with you, but it's against my better judgment."

Eiker understood Mifflin's natural reluctance. He, too, had instincts that whispered best when unencumbered by the views of others. Nevertheless, they had to go along with Herschel. Moreover, he was sure Mifflin was as impressed as he was by the fact that Herschel had found Falk.

Herschel offered his hand. "Thank you gentlemen. I'll see that you are notified as soon as Dr. Falk is in the city. We'll meet in a different location, of course."

Mifflin, who intrinsically mistrusted all who didn't have Cerberus as their base, smiled enigmatically and echoed, "Of course."

Less than five miles from the Dorotheum, on the third floor of Kanglerkrank-Zimmerstadt, in a nearly bare, dingy office, John Steele sat in a chair, leather straps pulled tight across his chest, arms and thighs. A guard was positioned on either side of the chair and Pasha sat on a stool facing him. The Arab's moist, clawlike hands held a leather shaving strop eighteen inches long and twice as wide as a normal shoelace.

Pasha, interrogator par excellence, ran his practiced eye over Steele. He analyzed his findings noting the stubborn chin— determined, even under sedation—and the hardened body that would take time to kill.

Pasha reached out and grasped Steele's jaw in a vise-tight grip. He waited until Steele's eyelids fluttered in pain then released him. Steele's legs jerked convulsively as the drug the men from the elevator administered still gripped him. Saliva ran from his mouth and dripped from his chin. A series of animalistic sounds began deep in his throat then died.

"My name…is…" he attempted but couldn't finish.

Pasha allowed an evil grin to split his parchment-like face, exposing ochre teeth to which threads of saliva clung. Leaning forward, he slowly slid the leather strop across Steele's face. "We want you to answer some questions…" Moving back, he raised his hand and brought the leather down across Steele's face with all the force he could muster.

Blood from the new wound oozed to the surface and streaked down Steele's cheek. "You are stupid, Steele. You were fooled by Switzer. You allowed Falk to escape and you were careless enough to be seen with a key. We want to know what the key is for and where you hid it."

Steele heard him, knew what he was saying but he couldn't function or articulate his thoughts. The pain in his face was excruciating. The humming in his head made him dizzy. He groaned and fell forward, the straps across his chest preventing him from sinking to the floor.

"Steele," Pasha said, "I'll make you talk. I've never failed. Use your brain…or die slowly."

Steele made a weak attempt to reply.

Pasha rose from the stool. "I'll wait one hour. By then the effects of the injection will have worn off. Then you'll talk."

The Judas List

Chapter 45

The crack of a rifle shot echoed and re-echoed in the utter, snow blanketed silence of the mountains. Falk heard the crackle of the bullet forcing its way through the frosty air as it passed inches above his head. A sniper.

He crouched low, his buttocks touching the top of the skis as they flicked and vibrated over the snow. Leaning forward, he rounded his shoulders until he was a compact mass, except for the poles tucked under his armpits, extending beyond his body like the wings of a diving hawk. He didn't dare look back. Instead he kept his attention focused on the tips of the skis and the oncoming snowscape, every fiber of his body tuned to survival.

Shifting his weight, he flashed past a half-hidden tree stump. No tourist run. This was raw, wild country and somewhere there was a hidden sniper intent on seeing he never made it to the bottom of the mountain. He dug his shoulders low, letting his poles skim the surface of the powdery snow as he navigated a sudden rise. He left the ground, flew through the air for twenty feet and landed with a thump, feet together. Had he outrun the sniper…gone out of range?

The second shot gave the answer as it crackled past, sending a spurt of snow skyward less than a foot away. Falk risked a quick glance over his shoulder as he leaned away from the slope and made a fast turn across the side of the mountain.

He only saw the almost suffocating vista of powder reflecting the early morning light. Ahead was a thin grove of trees—scrubby, wind twisted pines he could use for cover. He jammed his poles deep and headed for them as if they were the finish line at the Olympics.

The sound of the skis changed to a warning rattle that indicated he was on a sheet of ice. He shifted and slid into a skidding arc toward the trees. A branch flashed overhead as he swept into the dark shadows where the snow was thicker with less crust.

He felt the skis sink deeper but they were moving well, waxed perfectly to respond to each maneuver. He made it through the scrub pines and again was on the open mountainside. The landmarks Heinz had mentioned were straight ahead. He slowed and ventured a glance back toward the trees.

Then he saw him. A blur against the dark trees, a flash, a momentary glimpse that came and went in a second. Whoever it was was dressed to kill. White camouflage suit that let him blend like a mountain goat into the snow.

Suddenly a piece of Falk's jacket parted from his shoulder. It puffed, split and he felt the tug as the bullet went through the cloth and beyond. The next shot would be the last—the fucker had his range.

Falk twisted, jabbed the poles deep and slammed down the steep slope in front of him. Then he gasped! The ground fell away beneath him… For a split second he thought he had jumped off a cliff to his death. The wind grabbed and rushed at his body as he descended through seemingly endless space. Sky and earth floated before his eyes as he balanced, arms outstretched, leaning forward into the long, long fall. He glimpsed the snowbound earth, distant trees at the border. He became suspended between fact and hope.

As he landed, snow spun in a flurry around him and he gasped for air. His skis rattled, one pole ripped from his left hand and his knuckles gouged into the snow. He'd made the greatest jump of his life and no one was there to see it.

Had he outrun the ghost in the white suit? In the distance—too far distant to be his sniper—the faint discharge of a rifle sounded. The sound spurred him to renewed action. He headed toward the row of trees Heinz had indicated. He saw the scar of rocks and followed around the edge as instructed. Alert, he eased forward slowly, skirting the trees.

The world around him was soft, silent and white until a snarling, slavering canine demon broke from the trees and lunged at him. He only had enough time to see a gaping mouth of teeth, an expanse of shaggy shoulders and eyes blazing with frenzy. The fucking thing never even barked. Instinctively, Falk leaned into a turn but the brute never reached him. It was stopped in mid jump by a thin steel cable attached to its collar. The dog jerked in the air and dropped, then feverishly renewed his mute act of frustration. Falk realized that the cable was attached to an overhead haul line running through the trees and allowed the beast restricted lateral movement.

In seconds two similar dogs joined in the snarling, leaping performance.

Falk stemmed to a stop near a clump of berry bushes a safe distance from the dogs. They hadn't barked either. Then it came to him. The animals had been debarked for security reasons so not to bark at rabbits or other small creatures in the woods.

He reasoned that the movement of the lines would alert the guards, wherever they were. Guard towers probably were spaced throughout the woods along the border, each sector with its own early-warning dog system.

Something made Falk look down. Thank God he stopped when he did. Ten more feet and he would have tripped and been impaled on a row of wooden spikes buried in the frozen earth and partly hidden from sight by bracken and snow.

It would only be a matter of time before the border guards, alerted by the haul line, zeroed in on him. He edged forward cautiously, keeping out of the deep woods as advised and skirting the dogs, who still strained at the line and snarled for a piece of him.

The snow drifted like sand in the wind from the top of the ridge he was heading for. Another rifle shot rang out in the distance and the sound bounced across the mountains. The thought that perhaps he wasn't the only one trying for an early morning crossing heartened him. Topping the rise, he saw the stream and beyond it the road... and Austria. He could see freedom.

Three more rifle shots echoed off the mountain. They were farther away now. He inched forward, every nerve taut as a bowstring, breathing in shallow gasps as if taking a real breath would give away his location.

The next dog that came at him from the side was merely a blur in his peripheral vision. He spun in time to see it leap, eyes blazing, jaw nearly unhinged with ferocity. In the split second allowed him, he also noticed the dog didn't have a restraining collar and was free to rip him apart.

Dropping to one knee, he turned the tip of his grounded ski pole up like a lance. The hot canine breath was on his face as he felt the point of the pole crunch into the furred body at the base of its throat. The jar of its weight shuddered down the pole as the dog impaled itself with a sickening shattering of bone and sinew.

For a second, Falk looked into the eyes that glared at a freakish angle. The lips pulled back, revealing long, yellowed fangs. Then the full weight slumped on the ski pole and hung like a piece of meat.

Falk began to tremble like a man with the shakes. He struggled desperately to remove the bloody shaft that finally came free. He turned from the smell of warm blood in time to see two more unrestrained dogs bounding toward him, chest deep in snow. He realized these, and their fallen comrade, were the Komondors Heinz had warned him about. There was little chance of fighting off two of them. He started forward but knew it was too late to outrun them.

The Judas List

Chapter 46

Falk suddenly remembered the automatic. It had a suppressor and wouldn't give away his position. For a long, terrifying second he fumbled with the zipper. Finally it came open. He grasped the gun and released the safety. His hand shook as he aimed at the nearest dog and squeezed the trigger. The gun jerked with a *phutt* sound and the dog stopped in its tracks. The shot was good—directly into the brain. Dead.

The second Komondor didn't react fast enough. Falk fired again, hitting the poor beast in the side—a "gut shot" that crippled it in a flurry of snow and blood. Stricken, it made an attempt to regain its feet but its hindquarters wouldn't function, and it slithered along, etching a deep, scarlet trail in the snow. He wasn't proud of what he had to do. Since he was a kid, he had owned dogs, cared for them and loved them. His throat constricted as he moved closer to the animal. He placed the automatic behind its ear and fired then turned quickly and jammed the weapon into his pocket. Despite the cold, sweat oozed from his palms and forehead.

He took off, never stopping until he reached the stream and leaned against a slender birch, panting. Releasing the bindings, he kicked free and, working fast, stuffed the skis and remaining pole under the snow near overhanging bracken at the base of a tree. Crouching at the edge of the stream, he knew he didn't have any cover until he reached the other side, about two hundred yards away.

He stepped into the icy water and was soon up to his knees. He removed the automatic and checked the clip. Three rounds remained.

A movement on the far bank caught his eye. A man in a hooded parka stepped from behind a snow-covered boulder with a rifle aimed directly at Falk.

Falk stood motionless. After everything he'd been through and this close to Austria, he was going to die now with his boots on. The knuckles on his hand that gripped the automatic were white.

"Doctor Falk?" the man asked.

"Yeah, I'm Falk."

The hooded man lowered his rifle. "You look like a scarecrow, Doctor."

Falk's shoulders sagged with relief. Maria said there would be someone waiting.

"Come across, hurry," the man said. "I thought the dogs had you for sure."

Falk ran, sloshing, slipping, stumbling the last few yards to shore, nearly falling into the arms of the squat, broad-shouldered man with slightly bowed legs. Slinging the rifle onto his shoulder by its leather strap, the man stuck out a callused hand and his eyes actually twinkled.

"Welcome back to Austria."

Falk shook his hand and looked back at the sweep of dark trees on the other side and behind them the mountain. It was as if it was all a dream, one he would reconstruct in sleepless nights the rest of his life.

"Come," his companion said. He pointed to a car a few meters ahead on the road and they started toward it. He removed a stopwatch from his pocket and snapped a switch on its side. "You made good time, Herr Doctor. The package Maria gave you, may I have it?"

Falk opened his jacket and handed it to him.

"Good." He pulled away the oilskin covering and exposed a small plastic box the size of a pager. Three buttons protruded from one side. One by one he depressed them. "Ach, now it's safe, deactivated."

Falk's puzzled expression was too obvious to ignore.

"Sorry, Doctor. In our business we have to be very careful. It was a time bomb set to go off one hour from the time it was given to you... would have been triggered by a radio signal had you been apprehended..."

"Hold it!" Falk interrupted, "You saying I was programmed to self-destruct?"

"Only if you were captured or I saw that you had no chance of getting across. It would have been my job to..."

Falk didn't hear more. His adrenaline triggered a "fight or flight" reaction but he was through with "flight." He hauled off and landed a blow on the man's substantial jaw.

The poor fellow staggered back, more surprised than hurt. When he regained his balance, he studied Falk for a long minute, then burst into laughter. He rubbed his jaw and slapped Falk heartily on the back. "You know, I'd probably have done the same thing myself."

Falk walked toward the car. "One hour. How long did it take me?"

"Fifty-three minutes." He opened the passenger door for Falk. "Get in, relax."

Falk slumped into the seat; seven minutes. He had been that close to being splattered all over the mountain.

They covered a couple of miles in silence before the man said, "There's a flask of brandy in the glove compartment."

Falk opened the compartment. There was a flask of brandy there all right and it was sitting on top of the *Book of Hours*. Without taking his eyes from the book, Falk removed the brandy, unscrewed the top and took a long, slow, needed swallow then passed the container. His companion tipped it to the tune of three loud gulps and handed it back.

"It's okay. Take it out, leaf through it if you like. I understand you were interrupted the last time you were reading it."

Falk removed the missal and laid it on his lap. He turned to the driver. "What's your name?"

"Paul. Like St. Paul." He smiled as if pleased with the analogy. "We'll be in Vienna soon."

The heater was on high, the car warm. That and the brandy made Falk feel drowsy yet he couldn't relax. He wondered about Koski and Emma. God, he hoped they were safe. One thing he knew. Treasure be dammed, his number one priority when he got to Vienna was to locate the women. Falk unlaced his boots, kicked them off and flipped open the missal. What was it about this book? What exactly was its secret?

Chapter 47

Nikolai Youmatoff almost made it down the eastern slope of Caribou Peak before the storm broke. The sky that had been gray and loaded for days seemed to descend in millions of white, minuscule pieces. What began looking like sieved sugar on the ground became eighteen inches of snow that covered southeastern Canada.

Youmatoff dug in. He could do little else. Two days later he dug out, having taken shelter in the entrance to a cave. From the depths of his haven came the sound of slow, unlabored, bearlike breathing and protracted snores. He guessed he was eight hours out of Ottawa.

He took stock of his rations. One steak remaining in a jar of rolled venison steaks that Ann had preserved near the end of the season last year. One can of yellow eyes, also homemade and preserved. A good size dab of sweet butter. Some ketchup and one can of condensed milk. This would be his last meal. He quickly corrected his thoughts— his last meal in the Canadian wilderness.

He moved on a quarter mile southeast, making sure he wasn't downwind of the bear cave, and settled in a sheltered area. He cubed the steak with his knife, putting half in the bottom of his pannikin. Atop that he layered half the can of beans and a generous dotting of ketchup then repeated all, ending with his last bit of butter. He gathered some twigs that had drifted into a pile under a large boulder and made a fire.

While his concoction heated, he sat on his bedroll and marveled at the majesty of the snowscape in the thin winter sun. "Lovely," Ann would have said. Tree shadows of elderberry hue lay like lace on the surface of the pristine snow. They were, Youmatoff thought, as real as the still, sharply etched outlines they represented and as lovely. He found himself crying. A tear fell on the weathered, hide-like skin of his hand. He would move on the minute he finished his meal. Once he reached the main highway, he'd hitch a ride to Ottawa then catch a bus to the Soviet Embassy. He wondered if he would have to tell them everything: about that night in the vault-like room, about Goering, the book he filched with the blueprint in it and the wax impression of the damnable key. Those things seemed important when he took them. Hadn't Goering himself announced that the book was "the secret to our future?" In the end they all had become meaningless to Youmatoff.

After that night he was captured and returned to prison. Only the compassion of Lego Moyzisch had saved him. The Allies sent him here to Canada, allowed him to begin a new life. For the first time in years, Youmatoff wondered about the key. When he originally arrived in Canada he had a key made from the impression—an odd key in a shape he never saw before. He wrapped the book in brown paper to protect its extraordinary cover and it served as his prayer book for years.

He did the right thing, he reasoned, sending those things to Lego. Perhaps the blueprint to the Dorotheum, which Goering had declared "Uberholt," would help Lego find the treasures and he'd become rich. Youmatoff didn't want to become rich. He simply wanted to go home to Russia to die in his own land.

When he ate the beans they were perfectly mealy and swam in a thick, brown, buttery juice that made the venison more tender. These were Youmatoff's last connection to Ann and, hungry as he was, he could barely down the last mouthful.

In his dream of dreams, Youmatoff was with Ann and they had nothing to do with material treasures. He realized that over the years he became immune to thoughts of his homeland that now atrophied. He broke camp and started out with renewed vigor.

The Judas List

Chapter 48

Ahead, Koski saw buildings aglow with neon lights. Herman stopped and slid down his window. A draft of icy air swirled into the car. Beside him, Koski made an attempt at nonchalance as if crossing through security after escaping from a castle was an everyday affair.

A woman glanced at Herman's papers. "Head of security saw your car, Herr Lansfeldt. He asked me to convey his good wishes for another profitable trip..." She scribbled her signature on the documents. "He looks forward to seeing you personally on your next visit."

Herman nodded amiably.

Koski was certain she heard Emma's heart pounding above her own as the woman said, "There's been a prison break in Brno. We don't know who or how many have escaped. We're getting details from Colonel Zhilin's office at this moment."

"Sounds like you'll have a busy night," Herman remarked as he rolled the window up. "See you in a few days. Good night."

Koski slowly lowered her head against Herman's shoulder and his foot eased up off the brake pedal.

The woman stood back from the car as the window slid shut. Herman inched toward the gates beyond the neon glare and into the inky blackness of emancipation. Only when they were racing down the broad, smooth highway to Vienna did Koski sigh with relief.

"Herman, you were superb. I'm impressed."

"Ach, it was nothing." Obviously pleased with her compliment, he added, "I always see to it that the head man back there has the latest in home computers." She nodded her understanding. "When will we get to Vienna?"

"A little after daybreak. We can spend the entire day together my Liebchen."

Koski eased her head back against the headrest. She had succeeded in getting Emma and herself out of the Czech Republic. Certainly that was a victory. In the war she was fighting, however, the victory seemed more like an evacuation.

Churchill had said it after Dunkirk: "Wars are not won by evacuations." The real battle was the one waged wherever Falk fought for his freedom, one inexorably tied to her own. She knew she would go back willingly if it became necessary.

Rosie Wimmer found herself swept up and taken prisoner despite her knowledge of espionage. Such happenings do occur. John Steele, still partially drugged and strapped to a chair in the office where Pasha had taken him, had no answer to the incessant question.

"We have the key, Steele. Tell me what does it open? It's only a matter of time before we figure out its purpose and we don't have any time to waste." He brought the leather strop down across Steele's face again, lacerating the corner of his left eye.

"Don't be a fool, Steele."

"But it's true. I don't know."

"You go to the trouble to hide the key in a secret drawer, a key to... you don't know what?" He snorted. "You can do better than that. Evidently you don't put much faith in my powers of persuasion."

Steele glared at him and Pasha leaned in closer. "Brasinov and I have broken many men."

"Yea, like Hitler's Gestapo once did."

"Then you understand my potential. Now tell me about the key and you'll go free."

"Bullshit."

Pasha slid the leather strap slowly across Steele's bloody, swollen lips and turned and spat out a stream of Farsi to the guards. Within minutes the door opened and Rosie Wimmer was dragged into the room.

Steele couldn't believe his eyes. Rosie was alive. She didn't die in the car explosion.

The guards pulled her across the room and stopped in front of him. She struggled between them but it was evident that she, too, had felt the sting of Pasha's strop.

"We have this Interpol agent," Pasha said, smiling malevolently. "We will kill her first then you if you refuse to give us the information we need."

Steele was silent, his eyes fixed on the floor. He remembered Emma telling him that Rosie was Irgun, using Interpol as her cover.

Rosie suddenly lashed out with her foot and caught Steele across the kneecap. "Tell him about the key, you asshole!" She turned to Pasha. "I don't know anything about a key. If you think I'd protect this bastard you have another thing coming."

"Get that fucking traitor out of here," Steele roared. "And don't expect me to save her life. As far as I'm concerned, you can kill her."

Pasha put his hand to his cheek dramatically. "How touching. A lover's quarrel."

Steele groaned and slumped against his bindings. His head hurt.

He was bleeding and sick and his knee stung painfully. His resistance hit bottom. "Look, all I know about the key is that I was asked to hold it for safekeeping."

Pasha leaned closer. "By whom?"

"It was years ago. A man named Lego Moyzisch. He must be dead by now."

"Then he won't need the key. What did he say it was for?"

"I told you. I saw the man on the stairs in a hotel after we had met for a reunion in 1975. He handed me the key and asked me to keep it safe for him. When I asked what it was for, he shrugged and hurried away."

"That won't do, Steele."

"It's the absolute truth."

"He's a liar!" Rosie shrieked. She started to lunge forward but the guards restrained her. "He never did anything in his life unless there was something in it for him. That key must mean something and he knows what."

Pasha grinned. "My sentiments exactly." He motioned the guards to take Rosie from the room and she kicked and screamed all the way out.

Pasha turned back to Steele. "What makes you think this Moyzisch is dead?"

"Because he knew too much, probably knew what the key was for and wouldn't tell..." He stopped, aware that he had given the wrong answer.

"And where does that leave you in the order of things?"

Steele simply let his throbbing head fall forward and remained silent.

Chapter 49

In a noisy café on the Recht Wienzel, near the open-air vegetable market, Yakov of Czech Military Intelligence waited, seated at a marble topped table.

The café bustled with workers, stall owners and truck drivers. A thick haze of cigarette smoke filled the room and a constant chatter and clashing of dishes mixed with the smell of fried food and coffee. Yakov glanced at the wall clock. It was almost 6 a.m. He had arrived in Vienna three hours earlier, having thrown every available man into the search for Falk and Jan Michaelavitch. Sipping thick, sweet coffee, he looked around the room. Colonel Zhilin had told him that a local woman, an informant, would contact him.

When the door opened, a blast of cold air preceded a well-dressed woman. Yakov puffed a thin cigar and cursed inwardly. If she was the contact, it was a bad choice. Too many heads turned at the wild mass of red hair and the full, voluptuous figure.

Lisa Winkler scanned the room then went to Yakov's table and sat down. She lit a cigarette. "Yakov?"

He sipped his coffee. "If you prove to be other than the person I'm expecting, I'll consider this an attempt to blow my cover and I'll kill you."

Lisa took a long drag on her cigarette, reached across the table and dropped it into Yakov's coffee cup. "Look, I didn't ask for this job. Colonel Zhilin's people phoned me. I was assured I'd be well paid for my information."

"Were you followed?"

She was indignant at such a question. "I'm a professional, Yakov."

He was trying to make a point. "You took notes when you spoke to Zhilin's people?"

"I always take notes. It's my business."

"You wrote down this address?" Yakov's eyes narrowed.

Lisa nodded. "Date and time, nothing else."

"You have these notes?"

"Yes."

Yakov's fingers beckoned slowly. "Give them to me."

She thrust her hand into her raincoat pocket, pulled out a crumpled piece of paper and slid it across the table.

"Do you want me to eat it?"

Yakov took the note and placed it in the inside pocket of his coat. "First give me the information then we talk price."

"I know why the American, Falk, is in Vienna. I know he made a successful escape from your country. I can tell you where to find him, who his control is and what's going to happen when he finds what he's looking for." She relaxed against the back of the chair. "Does that interest you, Yakov?"

Yakov spoke softly "And the price for this information?"

Lisa's voice was almost a whisper. "One million American dollars in a Swiss bank of my choice."

"That will take time."

Lisa nodded. She eyed the room and wondered how many of Yakov's stooges were present.

Yakov's demeanor changed. "You also know where a man named Lego Moyzisch is hiding."

Lisa lowered her gaze and tapped on the table. "I don't understand…"

"Of course you do. You're a busybody who knows who, what, why, when and where about everybody who's anyone in Europe. You will leave this table, go to your car and drive to the place where Moyzisch is hiding. My men will follow. Once you're there, I'll be informed and will meet you. Perhaps with Moyzisch thrown in we'll have a deal." Lisa remained tight-lipped and silent.

"Go," he said levelly. "Do as I told you."

She scraped back her chair and left without looking back, cursing inwardly that she could do nothing to warn her Interpol cover. Walking to her car, she stopped to retrieve her key remote from her purse.

Kutna, disguised as a shabby merchant, came down the street pushing a handcart piled high with sacks of potatoes. He glanced at rooftops on his right and felt assured knowing that three of his best men were stationed there.

He had gone less than three feet when the roar of a high-powered engine shattered the quiet of the frosty morning and a black BMW careened down the narrow street.

Lisa was about to open her car door. She looked back as Kutna raised an arm to wave a warning. The car swerved from side to side across the narrow cobbled street, its rear wheels sliding in patches of snow.

Kutna dropped to the sidewalk. The cart tipped over and the sacks split, sending potatoes spilling into the street, across the cobblestones and under the wheels of the speeding automobile.

Three shots, like firecrackers, sounded and Lisa slumped, half turned against the side of her car, and slid to the ground. She was dead before hitting the street. The BMW screeched around a corner and was gone. The assassination took less than six seconds.

Kutna slowly beat his fist against the sidewalk in anguish and frustration. Yakov stood in the doorway of the café, his mouth agape, surrounded by shocked market workers. He was back to square one.

Chapter 50

When Eiker and Mifflin walked into Stewart's office in Grinzing, Stewart's first words were, "One of Interpol's best informants was killed on the streets this morning right under their protective cover."

Mifflin lowered his weight into a large leather armchair. "Who was it?"

"Lisa Winkler."

Eiker, who was in the process of sitting down, fell into the chair. "Jesus! How did it happen?"

"Drive-by early this morning in the central market area."

Mifflin frowned. "Do we know what she was doing there?"

"She had a meeting with a Czech named Yakov in a café on the Rechte Wienzel."

"Do we have any idea who the shooter was?" Eiker demanded.

Stewart answered, "Nothing yet."

"Who in the hell was in charge of the Interpol cover?" Stewart shook his head.

"Unbelievably, Kutna himself."

Eiker exploded. "What went wrong for Christ's sake?"

Stewart shrugged and Mifflin asked, "Can you get me Kutna?"

Stewart picked up the phone. "I need Interpol." He replaced the phone and asked, "How about a drink? I know your poison, Mifflin.

What about you, Eiker?"

"Scotch, no ice."

In his office at Interpol, Kutna switched the phone to his right ear, hunched his shoulder to hold it in place and rummaged through his desk for a cigarette and growled.

"Okay, Mifflin, what now?"

"Kutna, you and your people let a damned good contact get blown away today. What the hell happened?"

Kutna sat stiff-backed in his chair, eyes half closed, lips compressed. He took a deep breath and let it out slowly. "Don't try that hard-nosed crap with me, Mifflin. I'm not the new kid on the block. When it comes to screw-ups, I have enough on you to end your career and I'd get a reward for doing it, maybe the Nobel Peace Prize for ridding the world of an asshole."

Mifflin's voice grated. "Right now I need some answers."

Kutna was having a nicotine fit. He searched further through his desk drawers, flinging paper clips, rubber bands, crumpled cigarette packs, scraps of paper with phone numbers of people who were no doubt dead.

Finally he found a battered stub and scratched a match across the top of the desk. One drag on the butt and he felt better, but he didn't allow it to favorably distort his disposition.

"Listen, Mifflin, and listen good. Lisa Winkler was a friend. I want her killers as much... much more than you do. Let me know if you have a way to apprehend those responsible." He slammed down the phone and sucked the last centimeter from the cigarette. His hand shook as he ground out the stub in the ashtray.

He picked up the phone again and dialed Rosie Wimmer. He hung up after nine rings.

Chapter 51

An early morning mist hung low over the Danube as a barge trailing smoke from its battered tin chimney churned its way upstream and Herman's car crossed the Reich Brucke Bridge into Vienna.

Koski shifted her gaze from the river to Emma, who was half asleep in the back seat, her head propped against the side window. Herman asked hopefully, "Breakfast at your place?"

Koski twisted the rearview mirror and checked her makeup saying, "Coffee first?"

Koski knew she couldn't stall him much longer. "Schatzie," Emma replied sleepily, "A cup of coffee before we get to the apartment would save time."

He sighed. "It's too early for Demel's."

"I know a place in the Ringstrasser. Take the third turn on the left," Emma said quickly.

Indeed it seemed Herman really needed coffee. As they sat in the café he gulped down his first cup and signaled for another. Koski was antsy, afraid her rising anxiety would somehow manifest.

She had checked the restroom when they arrived. There wasn't a rear exit. Nevertheless, because she believed she would manage to devise a plan to break away from the two men, she made a quick phone call outside the restroom.

"Who'd you call?" Emma asked.

"Later," Koski whispered. Back at the table she wondered at her own audacity. She had made the call and now she must think of something. Koski glanced at Herman as he drained his cup and clunked it down on the table.

"Ready?" He rubbed his stout hands together.

Before Koski could answer, she heard a loud, querulous voice behind her and turned. At the next table, a man with dark hair and olive skin berated the waiter for dousing him with coffee.

"But, sir," the waiter protested, "it was you who..."

The customer stood and continued dabbing his wet slacks with a napkin. "Imbecile! Waiter indeed, perhaps you're better suited to be a Tyrolese sheepherder."

Koski watched a thin white line rim the waiter's mouth as he compressed his lips. He was a big man with an odd mixture of refinement and simplicity, one whose appearance evoked images of the Alpine Region the other had named. Now he thrust his hands on his hips, arms akimbo, enraged at what he obviously considered an insulting remark.

"I am no peasant," he said acrimoniously. "Furthermore..."

A voice at Koski's side interrupted. "My dear departed mother and father, may they rest in peace, were born in the South Tyrol, the Upper Leach River Valley to be exact." It was Marny, standing tall. His sharp Teutonic jaw was thrust forward, his mouth set determinedly. He walked over to the table and addressed the soaked customer. "And just what is wrong with being a Tyrolese shepherd?"

Koski thought she caught a glance in her direction and a nearly imperceptible flash of bemusement in the customer's eyes. If it in fact had been there, it was quickly gone. His face darkened and he let his napkin slide to the floor.

"Let's see," he said, "if the son of a peasant who sticks it to sheep can fight like a man." He took a step toward Marny and squared off. "Or is he chicken-livered?"

Emma gasped and Koski felt Herman rise beside her. However she regarded him personally, she figured Marny was neither a coward nor a pervert.

She was right. When Marny's first blow fell like a sledgehammer Herman joined in the fray. She decided not to wait around for the count. She grabbed Emma's hand and raced out the door.

As they reached the curb Emma asked breathlessly, "Where are we going?"

Koski nodded down the street. In the distance, a taxi turned the corner and headed toward them. "You asked me who I called."

"Yes."

Koski waved and the taxi stopped a few feet from them. As they hopped in, Koski gave an address to the driver and told Emma, "A cab of course."

As the taxi pulled away, Koski smiled at the nerve of that customer who had called Marny a degenerate. Months later she would reason he was an Interpol agent who deliberately started the fiasco then went directly to a phone and reported Koski and Emma's whereabouts. For now she was satisfied with the happenstance of colossal coincidence.

"Where are we going?" Emma asked.

"To the British Embassy."

"That's what I thought you told the driver, but why?"

"Best place for you."

"And if I refuse?"

"What do you mean?"

"Koski, I've come this far. I'm in this to the end."

Koski gave her a stern, maternal look. "Listen to me. I admire your spirit, but it's simply not a good idea."

"And I suppose quitting is?"

"I'm not talking about quitting. I'm talking about using our heads. At least if you're at the Embassy you'll be safe and I'll know where you are."

"But we make such a good team."

"Yes, but now it's time to go in."

Emma looked wide-eyed. "What about Joe?"

"Now that I'm back in Vienna I can do a lot to help him."

The cab came to a halt in front of the Embassy. Emma was about to swing her long shapely legs out of the car when she said, "I don't feel comfortable doing this. What am I supposed to do here? Sit and twiddle my thumbs?" She swung her legs out. "Forget it. I'll go find him on my own."

Chapter 52

Koski sighed and pulled Emma back inside the cab. "Tell the driver to circle the block once." As soon as Emma complied, Koski said, "I've something to tell you." Her voice was barely audible.

"I'm not a doctor of archaeology. Neither is Joe. We're FBI working with American security." She had decided to tell enough truth to satisfy Emma but keep Cerberus in the loop of secrecy. "So you see why I have to continue on my own now."

"No, I don't."

"I'm a federal agent, Emma!" She tried to whisper with emphasis. "I have a job, an official assignment to do. You can't be a part of that anymore. It was only by accident that you've been involved at all."

Emma's defiant expression turned melancholy and she stared ahead. "I'm going back to England."

Koski's head rolled slightly from side to side and her green eyes flickered skyward. "What does that mean?"

"I've never really belonged in Austria. I have no family, few friends...." She turned full face to Koski with tears in her eyes. "I thought we were friends as well as partners in this."

Koski fell silent, glancing down at her hands in her lap.

Emma looked ahead again. This time she held her chin slightly higher. "I also don't think I was cut out for the antiques business. It's too dull. I'm going into a different line of work, something more exciting. Maybe I'll go into P.I. work...some field I'm good at, like operating with certain *savoir-faire* in dangerous situations; knowing how to make connections to get another agent without a passport into the Czech Republic; using my womanly wiles to entice two strangers to drive that second agent back to Austria, thus saving that so-called friend's life...like..."

"Okay, okay!" Koski interrupted. The last thing she wanted was Emma running around town causing more trouble playing amateur detective.

Emma smiled and finished her previous sentence. "Like how to tell the driver to go to my place so we can pool our resources and regroup."

"Why didn't you tell me sooner?" Emma asked as she moved around her small kitchen, splashing water into a kettle for tea.

"I wouldn't have told you now if you hadn't threatened to take off and look for Falk on your own."

Emma sat down while she waited for the water to boil. Koski fell deep in thought.

"Emma, how much did your Aunt Louise tell you about this reunion group that met at the Romischer-Kaiser Hotel?"

"She told the story many times. It was almost like a bedtime story for me." Emma went to a small desk and removed a photo album. "Aunt Louise treasured this."

She laid a battered leather album on the table and opened the pages, revealing black and white photos, some going sepia and frayed around the edges. She pointed to a group picture. "I have an enlargement of this one downstairs in a silver frame. These are some of the original resistance members."

Emma pointed out who was who. Koski looked up when she mentioned the name Lego Moyzisch.

"That's the name Horidecki mentioned when we were in Spilberg. They have his wife under protection as he called it."

The kettle shrilled its whistle and Emma filled the cups.

"Horidecki also said Lego had gone missing," Koski claimed.

"Could he be in Vienna?"

"Anything is possible."

"Finding him might be the best way to either finish or halt this ridiculous hunt for treasure in its tracks." She stopped and sipped the strong, hot tea. "Think hard, Emma. Did your aunt ever tell you the group had any alternative meeting place? Somewhere other than the usual conference rooms at the Romischer-Kaiser?"

Emma was deeply pensive and then brightened. "Now that you mention it. I remember Lego said if any problem arose in the future, they should meet at a particular room at the Romischer-Kaiser, the room Horst Ekel, the owner, had used during the war to conceal refugees from the Germans. They called it simply 'the room on eleven.' I was a child when she told me. It made me think of Anne Frank."

"To your knowledge did any of the reunioners ever have occasion to use the room?"

Emma frowned. "Not that I know of, but I'm sure none would forget Lego's mention of it."

Koski immediately said, "Emma, I need you to stay here while I make a call from a public phone. Yours may be bugged."

"I have a disposable cell phone in my bedroom," Emma replied as she sprang from her chair. "I'll get it."

Koski sipped her tea and tried to recall the phone number Stewart gave Falk and her in the car at their second briefing. That meeting seemed so long ago.

She remembered part of the number but the last four digits... association usually worked...what had she... Ah, yes, she remembered now. Christmas, December 25. The last four digits were 1225.

Waiting for Emma to bring the phone, she flipped open the photo album and looked again at the figures in the picture. She was sure her hunch about Lego was right. People in old photographs only *seemed* to reside mutely in dust-collecting albums. In fact, they sent their souls through time and space and spoke to you.

Chapter 53

The room on the eleventh floor of the Romischer-Kaiser was small and ugly. With the exception of one chair—the one in which Lego Moyzisch sat—dustsheets covered what little furniture there was. Eerie silence and an air of dampness prevailed.

Lego was slumped in the overstuffed armchair, reading by the light of a low-wattage bulb from a small table lamp. Suddenly, like an animal that has caught the scent of the enemy, he tensed. His head tilted slightly as he listened then, hearing nothing, he returned to his book. He was tired and a white, three-day stubble covered his chin. His red-rimmed eyes tried to focus and comprehend the print.

He closed the book and pushed himself stiffly from the chair, rubbing his lower back with both hands that felt thick and alien to him. He slowly kneaded sluggish circulation through his body. Shuffling to the window, he saw the fringe of a new day brighten the edge of thick, brown velvet drapes laden with mustiness.

He recalled the words he had uttered at the reunion. "In time of need for a safe haven, remember the room on eleven. It has been a refuge for many in the past."

Lego shivered slightly, tugging a woolen cardigan closer to his body. He reached out and pulled the drapes aside, allowing thin winter sun to spill into the room. He turned. What was that sound?

Without taking his eyes from the door, he backed to the chair, reached under the cushions, extracted an old Walther P38 automatic and snapped off the safety. Now the only sound was his labored breathing.

Spinning, he faced the window as if expecting to see it shatter and admit an executioner. There was only sunlight, highlighting the crazed dance of dust motes on their stage between the window and worn carpet.

He lowered the automatic, his hand shaking. "You're too jumpy," he told himself and held his wrist until the shakes subsided, then reset the safety catch.

Nothing was as it used to be. He was old and hated the fact he had lived to discover his own fears and stumbling weaknesses. Returning to the chair, he positioned it so he could see both window and door. The gun lay in his lap. He ran his tongue across his dry lips. Dr. Benson, Louise and Steele had taken a vote and decided to hear his awful secret. Now they could all be gone, taken by the evil aftermath of a war they had survived.

He vowed he would wait here as long as there was a possibility that any of the assembly was still alive and would come. This was where they had sworn to return if their life as a group was endangered many years ago.

If any were left would they remember? He looked around the decaying room. The few tins of food were almost gone. He managed to postpone starvation by warming food on the old steam radiators he had coaxed into operation. There was no place to go. His wife would remain in protective custody in Brno until his government tracked him down and got what they wanted from him…or until he died.

He studied the gun, running his hand over the cold steel. One more day, he decided. Then he would end his waiting, perhaps place the dustsheet over both himself and the chair, leaving everything as he found it. Almost.

The Judas List

Chapter 54

Paul was silent as he drove Falk toward Vienna. Falk took this time to go through the *Book of Hours* resting on his knees. Page by page, he devoured every detail, scrutinized the colorful scrollwork, every loop and whorl of the magnificently formed letters. One particular picture caught his eye. It was a surreal scene of two greyhounds romping outdoors in a tiled courtyard of black and white diamond design. The spectacle was illuminated by a ray of sunlight slicing through a brilliant blue sky full of angels with raised trumpets.

The sunbeam held a dove in its saffron glow then diffused onto a fountain bordered by more angels. The light seemed to flow across the picture, touching birds, stars, jewels, silver leaves, blue feathers and small naked cherubs. One of them reached for a large Monarch butterfly. Another held a three-stringed whip on its shoulder and a sly smile played across its face.

In one corner of the picture, a cowled figure bent forward as if in prayer, head resting against the wall of the fountain. Scrolls in Latin and what looked like Arabic surrounded him. The picture was so absorbing that Falk had to force his eyes from it when the car slowed and Paul said, "Almost there."

Falk closed the book and leaned slightly to see his image in the review mirror. *My God!* he thought. A scrubby beard covered his chin and his face had cuts and scrapes. He hadn't brushed his teeth in he couldn't remember how long.

Paul swung the car into an alley behind the Kartendome and stopped. The back door of the restaurant opened and a man dressed in chef whites peered out and beckoned to them.

"Bring the book," Paul said.

As they walked to the door, two men came down the alley, got in the car and drove away. Inside, the smell of food made Falk realize how hungry he was. Fritz Lubbe bustled toward them.

"Come," Fritz pumped Paul's hand. "You two must eat."

Five minutes later Falk was scraping the bottom of the soup dish with his last slice of pumpernickel. Fritz smiled in satisfaction as if he, too, had finished the meal. "Feel better, Herr Falk?"

"Yes, thank you."

"I have good news for you. The two women are back in Vienna, your associate and the English lady."

"Where are they?"

"I'm waiting for the latest report but they are safe. You must feel better, I'm sure."

"Like a new man."

"Good." He checked his watch. "There's a taxi outside. You'll be taken to a meeting with Dr. Herschel."

"Dr. Herschel?"

Fritz, it seemed, suddenly couldn't hear. He extended his hand. "Good luck, Herr Falk. Paul will go with you." Falk thought he said it almost like he was saying, "Go with God." Fritz turned and hurried away.

Paul picked up the book as Falk said, "I have to go to the bathroom." Falk needed time out. He was back in Vienna and so were

Koski and Emma. He was determined to find them before he met with anyone.

Paul smiled. "Ja, sure, down the passage, last door on the left. I'll see you outside." Paul hurried from the kitchen to the waiting taxi.

As Falk jumped onto a moving streetcar a block from the restaurant, he envisioned Paul still waiting in the cab. Paul would find the restroom window wide open when he went to find out why Falk was taking so long.

The Judas List

Chapter 55

Stewart answered the phone on the second ring. "Koski, where are you?"

"Here in Vienna. We went directly to Emma's antique shop. Is there any word on Joe?"

"He's back in Vienna but I don't know exactly where yet." In the same breath he said, "Listen, Koski. I want you and Emma out of there. Are you using the phone at the shop?"

"No, a cell phone." Koski turned and looked at Emma as she continued. "I think I know where I can find Lego Moyzisch. I'm going to the Romischer-Kaiser, to a roo…"

"Listen to me. I don't want you going off alone. Do you understand? You'll need backup."

"I can handle it."

"I forbid it, Koski. That's an order. You and Emma take a cab to the Hotel Ananas, a place widely used by tourists. It's located near the city center, plenty of crowds to mingle with. There's a possibility you'll be followed and you'll have a better chance of losing a tail in a crowded area.

"Split up as soon as you leave the cab. Take one of the tour buses to the Belvedere Palace. They run every fifteen minutes. I'll have a blue four-door Volvo waiting for Emma outside the Ananas. The keys will be in it. She knows the city and can meet you at the palace. She'll be in the car park next to the terrace that faces the city."

He paused. "Eiker will be somewhere on the terrace. I'll contact him to watch out for you. He's up there following a lead. Don't show any signs of recognition when you see him. Just do as he says. Any questions?"

Koski had plenty of questions but they would have to keep.

A cold wind fluttered around the great stone building and the sky seemed undecided whether to rain or snow. Eiker stamped his feet on the stone terrace of the Belvedere Palace and looked at the great sweep of gardens and the city in the distance.

The view would be spectacular in summer. The message from Stewart made it clear he was responsible for the safety of the women. According to Stewart, Koski held an important clue, one that could possibly lead to the location of the missing loot.

Two tour buses turned into the parking lot alongside the building. Eiker watched as they disgorged their passengers in the graveled area. Some gaped excitedly, readying cameras. Others moved slowly as if bored to be at yet another pile of stone to be photographed and preserved in albums that would be consigned to gather dust. Some tourists huddled against the side of the bus and lit up, their little clouds of blue smoke shredded by the stiff north wind.

Koski was the last passenger off the bus. She ambled slowly, seemingly oblivious to the tall good looking Englishman. She thought she did an outstanding job of craning her neck as if she had never seen a palace before. She turned in a circle now and then, ostensibly to miss nothing. She stopped a few feet from Eiker, her back to him.

"You look well," he said softly, aiming his long distance lens toward the distant twin spires of the Votive Church.

Koski snapped a shot of one of the many large flowerpots bordering the terrace. "Last time I saw you, you were in Nevada hightailing it in a helicopter. Falk and I almost nailed your ass."

"Ah, yes," he mumbled. "I remember it well."

"I've got a tail on the bus." Her lips scarcely moved.

He swung his camera toward the palace. "Who?"

"See the woman in the wheelchair?"

"Yes."

"She's a spotter, not sure who the real tail is." Koski watched Eiker position himself between the handicapped woman and the palace's imposing facade. The shot would include Koski.

She wanted to be sure of one thing. "Stewart says Joe made it back?"

"He did, under Mossad protection. He's safe."

She felt a wave of relief pass over her and suddenly felt like the Energizer Bunny.

"Attention bus number twenty-nine," the guide from Koski's bus called out through a megaphone. "We're leaving for a lunch stop in five minutes then on to Schoenbrunn Palace."

"Where's Emma Lewis?" Eiker asked.

Koski snapped another picture. "She's in a blue four-door Volvo near the end of the parking lot. See it?"

Eiker pointed his camera in another direction. "Got it." He lowered his camera and looked around indifferently. "Lose the group when you get to the lunch stop. I'll be with Emma, watching for you."

When Koski boarded, Eiker was taking pictures at the far end of the terrace but he didn't miss a green BMW that took off after the bus. Casually, he crossed the terrace to the Volvo and got in.

"Miss Emma Lewis, I presume?"

Emma smiled. "Does that make you Dr. Livingstone?"

Eiker liked her right off. He grinned. "Rod Eiker."

She turned on the ignition and moved out of the parking lot.

Chapter 56

"Stay a few car lengths behind the green BMW," Eiker said. He saw the question in her eyes and liked that she didn't ask it; just followed orders.

As she navigated around a red and white, double linked streetcar, she gave Eiker a quick glance. "How did you get to Belvedere? I didn't see a car."

Maybe he spoke too soon. He believed most women talked too much. "I arrived by tram."

"Amazing," Emma said.

"Not really. I often use a tram, gets one around quite nicely in Vienna."

"No, I mean it's amazing how people communicate. Koski made one phone call and suddenly everything swung into well-oiled action."

"Not always well-oiled, I'm afraid." He nodded toward the road ahead as a car passed the BMW and suddenly they were closer. "Maintain at least two car lengths behind the Beamer," Eiker said and Emma slowed slightly. "Do you know the lunch stop the bus will make?" he asked.

"Koski said it was called Mannerheim's and that they served fine food."

"In Vienna they serve nothing else." Eiker pointed. "There's

Mannerheim's just ahead on the right." He knew Koski had no idea about the BMW. He would have to cover her.

"When we get to Mannerheim's, pull over and drop me off. Then stay in the car, facing the direction from which we came and watch for Koski. Don't worry about me and don't look back. Understand?"

"Yes."

"Good."

When Emma started to pull over, Eiker was out before the vehicle actually stopped. He moved between two parked cars and casually strolled along the sidewalk, tourist fashion.

He saw Emma drive into the parking lot and turn the car around as instructed. Koski's bus was unloading. The woman in the wheelchair was the first off, helped by willing hands.

Eiker moved near a parked VW and fiddled with his camera. Inside the green BMW parked across from the bus, he spied a swarthy, dark-haired man in the driver's seat. He also saw the man slide the window down. A gun barrel appeared and rested atop the glass.

Letting his camera hang from his neck, Eiker slowly walked to the rear of the BMW. Instinctively aware that the spotter had somehow alerted the driver, he stepped aside, crouched, turned and dropped to the sidewalk in one quick continuous movement. There was no sound of gunfire but the windshield of the VW beside him shattered in a sparkle of glass shards.

Eiker's first shot killed the BMW driver. Springing to his feet, he saw Koski make it to Emma's car. He rested his arms on the roof of a red Fiat next to him and squeezed off two shots that lifted the wheelchair occupant out of the chair in a whirl of limbs and skirts.

As he dashed to the moving car, Eiker caught a glimpse of the "lady's" lower body, clad in trousers, "her" wig three feet away from the disintegrated head.

Eiker exhaled and sank heavily into the seat, sweat standing out on his forehead. "Glad you mentioned the spotter, Koski. Otherwise we'd both be history."

Koski was about to tell Emma to step on it when the car jolted as Emma pressed the pedal to the metal.

Koski turned to Eiker. "How did you know the person in the wheelchair was a man?"

"I didn't." He tapped Emma's shoulder lightly. "Nice job. I'll take over from here. Pull over."

Emma joined Koski in the back seat as Eiker drove the Volvo into traffic. He pulled to the side of the road as two police cars and an ambulance rushed past them.

"As I understand it," Eiker said, "we're headed for the Romischer-Kaiser, right?" He glanced back but saw no one following.

"Right," Koski said. "I've a hunch we'll find Lego there."

"It could be staked out."

"I know," she replied calmly. "Any ideas?"

"Maybe if you and I were to go in together and they were expecting one woman or two women…we could throw them off."

Koski obviously liked the idea but that would leave Emma alone.

"Emma," Koski said, prepared for Emma's adverse reaction, "you'll drive to the British Embassy and stay there until we contact you, okay?"

When Emma silently nodded her assent, Koski admonished herself. She should have expected this mature reaction, should have realized that the retiring woman in the antique shop had grown into a perceptive operative of whom Quantico would have been proud. She sighed.

"Good. We'll drive once around the block and be sure it's clear. Then leave Eiker and me about two blocks from the hotel. We'll get a cab from there and you head back to the Embassy."

Emma nodded. "Well-oiled action." She shrugged at Koski's puzzled look.

"It looks clear," Eiker said. He and Koski exited the car and Emma got behind the wheel. He flagged down a cab two blocks from the hotel as Emma sped off.

Arm in arm, Koski and Eiker crossed the hotel lobby and went directly to the birdcage elevator. To an observer, they might have looked like a couple enjoying a lovers' tryst. Eiker slid open the concertina doors and Koski pressed eleven. "According to Emma, the eleventh floor is only used for storage now," she whispered.

Overhead, through the open lattice ironwork, Koski saw thick, black, greasy cables slide silently up and over the wheels, lifting them closer to another link in the entangled chain of events that began in the shadows of a world war.

"Koski, what if he's not here?"

The elevator lurched to a stop and they stepped into a dusty, unkempt hallway. As the lift jerked and descended out of sight, Koski whispered, "He's got to be here."

Chapter 57

Pasha, like a vile misrepresentation of a child, sat behind a desk too large for his needs in the third floor room of the Kanglerkrank-Zimmerstadt. He stared thoughtfully into space. If, as Steele said, Lego Moyzisch was dead, there was little Pasha could do to learn the significance of the key. Yet he was certain it held a clue to the puzzle he must solve.

"Come," he said to a knock at the door.

A tall, well-built man entered. He was light on his feet and had a disarming smile. Pasha had requested, and been given, one of the best hired killers in Slovakia. His name was Kraal.

Pasha waved him to a seat. "Report."

"When I shot the woman outside the café, I saw Kutna on the sidewalk dressed as a market worker."

"So?" Pasha hissed.

"I also saw Yakov."

Pasha tapped his knuckles methodically on the top of the desk. "Where is Dr. Falk?"

"The Israelis have him."

"Where are the British soldier of fortune and Dr. Koski?"

"He's very clever. He made contact with Doctor Falk's associate and they nearly eluded us. We trailed them to the Romischer-Kaiser

Hotel. I have men waiting for them when they leave."

Falk rode the tram five blocks and jumped off at the intersection of Schubertring and Johannesgasse near the Stadt Park without paying. He had no money, no ID, nothing since they had stripped him clean in Spilberg. He had to get in touch with Stewart.

Glancing around, he realized he was outside a florist shop and a middle-aged woman was busy arranging flowers inside. Without hesitation, Falk entered the shop.

"Excuse me. Do you speak English?"

The woman looked up and smiled. "Yes."

"I wonder if you can help me. I need to make a very important phone call and I don't have any money. Would it be possible to use your phone? It's a local call. I'll have someone pick me up then I can pay you."

The woman blatantly assessed him and he was self-consciously aware of what she saw. Commercial fishermen, even after showers, smell of tuna. Teachers, once they have retired, still retain the smell of chalk.

For most of his adult life, Falk considered himself a rather clean-cut, close-shaven, shoes-shined Norman Rockwell type of guy. At this moment, however, he was unshaven, disheveled, unvarnished and unclean. Did the scent of who he truly was linger discernibly around him?

The woman produced a cell phone from her pocket and smiled. "Of course."

Falk decided that one day he would ponder further on the phenomenon he had just experienced. It was like the woman in the apartment building in Brno who saved his life by advising him not to go to the rooftop.

Falk thanked her and quickly tapped the numbers to Stewart's office. He knew it was a safe number, impossible to bug. He gave his location and Stewart told him to wait in the shop entrance. Mifflin would be right along.

In less than five minutes the limo pulled up outside and Mifflin waved from the back seat. Falk crossed the sidewalk and yanked the door open. "Give me some money."

Mifflin looked stunned. He reached in his pocket. "How much?"

"Enough for a dozen hot-house roses."

Mifflin winced and peeled off several bills. "Damned expensive this time of year…"

Falk took the money, ran back into the store and pointed to a pail full of yellow roses that resembled spring sunshine. "Let me have a dozen."

The woman smiled. If she was surprised that an American who couldn't afford a phone call a few minutes ago now had a limo at his disposal and wanted to buy a dozen roses, she didn't show it. Falk laid the bills on the counter. "Will this cover the flowers and the phone call?"

"Yes, sir." She cradled the flowers in green tissue and a box. "Indeed it will."

Falk scooped up the box of long stems. "Thanks," he said and was out the door.

Mifflin shook his head as Falk slipped into the car beside him. "You can explain the roses to Stewart on *your* expense account."

Falk started to bring Mifflin up-to-date, including his fast departure from the café but Mifflin cut him off. "Save the details for Stewart's debriefing. Your sudden departure from the café has the Mossad highly pissed off. We've some fence mending to do. We need help from Interpol, some unit of security that knows the city inside out, despite the fact that the last person I want to ask for help is Kutna."

Stewart was sitting behind his desk when Falk and Mifflin entered. "Welcome back, Joe. You did well to escape alive."

"Tell me about it. Can you have someone put these in water?"

Falk slumped into the nearest chair. "Leave them on the table. They'll be taken care of."

Stewart turned to Mifflin. "Kutna's been trying to reach you. Call him from the other room. I want to talk with Falk."

As soon as Mifflin was gone, Stewart's voice grated. "What in the hell were you thinking when you gave the Israelis the slip?"

Stewart's eyes were hard. "They're on *our* side, Joe. They are the ones who got your ass out of the Czech Republic. You're supposed to be a doctor of archaeology, not 007."

"Sorry, Tom." He shrugged. "I decided to check in with you instead."

"Okay, well, I'll square it with them somehow but you must stay with them from here on out. The two real Smithsonian experts have been sent back to the States; too dangerous for them to be involved now."

Falk nodded. "Where's Koski?"

"She's with Eiker. They're checking out a lead on Lego Moyzisch."

Falk bristled. "Did they have to go together?"

"Yes. You weren't around," he said pointedly.

"Well, I'm back."

"I've arranged for you to meet with an Israeli by the name of Herschel. He and Eiker know each other. Seems Eiker worked freelance for him on a couple of jobs in Israel. Falk nodded. "Now,"

Stewart went on, "let's get down to details. Everything—from the moment you were abducted to the moment you got back."

"This is official business," Kutna said didactically when Mifflin returned his call. "Otherwise we wouldn't be on the line."

"Then get on with it."

"Interpol received information on a possible terrorist attack at the Dorotheum. All anti-terrorist precautions have gone into effect. In addition, Yakov was reported inside the building on several occasions over the last few hours. I'm reporting this information to you because I feel it's in the best interest of both our countries."

Mifflin was silent throughout. He understood the import of the message and that Kutna could have kept the information to himself.

"Thanks, Kutna. I'll take it from here."

"Understand we have sent Interpol agents into the building as a precautionary measure. They have been instructed that everything is to be low profile."

Kutna paused and lost some of his pomposity before asking, "Has Rosie Wimmer been in contact with you?"

"No, why do you ask?"

"I've had no contact for several hours. If she contacts you, I'd appreciate it if..."

"You'll know immediately."

"Ah, Mifflin...before, I didn't mean to sound..."

"It's okay." Nevertheless, he couldn't let him totally off the hook. "So you're a *human* bastard."

Kutna mumbled something and the phone clicked off.

The Judas List

Chapter 58

Alone in the musty storage room of the hotel, Lego gripped his automatic and faced the door. A shiver ran through his body as he listened: three soft taps, a pause then two. Crossing the room, he stood with his back to the wall next to the door, the Walther trained on the entrance. A woman's voice called his name.

"Lego, my name is Susan Koski. I'm a friend of Emma Lewis, Louise's niece."

He relaxed for a second then recovered. "Louise who?"

"Louise Fisher," Koski replied. "Hurry. Open the door."

"Is anyone with you?"

"It's not a trap. Rod Eiker with American security is with me. It's safe."

The woman knew of Louise. Should he take a chance?

"Lego, for God's sake, open the door! If we're caught in this hallway…"

"I'm going to open the door. I'm also letting the safety off my automatic."

Koski and Eiker watched as the door opened a crack then swung ajar for them to enter. Koski slowly pushed against it.

Lego was now in the center of the room, his gun aimed directly at them as they walked in. "Over there." He jerked his weapon toward the window. "Back against the window, arms above your heads. Face the center of the room." He backed against the door, shutting it with his left foot.

Alone, Eiker might have forced Lego into further interrogation but petite, disarming Koski immediately withered his defenses. He sighed. "I had to be certain."

Koski spoke softly. "You did right." She saw him sway slightly. "Lego, you're ill..." She glanced around the room and saw the evidence of his scant rations. "You're weak." Slowly she walked to him. "Here, sit down." She steadied his frail body as he lowered into the armchair.

Leaning back, he looked up at Koski. "Where is Louise's niece?"

"She's safe at the British Embassy. We'll take you to her."

"We also need your help," Eiker interjected somewhat impatiently. "We've made contact with an Israeli archaeologist, Dr. Yigal Herschel, who can possibly help us locate the stolen treasures Goering hid under the Dorotheum."

Lego nodded. "Ah, yes, the treasures." He pulled his sweater around him. "Herschel...was he once an army general?"

"Yes. You know him?"

"I know of him. He was a good general—good for Israel." Lego shrugged. "Then so was General Rommel, who was also an archaeologist—good for the Nazis."

"Lego, we'd like you with us," Koski said. "That is unless you fear you'd be risking your life..."

"I've no more time for fears, nothing left to fear. My wife was arrested by Czech security two days after I arrived here in Vienna. They confiscated a blueprint I had that they think I can interpret."

He sighed wistfully. "I wish she still had the prayer book. It would be a great comfort to her."

Eiker stiffened. "Prayer book?"

Lego smiled. "Ja, a beautiful book. When I packed my bag before I left for the reunion in 1975, I put it in my suitcase along with the key. I doubted I'd ever live long enough to make it to the next reunion."

Koski was saddened, watching him relate his innermost feelings, still affected by loyalties formed in the latter days of the war. "Lego, you must go back…your wife…."

"They won't harm her…yet." He straightened as if calling on some lagging determination.

Koski was curious about the book. "This prayer book, was it in your family a long time?"

"Many years. I remember it came in the mail from Canada about 1955," he rubbed his chin. "There was a key taped inside."

"Who sent it?" Koski asked softly.

"The Russian Youmatoff, Nikolai Youmatoff."

"I remember," Koski said, "the man you helped to escape during the war."

Lego looked plaintively off into space. "My wife loved that book, the colored pictures…she took it with her to church every day."

Koski put her hand on his fragile shoulders and patted lightly.

"When you received it," Eiker questioned, "was there a return address?"

"Nothing."

"Then how could you be sure it was from Youmatoff?"

"Inside the cover were three Xs drawn in pencil in a row with a line through them. It was our way of signifying 'prisoner of war.'"

Eiker nodded. "What about the key? What was it for?"

"I don't know. It was a mystery to me." He shook his head. "It was small and odd-shaped. I tossed it in the back of the knife and fork drawer in the kitchen where we kept old keys."

Koski frowned. "Weren't you curious about the key and the book?"

He shrugged. "It was a long time ago. I suppose I was, but what could I do? The book made my wife happy and that was all that mattered."

Koski believed him. She also admired a man who could toss a key into a drawer and find it ten years later. "You say you took them with you when you came to the reunion here in Vienna back in 1975?"

"Yes."

"You didn't mention the book and key to the others when you told them about Goering's hidden treasure?"

"No. I wanted to ask Dr. Benson what he thought."

Koski saw that Lego was tired but she needed a few more answers. "What happened after the reunion?"

"On the way to Dr. Benson's room I met John Steele coming down the stairs. He said Doctor David had gone to bed. I asked him to keep the key for me as I was always losing things when I traveled.

"I said I'd retrieve it at breakfast. We said good night and I went to my room. In the middle of the night I heard someone in my hotel suite, outside my bedroom. I slipped out of bed, grabbed my clothes and went down the fire escape. Had I stayed, I know I would have been killed. I never saw Benson or Steele again."

"Did you take the book with you?" Eiker asked before Koski had a chance to frame the question.

"No. I left everything."

Koski thought the package Youmatoff sent in 1955 was the book and key. Somehow they tied in with the blueprint of the Dorotheum and pointed to the exact location of Goering's cache.

Steele had the key. Who had been in Lego's suite? Whoever it was must have found the book.

The Judas List

Chapter 59

The sky was high blue without a cloud the day Youmatoff got off the bus and walked through downtown Ottawa. His cheeks were burnished from the wind and snow and burned more intensely with the fire from within. He had buried his snowshoes before reaching the highway and shed his wool cap and gloves since the weather had turned slightly warmer.

Was it possible he had eluded the Mounties? He was bothered by people as they passed and made him aware of himself, skittish, the city lacking the fraternity he had formed with the woods.

As the seashell held the roar of the sea, Youmatoff was certain of the smell of forest. Years ago, he heard that people who spent blocks of time in the extreme solitude of the forest become "woods queer," forgot how to act around others. He once knew a trapper who went stark raving mad in the woods. Youmatoff, caught in the maelstrom of civilization himself, moved uneasily along the sidewalk, feeling mental discomposure, out of step with unsympathetic vibrations that rose from the city.

He ran a great weathered paw through his hair that was the umber of withered fern and as dull. He was getting closer. In answer to Youmatoff's stuttered question, the bus driver indicated a building on Charlotte Street, Number 287. Youmatoff quickened his pace, knowing that the Russian Embassy—a piece of his homeland on Canadian soil —was near.

Chapter 60

When Lego, Koski and Eiker left the Romischer-Kaiser Hotel, the weak sunlight was gone and snow fell in heavy silence, muffling the sound of late afternoon traffic. Cars passed with headlights on, windows steaming, windshield wipers slashing a triangle of visibility.

Lego looked skyward, squinting against a bombardment of flakes and turned up his collar. "Ach! The city traffic will be snarled before evening."

Koski looked down at a small whirlpool of snow that swirled around her feet. "We should have called a cab, Eiker."

"I did. Called from the desk and told him to meet us around the corner just north of the entrance."

"There was a man watching us as we left," she said, impressed with Eiker's forethought.

"I know. Main reason I wanted the taxi around the corner."

Kraal, observing the three from an upstairs window of a building facing the hotel, smiled as he watched them turn the corner. As he hoped, they had led him to Moyzisch and he would be on their tail in minutes. He glanced across the street at the man he had stationed in the doorway.

Kraal was sure the threesome made his man. When Koski looked over her shoulder, Kraal toyed with various entertaining methods he might deploy to kill her when the time came. He saw his man step from the doorway and go to the curb to meet a black Volvo that was to pick him up. Kraal turned from the window and hurried downstairs to join him.

As he reached the front door, Kraal stopped and flattened against the wall in the hallway, pulling a Marakov 9mm from his shoulder holster. Through the shattered glass panel of the door, he saw that the Volvo was gone. His man sprawled across the sidewalk, his head in a pool of blood.

Then Kraal saw something that sent him racing back down the hall with only seconds to get to the rear entrance and out of the building. A hand grenade had been tossed through the broken glass panel.

He ripped open the back door and flung himself from the building as a roar and the heat of the explosion drove through it like a blowtorch and slammed him into a sooty snow bank beside a row of battered trash cans.

An admixture of the ugly stench of cordite and acrid smell of wet, smoldering wood filled the air. Wisps of smoke curled from the glassless windows of the building opposite the Romischer-Kaiser. Water from fire hoses turned to ice and slush beneath firefighters' feet.

An ambulance with its back doors open was angled to the curb. Captain Vlad of Austrian Military Intelligence flipped a sheet over the man on the stretcher then let the paramedic close the doors.

"No need for the siren with a dead man on board," Vlad remarked as the ambulance yodeled its way into the distance.

Beside him a sergeant muttered. "They want to get back for their coffee break."

Vlad was about to concur when an excited fire chief rushed up to him.

"We've found a man behind the building," the chief said. "He's pretty badly injured but alive."

Vlad pushed him aside and went to the back. Kraal was sprawled on the ground, out cold, the back of his head burned raw. A lump on his forehead indicated a possible concussion and his left foot was blown to a bloody pulp. He still gripped the Marakov.

"I want him kept alive," Vlad said after assessing Kraal's condition. "Quick. Get an ambulance."

When the ambulance arrived, Vlad climbed in the back with Kraal and removed the Marakov from Kraal's grip. He was intrigued. The Marakov was a crib of the German Walther PP automatic, a dangerous one for anyone not thoroughly familiar with it.

It looked identical to the Walther except for one small detail: the safety catch worked in reverse. Vlad pulled down the trigger guard, snapped the slide back and up and the recoil spring slid out. Once assembled without the spring, he slid it into his own pocket. Seated next to the sedated Kraal, an attendant watched with rapt attention.

"This is military security business," Vlad said pointedly. "No mention of what you've seen. Understand?"

The attendant nodded emphatically.

The Judas List

Chapter 61

Mifflin rapped on Stewart's office door and entered as if, once in, his presence justified his lack of decorum. "I had a call from Vlad of Military Intelligence; could be a break for us."

Stewart eased back in his chair. "Tell me about it."

"Vlad has a man in a military hospital...thinks he could be a Muslim terrorist. He feels I might be able to find out more about him."

"They have their own people. Why call you?"

"Vlad knows I've worked Eastern Europe, on and off in Bosnia-Herzegovina. Special assignments 1992-1995 and I know how their minds work."

Stewart nodded. "Go over there and talk to Vlad."

Mifflin was perched at Kraal's bedside when the latter regained consciousness.

"What's your name?"

Kraal remained unmoving except for a flicker of his eyelids. Mifflin rasped a sentence in Farsi and Kraal opened his eyes and turned toward him. He immediately shut his eyes.

Mifflin reached out and grabbed one ear that protruded between the layers of bandages around Kraal's head. He jerked it hard and Kraal let out an agonizing moan.

"What's your name?"

"Kraal," he moaned.

"Who are you working for?" Mifflin felt the man quiver, reacting to pain and drugs. He wondered if this Kraal was the type who would rather die than tell what he knew.

"Listen," Mifflin said, leaning close to Kraal's face. "I can pump you full of drugs that'll make you tell me anything I want to know." Kraal was silent. "One phone call and I can have you shot up with so much shit you'll tell me when you had your last hard-on."

"Or," he jerked again on the ear, "you can tell me what I want to know right now and you'll stay nice and safe with the Austrians, who will most likely fly you home first class when you're well." He released his grip on Kraal's ear and smoothed the man's nightshirt over his chest. "What's it going to be, hmm?"

Kraal looked long and hard into Mifflin's steady gaze. Kraal was a terrorist. His sophistication lay in surprise, ambush attack. His role was to inspire fear. If required, to die instantly and gloriously, not slow and painful.

"Pasha," he muttered.

Mifflin brightened at the name. "That little shit! Where is he?"

"The Dorotheum," Kraal said weakly.

"That place is more popular than Disneyland these days. What's he doing there?"

"He's under it looking for Nazi treasures." Sweat glistened on Kraal's upper lip. "That's all I know."

Mifflin pushed back his chair and rose. "Just out of curiosity, Kraal, what's your cover here in Vienna?"

"Wein Neustadt, cotton exports."

"U.N. trade mission?"

Kraal nodded slightly.

266

Mifflin shook his head. There was something wrong with a system that allowed men like this to move freely, creating problems under the cover of a United Nations' trade mission. He looked at his watch. "When were you to report to Pasha?"

Kraal's face twisted in pain. "What time is it?"

"7 p.m."

"Then I am three hours late."

Mifflin turned and left the room. Outside, he said to Vlad, "When you're finished with him it'll be the end of the line. We don't want him back on the streets—ever."

Vlad smiled. "Nice working with you Herr Mifflin."

The Judas List

Chapter 62

Stewart picked up the phone and heard, "This is Kutna, Interpol. I have a message for you."

"Go ahead." Stewart wrote as he listened. *POSSIBLE TERRORIST ACTIVITY INSIDE DOROTHEUM IMMINENT. YAKOV ALSO SEEN.*

"Where did the Intel come from?" Stewart asked.

"Interpol's computer," Kutna said, "and one of our people who's been covering Yakov."

"What's Yakov doing?"

"I don't know. Interpol security forces and the Austrian police are going down there now. We're trying to keep everything as low-key as possible."

"Wouldn't it be wiser to evacuate the place?"

"Not at this time. If it's a false alarm, we'll tip them off that we got word of their plans, which could mean hostage taking…and God knows what else."

Emma was seated in a high-backed chair beside the fireplace in the British Embassy's reception area, reading a copy of the *London Illustrated News*. She looked up and glanced at an old grandfather clock in the corner. It had been over three hours since she last saw Koski and Eiker.

It was another fifteen minutes before the duo arrived with Lego. Koski went directly to a phone, called Stewart and learned Mifflin had gone to the Dorotheum following a message from Kutna.

"Any news about Youmatoff," she asked.

"Contacts in Canada report they still don't have Youmatoff in custody." Koski swore under his breath. If Youmatoff decided to go back to Russia, he could throw a monkey wrench into the works. Cerberus needed him *and* the first-hand information regarding the location they believed only he could provide. Koski hung up and joined the others.

"Ready to go?" she asked. "We have a meeting of the minds. Stewart's sending a car for us."

Koski was the first to enter the room when Stewart answered the knock. Eiker, Lego and Emma followed. Koski went straight into Falk's arms. She felt his warm breath against her ear as he bent and hugged her.

"Susan...Susan," he whispered.

They stood interlocked as the others skirted around them. She pulled back and looked at him. Handsome but older, thinner, sun and wind burned...creases at the corners of his eyes slightly more pronounced...parentheses on each side of his mouth deepened beneath a meandering mass of brown facial hair with familiar red highlights... dear...beloved...

She grabbed him again, hugging him fiercely. "Are you okay?" she asked when she finally disengaged herself and his arms reluctantly released her.

He nodded, fingering a tendril of her hair at her temple. He tenderly traced the line of her cheekbone and jaw, taking in the emotions she knew were blatantly evident in her eyes. "Thank God you're safe," he said huskily.

She sighed, suddenly aware of the others, wound one hand in his and held the other out to Lego. "Lego, come meet Joe Falk."

Lego took Falk's hand between his frail palms. "I'm happy to meet you."

Stewart ordered a hot meal for Lego and called everyone to be seated. Once he had their attention, he laid out the next move that included joining forces with Herschel.

"Falk, you and Koski will go on ahead to meet with Herschel," he said. "At some point Mifflin will join you. Due to security considerations, Emma and Lego will remain with me until cleared to join you." He glanced at Eiker then back to Falk. "Eiker will be along shortly. We have some minor details to discuss."

Beneath the Dorotheum, Pasha and two of his men led John Steele to a cell that was once a storage room, one of hundreds throughout the building.

Steele entered, walked a few feet and stopped. The first thing he saw was Rosie Wimmer.

Pasha, master of the garrote, had strangled Rosie with the leather shaving strop he used when questioning Steele. Stiff and cold, she looked almost obscene the way she was placed in the straight wooden chair. Her hips thrust forward, hands folded between her legs, head tilted back at a grotesque angle. Next to the chair was a small, wooden table with a flickering candle positioned to allow shadows to fall across Rosie's waxen face. Pasha made a sweeping gesture as if presenting her, obviously admiring his own handiwork.

Steele turned away from the final agony he saw reflected in Rosie's face.

Pasha laughed. "We completed the job you failed to do. When I set out to kill, I don't fail." He took the candle and walked to a dark corner. "I have something else to show you." With a flourish, he illumined the lifeless body of *Faux* Monk, who was sprawled on the floor, mouth agape, two bloody sockets where his eyes had been.

"Jesus!" Steele said. "That was the man who led me to the crypt —the only person who could find his way through the passages. Without him I'm nothing to you!"

"I couldn't have said it better myself." Pasha set the candle down. "We'll let the Mossad lead us to the treasures." He walked to the door. "Yes, Steele, you're about to become nothing but unnecessary baggage —a walking time bomb to be exact."

Steele heard one of Pasha's men behind him a second before he felt the blow to the back of his head that sent him reeling into darkness.

Chapter 63

Yakov, with signs of a head cold drooping over him, stood inside the main entrance to the Dorotheum as an early afternoon crowd streamed steadily in. He stamped his feet and turned up his coat collar against the icy blasts of air that hit him each time the door swung open.

"No sign of anything, sir."

Yakov turned slightly toward the voice of one of his men in a long, leather overcoat and *astrakhan* hat. Yakov removed a cough drop from a box in his coat pocket and popped it in his mouth. "I want every inch of the building searched for possible explosives," he snapped. "Basements, storage areas, yards, sheds, offices…everything. And check every porter's ID."

Suddenly Yakov realized that the head porter was waving to him from his small glass cubicle. Yakov refocused on his present situation. He cursed and crossed the wide hallway, shoulders hunched. He had no wish to die in a pawnshop—large or small.

The porter was Helmut Sten. Yakov had told Sten that he and his men were here to cover a story for a Czech Republic magazine. Sten held up a steaming mug of coffee as Yakov reached the cubicle.

"Please," he said as Yakov approached, "join me." He closed the door to the small, overheated office.

273

"Thank you, Herr Sten." Yakov pulled up a wooden chair, positioned it facing the entrance through the panorama of glass and sat down with the mug.

"Is there anything else I can do?" Sten asked eagerly.

Yakov nodded. "As a matter of fact, yes. I was about to ask if we might see how the antiques are stored and cared for prior to being placed at auction. We'd like to view the storage rooms and the underground facilities. These would be of great interest to our readers."

"No trouble. I will arrange for some of my people to guide you."

Yakov shook his head. "My men and I wish to go alone, unencumbered, so to speak. It will make for more candid shots."

"That's against the rules. No one is allowed beneath the Dorotheum without permission and a guide."

"I understand but we don't want you to go to any trouble." Yakov set his mug on a nearby table. "Just give me the keys. We'll look around, take a few pictures and be back in no time. No one will be any the wiser."

"Sorry." Sten's face reflected his uneasiness. "It can't be done."

Yakov moved quickly and Sten was facing the barrel of an ugly 9mm automatic.

"I'm out of time." Yakov spat, his gun gesturing to a row of keys on the wall. "Get those keys."

Sten's hand shook as he comprehended the situation. He handed the keys to Yakov then backed up against the wall.

"Perhaps you're right," Yakov hissed as he opened the office door. "We should have a guide. Walk ahead of me as if nothing's wrong. No heroics."

John Steele was inside a large, wooden crate labeled "Glassware" that stood in a remote warehouse area of the Dorotheum. It was coal black inside and Steele was bound hand and foot with a thin wire. One portion of it ran around his jaw and across his mouth, jamming his tongue against his lower teeth like the bit of a bridle. He breathed slowly, easing each hiss of air out between bloody, swollen lips. Steele heard someone outside the crate, a scraping sound then a click and the side of the crate snapped open and widened. It was Ali, one of Pasha's henchmen, who whispered, "I'm going to check the area."

Steele heard a sound like an old-fashioned wind up alarm clock being wound. "I'll be back before the detonator makes contact. If I'm detained, you'll die a peaceful death because the detonator will release a gas. You'll simply go to sleep." Steele felt the man pat his shoulder. "No doubt I'll return before the spring reaches contact."

How reassuring, Steele thought, as the man eased the side of the crate down and clicked it shut.

Alone with the ticking timer, Steele heaved against his bindings but the movement only caused the wire to saw more deeply into his lips. Breathing heavily, he rested his head against the rough wood of the crate. The ticking was like thunder in his ears. He had no idea how much time he had. Whatever happened, if he did get out of this he'd get that piece of shit Pasha.

The Judas List

Chapter 64

Kutna was already at the Dorotheum when Mifflin entered. He looked the part of a bargain hunter equal to any Viennese his age down to the battered briefcase he carried. With no wish to repeat the fiasco at the vegetable market, Kutna glanced around to make sure his men were in place. He watched Mifflin plod through the hallway, glance toward the porter's cubicle then pass from sight.

Kutna turned his eyes to the porter's office and tensed. Gut feeling told him something was wrong. He saw the porter and another man with his back to the window. The porter's face registered fear. There was something about the other man...then Kutna knew who it was.

The caretaker, followed by Yakov, left the cubicle and walked toward a door in the hall. Kutna was about to signal his men when a quiet voice beside him said, "I have a message from Mifflin." Kutna swung around to face a slim blonde in her early thirties. "Mifflin says you're to remain in place. The head porter has been taken hostage."

"I *know* that!" Kutna hissed between clenched teeth. "Tell Mifflin that I..." The woman was gone before he could finish, lost in the crowd.

A squad of soldiers, whose uniforms identified them as Austrian Military Intelligence, slowly walked the width of the hall with leashed

German Shepherds, moving the public steadily toward the front doors. They closed and locked them without fanfare.

Kutna had no doubt similar squads were securing other doors. He cursed. Mifflin must have arranged it and Captain Vlad executed it. Once again he and his department were relegated to mere guard duty.

Kutna spun around and waved to one of his men at the top of the curving staircase. The man ran down the wide, marble steps and stopped in front of him.

"Get some of our people into the *Josef Saal*," Kutna ordered. "Leave enough to cover this area."

The man looked up the stairs to the tall, ornate doors of one of the auction rooms known as *Josef Saal*. "The door is closed," he said. "The auction is about to begin."

"Very well. Leave two men at the door. Detain anyone who tries to leave before the auction ends." The man scurried back up the curving staircase. Signaling to two of his men, Kutna walked to one side of the hallway.

"Knoph," he said, "stay close to me. Reinhart, I'm going to find out what's going on...cover us." Followed by the men, he went through the door off the hall into a dimly lit stairway where Yakov and the porter had disappeared.

Silently they descended three flights of stone steps bordered by a wall on one side, iron railings on the other. Reinhart, who had removed a Lugar from his shoulder holster, remained a few feet behind the others. Kutna and Knoph, crouched low, cautiously rounding each landing, alert to danger.

It did them no good. The first shot caught Knoph at the hairline, lifting his scalp like a saucer and tipping it to the back of his head. He fell on the spot in a cascade of blood and matter. A second shot, sounding almost before the first had ceased reverberating, passed Kutna's shoulder by scant inches and entered Reinhart's right clavicle, shattering his shoulder blade. As he fell to the steps, he emptied his pistol in the direction of the shots. Before he passed out, his trained reaction was rewarded when he heard a cry and the unmistakable gurgle of death.

The overhead lights went out. Cordite and the smell of insufferable closeness mixed with a sudden silence that fell on Kutna like a cloak of death tossed across a coffin. He curled into a tight ball and pressed against the stonewall.

His men were hit. He must remain silent or die. He listened, certain that Yakov and his men were there somewhere. The only sound was Knoph, taking his last breaths a few feet away. Kutna felt compelled to move. Easing away from the wall, he snaked on his belly to the center of the passageway. The sudden stuttering blast from an Uzi on full automatic filled his ears and chips of stone flaked from the wall where he'd been moments before. His instinct to move had saved his life. He would continue to play the fox. Quickly he removed his shoes. Then with a muffled yell, he let his .45 drop to the floor. He had seen the flash from the machine gun and had a good idea where the gunman was.

Scooping up the .45, he hurried silently on stocking feet to the opposite wall where he remained still, hardly daring to breathe. The weapon in his right hand was rock steady, aimed at a level two inches higher than his own belt buckle. A few seconds later he heard a slight shuffling sound. He closed his eyes to listen better. There it was again —a shoe sliding along an uneven stone surface.

He felt certain it was one-on-one now or aspects of the attack would have been different. Opening his eyes, he turned his head in the direction of the sound. He only had one chance. His finger tightened on the trigger and he stared into utter blackness, ready to squeeze off a round.

The sudden stabs of an automatic's yellow flame didn't come from his gun but from the stairs behind him! He flattened against the wall, spun his weapon upward as the lights came on.

A familiar voice said, "Okay, Kutna. Relax." But he saw no one capable of speaking. The stairwell was a scene of carnage. Reinhart, barely breathing, was draped over the stairs in a puddle of blood. Knoph was slumped grotesquely in a corner, his dead features hardly recognizable.

One of Yakov's men was propped against the wall as if taking a break. He had achieved eternal rest, eyes gazing up toward the hole in the center of his forehead.

Yakov wasn't three feet from Kutna. He wore the same forlorn expression in death that he bore in life. Beside him, head porter Sten laid still, head in an ever-growing pool of blood. He would never again drink coffee in his small, glass-enclosed office in the Dorotheum.

"Okay, Kutna," Mifflin repeated from the head of the stairs and showed himself. "It's safe to come out now."

Kutna snapped the safety on his .45 and jammed it into its holster. "Damn!" was all he could think to say and it didn't begin to cover it.

Chapter 65

The meeting between Falk, Koski and Dr. Herschel took place in the back room of an abandoned tailor shop. Koski's nose wrinkled at the smell of old wool and the faint decay of an unused area. A scowling "Saint" Paul, still unhappy about losing face at the restaurant, had ushered them in. He departed unceremoniously and slammed the door behind him.

"Delighted you made it back." Herschel got up from behind a table piled high with books and maps and walked toward them, hand outstretched. After the usual introductions, he pushed a chair to the table for Koski while Falk got his own. They sat facing the doctor.

"We shall go over the maps together," Herschel said. He set out the largest, showing details of underground sewers and passageways beneath the central part of Vienna. "We are here." He stabbed his finger at a point on the Spiegelgasse close to the Capuchin Church.

"We'll go underground near the corner. I've arranged for us to use a City Water and Power truck. We'll wear official coveralls, set up the usual caution signs around the manhole and go down under the city using the catwalks."

"The city has agreed to let us do this?" Koski questioned.

"No but by the time anyone begins to wonder about the barricade and tent over the manhole we'll be through, which could take days the way the city bureaucracies work."

Falk nodded. "Once underground then what?"

"We follow this gallery, see." He tracked the route with a finger. "It runs deep beneath the foundation of the Capuchin, cuts across and passes the east side of the underpinning of the Augustinian Church. I feel the location we're looking for is either directly underneath the Dorotheum or somewhere between the two churches." He reached to another table, pushed aside a dusty pile of fabric and produced a book.

Falk was astonished. *"The Book of Hours,"* he whispered.

Herschel nodded. "Do you think it really holds a clue for us?"

"It's possible. I need to study it more."

Koski tapped the map before her. "The Capuchin Church has the Habsburgs urns, correct?" She looked from Falk to Herschel.

"Yes," Herschel said. "Fifty-four of them if memory serves me. Why?"

"Sadistic irony if Goering decided to conceal his blueprint for the heart of the Fourth Reich beneath the church of the Habsburgs."

Herschel's eyes brightened. "I intend to leave no possibility unexamined."

Falk studied the map again. A few hundred feet separated the churches. The passageways and galleries used by the Water and Power were well detailed down to each piece of conduit that carried cables and electrical wiring under the city.

Herschel tapped a spot beside the Capuchin. "When we arrive here I'll send one of my divers into the sewer system. You will note the waterways run parallel with the gallery. It's all part of the Danube Canal system that runs deep and fast this time of year."

"Why at that point?" Falk asked.

"I understand you were taken to a crypt beneath the church not long after you arrived in Vienna. You were left with a monk and this *Book of Hours*, correct?"

"How do you know that?"

"I have ways."

Yes, Falk thought. What the Mossad doesn't know it has ways of finding out.

Herschel continued. "Did you hear water running when you were in the crypt?"

"Yes, and the walls were wet in places."

"Good." Herschel flipped some pages back and forth, deeply engrossed, tracing, measuring and making notes.

Falk glanced down at the map in front of him. His eyes caught sight of rows of lines winding like vines. Checking the dated legend at the bottom corner, he discovered the lines represented electrical conduits. The map was less than ten years old.

Conduits. Falk let the word linger in his mind. He stared at the map, his heart suddenly beginning to thump wildly. Latin, *Conductus* —from *conucere*—to bring forth. Vienna was a city of fountains. The *Book of Hours* pictured fountains, birds, angels, monks, churches— holy things. Good God it had been there all the time in bright, Holy Roman color! Reaching across the table, he pulled the prayer book toward him.

Koski noted the move and was about to say something but Joe quickly shook his head. At the same time his facial expression indicated that she remain silent. Koski nodded her understanding and went back to her maps.

Falk quickly checked the chart for fountain locations in the inner city where the search would take place, especially noting the area around the Dorotheum and both churches. Now the prayer book began to make sense. He flipped the pages, seeing illustrations beautifully drawn, colored pictures of monks kneeling at prayer beside fountains.

Falk's mind was racing. Was the hiding place secreted beneath a fountain? Smiling cherubs, some with whips…

A cherub, Falk thought, *is a member of the second order of angels, distinguished by knowledge and often represented as a beautiful, winged child.* Was he crazy? Goering had been master of the German Luftwaffe. A winged child indeed!

His roving index finger returned to the atlas and stopped at a fountain, bounded by both churches and the Dorotheum. "Providence Fountain," the legend indicated, "By George Raphael Donner, built 1737-1739, more commonly known as the Donner Fountain." Reading the Water and Power notes further, Falk discovered that the Donner Fountain was sealed and capped in 1914. Beneath the fountain, clearly marked, was a stone vault dating back to Roman times and once used as a cistern, fed by a natural spring.

According to the notes, capping the spring had been necessary due to constant seepage that threatened to damage other building foundations in the area, including both churches. A more up-to-date system was presently in effect for circulating water but the cistern, a vault-like room, narrow and about thirty feet long, was still there.

Falk read more notes that were apparently prepared for the benefit of tourists. Four graceful angels, one on each corner of the fountain, represented four rivers: the Enns, March, Traum and Ybbs.

At first the river names meant nothing. He read them slowly, looking for a clue. He remembered that he had heard water on the sloping walk to the crypt, had felt it on the walls. Perhaps river water still ran through the cistern.

Was it possible it had been uncapped and the vault filled, ready to burst if anyone attempted to enter? He cursed silently. Another damned obstacle to overcome. How could he be sure if the cistern was empty?

Staring at the paper, he reread the names of the rivers, trying the most elemental formula—the first letter of each. Could it be that easy? E-M-T-Y. Empty. Yes! Imperceptibly Falk pumped his fist. Goering must have known. That's why he hid everything beneath the fountain and above the passageways. Falk felt a rush of adrenaline and scarcely prevented himself from shouting aloud. He had to get *inside* the cistern to be sure.

Herschel lowered his pencil and stretched his arms above his head. "I'd like you both to examine the route we'll be taking. Check it out, point out any changes you think we should make. Let's go over this from the minute we descend below street level."

The trio bent over the charts and maps. It was almost an hour before Falk and Koski sat back, fully satisfied with the plan they had mapped out with Herschel. The charts of passageways maintained by the Vienna Water and Power were in perfect detail down to individual light switches that were numbered and named.

Falk was careful not to let anything slip about his plan to get into the cistern beneath the Donner. He felt confident he was onto the hiding place and was ready to inform Koski when he got the chance.

Herschel still favored a location beneath the original wing that was destroyed during the last days of the war and subsequently rebuilt. Falk was unconcerned. He pondered how he and Koski could shake loose from the rest of the team and follow-up on his own lead without tipping his hand.

"I had expected the others would be here by now," Herschel remarked.

"Yes," Falk said. Although he didn't relish tramping through the sewers of Vienna with this "crew," he was antsy to get moving.

Slowly he began to formulate his exact plan. Herschel had drawn his pencil along the passageways beside the fast flowing water in the main sewer channel. The first leg ran straight then turned left for two hundred feet before hooking at a forty-five degree angle. He noticed light switches placed exactly at two hundred foot intervals. He would turn off the lights in the passage as soon as they made the right turn then and he and Koski would make a run for one of the galleries intersecting the main passageway.

Falk knew the gallery he wanted, on the right, the second one after they made the turn. Given the sudden darkness and confusion, he and Koski had a good chance of making it. The others would have to search all the galleries to find them.

Herschel excused himself to go to the bathroom and Falk took the precaution of ripping a page from the map book. It had nothing to do with the Herschel route but rather depicted details of the cistern under the Donner. Quickly he briefly outlined his plan for Koski.

Now that he had the arrangements worked out in his head and Koski was aware of their next move, he relaxed somewhat. He could afford to play Herschel's game.

"Well, Doctor," he said when the general returned, "we're in your hands. We can't really argue with your strategy."

"I'm glad we're a team." Herschel smiled a broad, genuine smile. "Remember, Emma and Lego will be safer with us than in the city. There are some people who'd like to see them as prisoners again."

They turned toward the door at the sound of voices.

Chapter 66

After what seemed like hours, Steele heard a click and the crate that enclosed him snapped open.

"You get to live a little longer," Ali said as he turned off the timer he had set earlier and pulled Steele from the crate. "Steele, you look like a fooking scarecrow."

From somewhere in the warehouse Steele heard a forklift whining toward them.

"Now we go places," Ali exclaimed and released the wire from Steele's mouth. Steele spat a bloody tooth onto the floor.

"What about these?" Steele asked and turned his wirebound wrists toward him but Ali shook his head.

The forklift, two steel fingers jutting like tusks of a long-forgotten prehistoric animal, came in from the shadows and across the wide expanse of warehouse. The whine died as the driver came up beside them. He and Ali exchanged a few words and the two tossed Steele onto the stubby rear deck of the vehicle. Ali stood at the base of one of the tusks and the driver turned the yellow machine in a tight circle and set off into the shadows of the subterranean shipping area.

If one were to draw a line through the floor from where Mifflin was standing, it would have come out within three feet of the small dingy room once used as a shipping office in the lower level; the door to which Pasha opened slightly at the sound of the approaching forklift. Satisfied it was safe, he pushed the door open and stepped out. Steele, his wrists and ankles still bound, was hauled from the machine and dragged toward Pasha.

"Good. My bait is still alive." He stepped close to Steele. "I have one more job for you."

Steele raised his head and spat. The spittle, laced with blood, hit Pasha full in the face. Ali raised his automatic, its butt ready to strike.

"Don't!" Pasha's voice trembled with rage. "You have little time to live, Steele, but I promise it will be long enough for you to regret what you just did."

Steele sneered and his bloody, swollen upper lip cracked. "Then get on with it."

Pasha wiped his face on his jacket sleeve. "Get him ready."

Ali removed the wire from Steele's wrists and ankles and snapped his wrists in handcuffs behind his back. His shirt was pulled down to his waist and a misshapen cloth bandoleer filled with explosives was strapped tightly to his body. Ali smiled malignantly as he rebuttoned Steele's shirt.

"You're primed, Steele," Pasha purred. "You're now a suicide bomber." He circled Steele like an army sergeant inspecting a new recruit. "Fits the body well." He turned to Ali. "You're certain of the range?"

"Range of the transmitter to the subject's receiver," he tapped a spot in the center of Steele's back, "is sixty meters. I intend to be a little closer."

Pasha nodded. "Remove the handcuffs. Bring him into the office." Ali took off the cuffs and he and the forklift driver shoved Steele forward.

"Here." Pasha tapped the top of a scarred wooden table. "Place his left hand in the center." Steele tried to pull away but the driver grabbed his arm and slapped it across the table.

The corners of Pasha's mouth turned up slightly. "I warned you that you'd regret spitting in my face." He reached beneath the table and came up with a thick, heavy, three-legged stool. It took both Ali and the driver to hold Steele and his hand on the table. In one swift sizzling arc, Pasha lifted the stool over his head and brought it down. The crunch of bones sounded like dry twigs being ground underfoot. Steele fell forward across the table, out cold.

"When he comes to, put that hand in his pocket. He won't need it again." Pasha replaced the stool and smoothed his shirt.

Steele was back on the forklift when he regained consciousness. His mangled left hand in agonizing pain throbbed and stabbed up his arm like a red-hot poker.

"The fooking scarecrow's awake." Ali grabbed the purple, misshapen mass that had once been Steele's hand and roughly jammed it into Steele's left pocket. A wave of nausea hit Steele and his brain fought to remain conscious.

"Take him to the gallery," Pasha ordered. "You know what to do."

"What do I do if he refuses to get close to the passageway?"

Pasha's eyes narrowed until the flesh around them threatened to engulf them. "Ali, we're men with a mission for Islam. Carry out my orders."

Ali nodded and he and the driver mounted the forklift. The electric motor spun to life. In exactly that moment, Steele came back from a hazy, REM-like void and caught sight of the one thing he coveted most in the world at that moment: Pasha's throat. When he lunged, his will denied his weakened condition, his quivering knees.

With what remained of his left hand and with an almighty effort, his good right hand shot out and clamped around the scrawny throat in a bulldog grip. A gasp was the only sound Pasha made, his eyes round with fright as they shot to Ali.

"Move a muscle and he's dead," Steele rasped.

Ali hesitated at the cold, calm edge in Steele's voice. Steele dragged Pasha closer until the scrawny Arab was tight against him. In a quick shift, Steele released his grip and immediately replaced it with an arm lock around Pasha's neck. A surge of strength flowed through Steele's body. He was a Canadian paratrooper once more, oblivious to pain with the enemy firmly in his grip.

He waved his fingers for the remote Ali held in his hand. "Give me the transmitter, now. Tell him, turtle piss."

Pasha made a croaking sound. Ali leaned forward and passed the transmitter into Steele's fingers. Steele grinned, showing a gap where a tooth had been. "Throw down your weapons or I flip on this remote and we all leave…abruptly." Ali and the driver let their guns clatter to the floor. "Now," Steele said, "we get the hell outta here."

"The building is full of police and military security," Ali noted. "Better we take the galleries above the sewers."

Steele pushed Pasha ahead of him and stepped onto the base of one of the steel fingers of the forklift. "Drive real easy. I don't want to get nervous and hit the switch."

As they moved slowly toward a freight elevator, Steele listened to Pasha's harsh breathing and the soft hum of the forklift motor and thought that perhaps the life and times of John Steele were running out.

Chapter 67

To Nikolai Youmatoff, having emerged from his long woodland trek, Ottawa's sidewalks seemed the busiest he'd ever seen. It was actually a slow day, considering the approaching holiday, with relatively light pedestrian traffic. The area of the Russian Embassy was particularly deserted.

Youmatoff spied Charlotte Street ahead and he started down a side street that intersected an alley. As he passed the dark, narrow cavity between two buildings, he stopped in mid-stride. He didn't turn but looked straight ahead. He knew instinctively that a pursuer had found him and that a gun was pointed precisely in his direction.

If he twisted toward the alley, he'd be looking at his past and his future no more than six feet away. They always got their man, Youmatoff thought, and almost laughed at the irony of it all.

He waited. Apparently the Mountie was not prepared to kill him —perhaps wound him if he resisted. Youmatoff wondered, however, why the man said nothing, did nothing.

Had Youmatoff turned and looked into the face of Sgt. Christopher Pullbrook, he still wouldn't have the answers to his questions but he might have had a glimmer of what was to come.

Sgt. Pullbrook was a graying man. He had served most of his life as part of that vast constabulary of Royal Canadian Mounted Police known as the Canadian Security Service.

From the day he entered, at less than twenty, he'd looked forward to the excitement of investigating espionage and subversion. At the time, he was six-three with a bulldog physique that bespoke his youthful determination.

Unfortunately, Sgt. Pullbrook broke his ankle during his first week of basic training—a fracture that, due to diabetic complications, never healed properly—and spent more than thirty years consigned to liaison duties requiring little involvement.

In fact, today, less than a year from the date of his planned retirement, he was doing "gofer" work, delivering a routine message to the Soviet Embassy when he saw Youmatoff. He had just come from CPIC headquarters where he saw Youmatoff's file. He noted the picture of the Russian that came over the net from Photo Service Information Center.

On one hand, Sgt. Pullbrook saw the years left to him as deserved things—ample compensation for unlived life. On the other hand, Sgt. Pullbrook, who had never mounted a horse, who—although he was issued a handgun that he usually kept holstered against his left armpit —had never gone out on what he considered a legitimate assignment, saw Youmatoff as his first and last chance for undying glory.

Chapter 68

Herschel greeted Eiker as the tall Brit led Emma and Lego into the old tailor shop where Falk and Koski waited. Shaking hands with Herschel, Lego said, "I'm honored to meet you, General."

Herschel reacted with surprise. "Thank you but that was a long time ago. I'm no longer in the Army." He greeted Emma and guided her and Lego to a couple of easy chairs, noting that Mifflin had yet to arrive. "I've been over the details with Doctors Falk and Koski. I'll take a few minutes to bring you up-to-date. I also have questions for Lego that might be vital to our operation."

Falk was disturbed they had been searched prior to entering the room and all weapons temporarily confiscated for "safekeeping." He took note that Koski nearly got by with a Beretta in her purse, no doubt issued by Stewart since her return to Vienna. She was patted down, although there was no female guard to thoroughly examine her person. Eiker, Falk noticed with surprise, readily obliged the search, dutifully emptying his pockets, offering his weapon, retaining nothing but a pack of gum and a Cartier lighter.

"Dr. Falk, Dr. Koski and I," Herschel began, "have gone over plans, charts, tourist books, blueprints and maps of the area beneath the Dorotheum and adjoining buildings, including the Capuchin and Augustine churches." He crossed to a blackboard and drew a horizontal chalk line across the center.

"Let's say this is the surface at street level. We're going under the streets and buildings by the same method the city's Water and Power people use. You'll be issued regulation coveralls, hard hats and flashlights so if you're seen no one will suspect you."

He drew a second line a foot below the first. "Here's the sewer system's main gallery. We'll be walking in this direction." He drew a dextral arrow. "The galleries are lighted but beware: The surface could be slippery in spots. To our left will be the water from the Danube Canal, three to four feet below the level of the gallery. It runs fast and deep and at this time of the year is damned cold."

"Earlier you mentioned something about a diver?" Falk asked.

"Yes, coming to that. We'll be in two separate columns. You'll get your positions later. The first leg will be a little under a mile and will bring us directly under the old section of the Dorotheum—the wing that was destroyed in the bombing."

He placed a large X on the board and erased part of the line to make room for his next drawing. "This is the Capuchin." He drew a short line, another X and another line, continuing almost off the board. "Sorry. My scale isn't too good. This," he pointed to the second X, "is the Augustine." Finally he drew a wobbly oval to enclose both Xs. "It's my belief that what we are seeking lies within this area."

He turned to Falk. "The diver will enter a small tributary that cuts under the Dorotheum here. As you see, it crosses from the main stream, curves under the buildings and rejoins it near the Capuchin. The only other possible way anyone can get into the area we'll be searching is to follow that tributary. The diver's job is to be certain no one does. The entrance we descend will also be covered as will all others in the immediate vicinity."

"What about the city?" Eiker asked. "They could conceivably need to be down there."

Herschel nodded. "We've checked the maintenance schedule. No one will be in that section for the next three days. As you know, an Austrian schedule is exact. Nothing short of an all-out emergency can change it."

"When do we start?" Koski asked.

"Midnight, by which time Mifflin should be here." Herschel ran a hand through his thinning hair. "I suggest everyone get as much rest as possible."

He went to a door that opened onto another room. "There are comfortable chairs in there. Perhaps you can relax a while." He turned to Lego. "May I speak with you alone a moment?" Lego shrugged and they went back to the table.

The second room was once the living quarters for the family who ran the tailor shop. It contained a couch, three battered armchairs and a coffee table. Koski and Falk sat together on the couch, his arm protectively around her shoulders. Emma and Eiker faced each other in armchairs.

"Seems like a good plan," Koski said a little too loudly. She waved her arms in a gesture that indicated the room could be bugged. She continued. "Looks good on the blackboard anyway." She got up. "I need to visit the restroom. Be right back." She disappeared into the small adjoining bathroom.

When she returned Koski sank down next to Falk, pressed against him and surreptitiously slipped one hand into his jacket pocket. "So you won't feel naked," she whispered then lightly kissed his cheek.

She withdrew her hand. The weight where it had been remained and he knew the source.

"How…" he began.

She scowled to stop him and softly brushed his cheek. He felt the reverberation of her words against his skin, more than heard them. "Plastic."

His lips unmoving in a fashion that would have made a ventriloquist proud, he softly hissed, "Where did you hide it to get it past the guards that searched you?"

"You don't want to know."

He pulled away slightly and let his vision slip into those deep green pools of speckled light. "Don't be too sure of that."

She leaned her head against his shoulder and they both closed their eyes. For nearly an hour, Falk felt like they were alone in the world.

Eiker suddenly blurted out, arousing the others. "Where the fuck is Mifflin? It's getting late. I want to get this show on the road."

Chapter 69

Kutna and Mifflin stood face to face at the top of the stairs beneath the Dorotheum. Kutna wiped the back of his hand across his forehead and said halfheartedly, "Thanks."

Captain Vlad walked up to them. "What happened?"

"Yakov and his people kidnapped the head porter," Mifflin said, "nearly killed Kutna here. Any news of other possible terrorist activity?"

"A fellow in the warehouse reported his forklift missing," Vlad replied. "We're checking it out, nothing else."

The three walked back toward the front entrance. Everything looked like business as usual, the soldiers out of sight.

"Look, Kutna," Mifflin said, "you and Vlad can take it from here. I'm late for an appointment."

Kutna nodded. "Mifflin…" he started to say but the big man waved away his thanks.

"You're welcome."

Kutna watched as Mifflin nodded to Vlad then plowed massively across the entrance hall and out the front door. Turning back toward the main hall, Kutna wished he had some news on Rosie.

The Judas List

Chapter 70

Steele felt the quiver of fear running through the thin body of the man he held in a death lock. The forklift hummed at a cautious pace, the driver afraid the least bump or jar would cause the explosives strapped to Steele's body to detonate.

"Steele," Ali called, his voice low and submissive now. "I know a better way. We can stay alive...Let's make a deal..."

Steele turned his head slightly and looked at him. "No fooking deals, chum." He tightened the grip on Pasha's neck. "It's bye-bye for all of us." Pasha squirmed against him and Steele felt the bulge of a gun pressing into his side. The bastard was packing!

"Is that a gun," he questioned, "or are you just happy to see me?" He took a deep breath and jammed Pasha's head down between his legs in a leg lock that threatened to crush the man's trachea. He slid his right hand into Pasha's pocket and came out with a Beretta 9mm automatic. "How sweet it is," he said then thumbed the safety, turned and blew a hole in Ali's face. The bullet entered just above his top lip beneath the right nostril. Ali jerked back, spun sideways and was gone. As he hit the floor two feet behind the forklift, Steele shifted his eyes to the driver, who was terror-stricken.

"Nice and easy," he said, "over there next to the freight elevator." The driver headed cautiously in the direction indicated. "When we get there," Steele continued, "you get off, open the doors then drive this rig on." He grabbed Pasha by his thin straggling hair and pulled him upright to be sure the man was witness to his own execution.

He placed the barrel of the gun in the little man's ear and pulled the trigger. "Allah Akbar." Bone gore and brains splattered across the forklift and Pasha slid down and arched across the steel tusks.

They were at the freight elevator. The driver was shaking so violently he nearly fell off the machine. He opened the elevator doors, remounted the rig and slowly drove onto the large wooden platform.

Steele painfully eased from the forklift and off the elevator. He stood aside while the open latticed doors began to close. The terrified driver's face looked directly into the first bullet that took him out of his terror as the steel jacketed slug tore into his right eye. The second clipped the lobe of his left ear as he fell sideways from the driver's seat. Steele lowered the gun, reached through the lattice and jabbed a button on the panel.

"Going up," he said and headed for a side door as the elevator began its ascent.

The door led to an iron walkway known as a gallery that ran over the passageway beside the running waters of the Danube Canal and the Vienna sewer system.

At that moment Steele was three hundred feet ahead of where Falk had decided he would turn out the lights and make a run for the cistern of the Donner Fountain. Steele needed to hide, to rest. He knew his life was near its end and just once he wanted to look upon Goering's damnable stolen treasures.

If only Dr. Benson had listened to him this wouldn't have happened. They could have worked together and found the loot. It all could have been so simple. A stab of pain shot through his arm from the mangled hand. Thanks to Pasha's beatings, his head hurt and his mind weaved in and out of clarity. He reached for support but slid down the wall in a crumpled heap onto the cold iron grating. Above him, rusty iron conduits sagged like snakes. Despite his deteriorating condition, he remained filled with resolve. "If I can't have the treasure, no one will. I'll wait and when the searchers come through the passageway below me, I'll take them all to hell with me."

Five minutes after Mifflin left, Kutna glanced up the broad, curving staircase leading to the Dorotheum's upper rooms and saw Vlad double timing down the stairs. At the same time, one of Kutna's men came up to him with a startling report.

Not wanting to arouse suspicion, Kutna followed his man at a half walk, half run toward the back of the building. They made their way through endless rooms of antiques, paintings and tapestries to a freight elevator where a gathering of warehouse workers huddled. Vlad caught up with him as he stopped in front of the open freight elevator.

"Get everyone back," Kutna shouted, "but don't let any of them into the main building." Together the two men walked into the elevator. Pasha's twisted body lay slumped across the bloody steel shafts of the forklift.

The driver was slumped on the floor. The thought that flashed across Kutna's mind was that he knew something Mifflin didn't. What was it exactly and how could he use it to his advantage?

The Judas List

Chapter 71

When Mifflin alighted from the cab that brought him from the Dorotheum to Stewart's office he sensed things were moving fast and he was falling behind.

"What's happening at the Dorotheum?" Stewart asked calmly.

"Kutna and Vlad are handling things. Yakov and his Czechos were caught in a cross fire. Yakov's dead along with several others."

Stewart pinched the bridge of his nose and lowered his head. "There's a car waiting to take you to see Herschel. He arranged it."

"Good. Now I can catch up with Eiker."

"You can catch up with everyone."

"I'll have a tail so you'll know where Herschel and his little band are taking us."

Stewart nodded. "I'll know where you are at all times."

"Fine. I'll be in touch."

After Mifflin left Stewart leaned both elbows on his desk. He was looking forward to the end of this episode.

When he arrived Mifflin was searched and ushered into the back room.

"Glad you could make it, Harold," Herschel said. "I was beginning to think we'd have to go without you."

"Unavoidable," Mifflin muttered as he was introduced to Lego and the three joined the others in the next room. Eiker, pacing the floor, turned at their entrance.

"What took you so long, Mifflin?"

Mifflin knew there was too much to tell. He simply said, "Christmas traffic."

Herschel quickly took center stage again. "I want to run a few final details by you before we go down. Lego has given me information not shown on any of our maps or other drawings."

Two men entered carrying Vienna Water and Power coveralls and hard hats and interrupted him.

"Thanks. Put them in the corner." Herschel waited until they left to continue. "We'll form two single file teams. I'll lead one, Dr. Falk the other. My team will consist of Lego, Miss Lewis, Mr. Eiker and one security man. Dr. Falk will lead Dr. Koski, Mr. Mifflin and a security person. The reason for the two teams is, of course, security.

"My team will go first with a quarter mile separating us. We'll be able to assist one another if an attack occurs. Are there any questions?" Since no one responded, he continued. "Very well. When my team reaches the section where a small tributary runs off from the main stream, I'll signal for the second team to join us.

"Then we'll descend below the main gallery. This could be the most dangerous part of the expedition—a descent of about sixty feet on a vertical iron ladder."

Falk was fascinated. Perhaps Herschel was onto something. Perhaps his theory was off-the-wall. No, he had to try his way. If it turned out that the fountain wasn't the place…well, he'd deal with it.

"I'll go down first to be sure the ladder's safe," Herschel explained. "When I get to the bottom, I'll flash my light three times for you to join me. It's my firm belief that we'll find the hiding place under a room that was destroyed by bombings during the war."

Mifflin snorted. "I still don't see how the room wasn't discovered at the time of the rebuilding."

"I have no idea, Mr. Mifflin. Perhaps it was. To the workers, however, it was nothing but the remains of a bombed-out building. We must assume the treasures weren't sitting in full view. The room was once the main shipping office for everything leaving the Dorotheum.

"In addition, the room was built over an old wine cellar. Most of the world knew that the wines—some of Europe's finest—like most of the riches in the Dorotheum, were removed by the Nazis and hidden in the Bavarian Alps. When the demolition crews and builders started to rebuild they figured there was nothing to find."

"Yet you expect to find the loot after all these years?" Mifflin insisted.

"Yes, I do."

"There literally must have been tons of rubble. How will you locate the room?"

"I intend to go directly to the cellar through the wall that faces the level at the bottom of the ladder."

Mifflin rubbed the back of his hand across his mouth. "It still sounds like a wild goose chase to me but..."

Herschel replied, "I had a plan where I was headed but I couldn't pinpoint the cellar until I spoke to Lego and I had to wait for him to be delivered to me."

"What do you mean?" Falk asked.

"Lego related to me how he remembered the original building, how it looked and where the shipping office used to be. I checked my plans and, knowing how Goering's mind worked, I decided it was the most likely place."

Falk shifted uneasily. Either Herschel was off by a mile or *he* was. Herschel checked his watch.

"Our transportation will be here soon. Time to get in to our coveralls." He picked up a set, checked the size and handed them to Koski. "We have small, medium and large. As you leave you'll each be given a regulation belt that contains a tool pouch and an industrial-sized flashlight. These, along with the hard hats, should let us pass easily as Water and Power workers."

Falk was the last to leave the tailor shop, following the others into a small courtyard. It was dark and a sift of snow was falling. Light suffused over the area from an old-fashioned, wrought iron lamp above the door. He buckled his tool belt and climbed into the Vienna Water and Power truck.

Herschel hurried everyone aboard. Inside they faced each other on long wooden benches. The security men sat nearest the tailgate. Herschel went up front next to the driver. No one spoke as the truck moved from the yard and turned onto the street. All were alone with their own thoughts, Falk certain that he had the most at stake.

Chapter 72

Steele's cheek lay pressed against the cold iron railing. He shivered and slowly eased to a sitting position despite the excruciating pain that shot through his hand to his shoulder. From his perch on the totally dark catwalk he heard the gurgle of water swirling its way beneath the old city, branching off into a narrow tunnel and out of sight. What faint light there was came from the main gallery below.

His eyes were fixed on the water. Something moved. The surface rippled, bubbled and foamed and a black glistening form rose with a hiss of air.

Steele was transfixed. He'd heard of sewer rats—but this! Then there was the glint of glass as the diver pushed his mask back. Heart thumping, Steele watched the diver climb from the water, remove his mouthpiece and shrug off his air tanks and inflatable vest. A metallic clank resounded as he set them on the stone floor.

Hardly daring to breathe, Steele pulled back into the shadows as the man removed a flashlight from his belt, aimed it down the gallery and pressed the switch three times in quick succession. Seconds later three stabs of light answered. A rendezvous in the making and Steele had a grandstand seat.

Within five minutes of the truck arriving at the manhole, Herschel had everyone down the ladder to the first level. Falk had noticed road warning signs, the tent over the manhole, reflectors. Everything was set up exactly like city crews would have done.

"We have two levels to go," Herschel said. "The next is thirty-five feet; the last fifteen. That will put us on the main gallery level one hundred and ten feet below the street. Watch your grip on the ladders, no time for accidents."

The only sound was footwear scraping on the ladder rungs as they slowly descended to the main gallery. They heard the rushing water before they saw it. Finally they were grouped beside the gallery's stonewall.

"It's like the London Underground without the train tracks," Emma whispered to Lego.

"And a damn sight colder," Eiker replied.

"Dr. Falk, get your team together. Once we start I don't want anyone using flashlights. We'll rely on gallery lighting only."

The dim lights were built into the stonewalls and covered by metal grillwork. Falk checked for the light switches to be certain he had their exact location in mind when he and Koski made their break.

Herschel checked his watch. "Dr. Falk, I have six-thirty...mark."

"Check."

"Good. When I move out give me seven minutes and then follow. I want a safe distance between us. One of my men will be at the end of your line, a sort of 'Tail End Charlie'."

Falk shot a quick glance to Koski and received an almost imperceptible nod. They both knew the team's security man was for Herschel's safety, not theirs. It was up to Koski to take care of Tail End Charlie.

"You remember the signal?" Herschel questioned.

"Of course," Falk replied. "Three flashes and we move up and join you for the final descent below this gallery."

Herschel shook Falk's hand. "Good luck." He turned and started moving. Lego, Emma and a security guard followed.

"Damn!" Stewart slammed his phone down and drummed his fingers on the desk. Mifflin had gone to meet Herschel and now he had no way of knowing where Mifflin and the others were. One of the men following Mifflin reported he'd lost him in traffic. A few moments later a second call informed Stewart that Mifflin's backup tail was found sitting on a bus bench with his throat cut.

The Judas List

Chapter 73

Mifflin puffed along, following Koski, who followed Falk. Falk heard the Mossad security man bringing up the rear. Whoever was trailing me from Stewart's office, he thought, did a damn good job. I never saw anyone.

Three stabs of light flashed up ahead. Falk turned and softly called an order to stop. "Crouch down close to the wall and stay still." He blinked a response.

Mifflin heard the metallic click of a safety catch from the security man's weapon followed only by the sound of their breathing. An icy coldness drooped around them.

Herschel beamed the answering signal. "Let's move forward, slowly now." He stood as the others in his team passed. Herschel returned to the head of the column, his voice tinged with excitement. "We're getting closer to our goal. So far all is clear."

Lego slowly shuffled forward, his mind drifting back over the years to when Nikolai Youmatoff gave him the information that had dogged his life ever since. The Danube Canal rushed along at his side as if it was the years passing. He reached back with one hand and Emma grasped it. Together they were nearing the end of a mysterious journey that, for Lego, started over a half-century earlier.

After Falk responded and they started moving ahead, he knew

Herschel was intent on making his way to his contact. Falk had to make his move now. They were making the right hand turn. He whispered to Koski, "Ready?" Before she could respond, he fell to his side and grabbed his ankle.

"My ankle," he moaned. "I think it's broken."

When "Tail End Charlie" moved up beside him and bent over Falk, Koski hit him across the back of the neck with her flashlight just below the rim of the hard hat. He folded forward without a sound. Falk and Koski were up and running in the direction of the second gallery on his right. Within seconds, Falk flipped the lights out and Mifflin was alone in the darkness.

The tantalizing thought that he was getting closer to his objective made Herschel increase his stride. He arrived at the location where he was to meet the diver minutes ahead of the rest of his team.

The diver snapped a salute. "All secure, sir."

"Good. Prepare the descent."

The diver knelt on the stone floor and scraped at a film of dirt and grime until he located two recessed handles in an iron manhole cover. The rest of the team arrived and Emma, Eiker and the security man formed a semicircle around him. Lego was off to one side in the shadows, leaning against the wall to gather his strength. The diver rounded his shoulders and pulled at the handles. Nothing happened. Shifting his grip, he tried again, his neck muscles bulging with the effort. He let go and looked at Herschel. "I need something to pry..."

He gasped, his vision focusing beyond Herschel's anxious face. A peal of maniacal laughter rang out. It echoed off the curving walls to join the omnipresent sound of rushing water and sent a stab of fear through the group. Herschel turned fast, a gun in his hand. The security man crouched beside him with his Uzi whirling in all directions, seeking a target.

One face stood out to the man in the grandstand seat. "Emma, you bitch!" Steele shouted. "I should have killed you when I had the chance." The voice seemed to come from heaven and all eyes turned upward. "You two with the guns," Steele hollered, "drop them or we'll all go up together. I'm wired with explosives."

Herschel and the guard hesitated, not sure if whoever was up there was telling the truth. They raised their flashlights.

"Steele!" Emma gasped as the powerful beams illuminated his haggard face.

Steele ripped open his shirt to reveal the bulky explosive package enclosing his upper torso. His hand also held the remote transmitter, glinting in the light. He raised it over his head. "In person...I press a button and zap..." He grinned like a lunatic.

"Do as he says," Herschel commanded and the guard let his Uzi clatter to the floor. Herschel reluctantly tossed his automatic aside. It, too, resounded as it landed in the nearby shadows.

"Emma, move closer, where it's lighter so I can see you," Steele ordered. Emma did as she was told, prepared to buy some time on the chance that Falk and Koski soon would be there to help.

"You know, Emma, we could have done this together and got away with it. Just you, me and the Yank...where *is* the Yank?"

"He's not in Vienna."

"Bullshit."

"It's true. He's not here."

"Where the hell is he?"

"Last I heard he was in the Czech Republic. We escaped."

Steele snarled. "We?"

"Susan Koski and I. You remember Susan, don't you?"

"Yeah. I should have killed her, too. You see it seems killing is my forte. Took them a long time to figure out how I killed our friend, Dr. Benson."

Emma gasped and staggered back a few steps.

Lego, hidden in the shadows, stared up at the man he once called a friend. A low, animal sound escaped from Lego's lips. Driven by feral instincts stronger than reason, Lego scooped Herschel's discarded automatic from the floor. Using a two-handed grip he extended his arms forward until Steele was centered in his sights. He sucked in a deep breath, held it and squeezed the trigger.

In the same instant Steele caught the movement in the shadows. One perfect shot sang into Steele's head, the bullet plowing between his top lip and nose, but not before his thumb depressed the transmitter button.

The sound of the shot didn't fade when the roar of the explosion hit the confines of the catwalk with an intensity so strong the shock wave shuddered against the walls and through the water. It caused a waterspout to rise and meet the catwalk as it crumbled in a twisted mass of iron, wood and concrete.

Yards of metal sagged, pipes split, debris showered down onto the gallery and into the water. Herschel, the security man and the diver vanished under the initial mass of falling masonry, crushed like ants underfoot. Before a chunk of flying concrete hit him, Lego lived long enough to see bits and pieces of John Steele rain down and mix with the waters of the Danube Canal.

Chapter 74

Emma survived only because Eiker had pushed her against the curving wall, protecting her with his body.

The concussion flattened Falk against Koski and she clung tightly to him. The shock wave hit the dark, narrow passage. A hot blast of air rushed down the gallery and for a moment the floor shook. The shaking stopped, replaced by an awful stillness, and the gallery filled with billows of acrid smoke.

"We're still alive," Falk rasped, spitting out sand and grit. "But we've got to go back—Mifflin..."

Making their way through the rubble, they arrived back to where Koski had struck the guard and found Mifflin flat on his back, the dead guard beside him. Falk rolled the dead man into the water. The body swirled in the stream, hit the wall then, with one arm raised as if in farewell, sank from sight.

Mifflin groaned. Koski knelt beside him, rubbing his hands and checking him for wounds. "Are you okay?"

Mifflin opened one eye. "What happened? Where the hell did you two go?"

Falk pulled him over to the wall and propped him up. "You took so long getting to the meeting I didn't have time to fill you in on our plan."

"Thanks." Mifflin stretched, testing his body for injury. "My right inside pocket..."

Falk reached in, removed a flask and passed it to him.

Mifflin took a long swig then offered it to Falk.

He refused but Koski took a deep swallow.

"I've got to get up ahead and see what the hell happened." He turned to Koski. "He's still groggy. Stay here with him. I'll be as quick as I can."

The explosion had jolted all levels of the Dorotheum. Vlad cursed inwardly as he raced to meet his men in the main hall. He knew he should have evacuated the building earlier. "Cover the exits," he instructed his men. "Avert panic and make an orderly exodus."

Kutna appeared at his side, his eyes betraying his inner fears. "Terrorists?"

"Don't know yet," Vlad said. "If so they'll make demands."

"Need any help?"

"No, thanks. City police are on the way. They'll handle things outside. We're staying in the building to make sure the place is fully evacuated."

Kutna nodded and left to return to his office. He knew without a doubt that the phone lines would be overloaded with calls from around the city.

Chapter 75

For a moment Emma thought Eiker was dead. She was pinned beneath him and the pain in her leg indicated it was broken. She fought to remain calm when a small avalanche of bricks crashed to the gallery floor inches from her head.

Some lights were still burning but the dust was thick and she could only see a few feet beyond them. Her face flushed and panic began to rise within her. She stirred against Eiker's weight. "Eiker... Eiker," she coughed.

He grunted and came to full consciousness. "Bloody hell!" he rasped as he rolled onto his side then back against Emma. "Don't move. There's no floor beyond us!"

Emma groaned. "My leg is broken."

"Which one?"

"Left," she replied through gritted teeth.

"Okay." Breathing heavily, he paused, spitting out dust and grit as he quickly assessed the situation. "There are only a few feet of floor between us and the water. I'm going to move. Your left leg is against the wall. I'll do all I can to avoid it."

Another rumbling of rocks crashed into the water to their right. They both fought the smothering fear that any minute the walls, ceiling or both would bury them. He groaned in sudden pain as he eased over her body.

"Eiker, are you all right?"

His feet searched for more ground. "I'm fine." Emma was in so much pain that she decided to believe him.

The toes of his shoes found solid stone. "There's some floor remaining," he grunted. He slid onto the cold stone and fingered the floor to his left a few inches…then nothing. Unhooking his flashlight, he thumbed it on and swept the beam around the small confine. He now realized they were marooned on a shelf no more than four feet wide jutting out over the swiftly moving current. He pointed the beam down the gallery beyond his feet. What Emma saw nearly made her heart stop.

The shelf ended abruptly, blocked by a slide of rock from ceiling to stream.

"We can't just stay here," Emma groaned. "There has to be some way out."

"Your leg is broken. What do you suggest?" Emma noticed his labored breathing wasn't subsiding.

"Could we swim?"

"You wouldn't have a chance."

She knew he was right but to lie there doing nothing… "At least try signaling with the flashlight. Do something, for God's sake."

"I'm going for help. You'll be okay as long as you stay still. Don't move at all. Understand?"

"Yes."

"Good, now listen. I'm going to remove my coveralls and shoes, attach the flashlight to my hard hat with strips torn from the coveralls. I'll turn it on and swim back upstream until I find a spot where I can get out… find help."

He paused and winced but continued. "It's possible the authorities already have teams out looking for the cause of the explosion and hopefully will see my light." He reached over and found Emma's flashlight. "Here. If you see or hear anyone yell like hell and signal them with the flashlight beam. Got it?"

"Yes."

Slowly, hardly daring to move in case he disturbed more rocks, Eiker eased out of the coveralls and slid off his shoes. As soon as he was satisfied the flashlight was secure to his hard hat, he gave Emma's shoulder a reassuring pat. "Remember now, lie still. Everything will go like a well-oiled machine."

Emma smiled weakly despite her pain and discomfort. Seconds later she heard a splash and was alone on the ledge.

The Judas List

Chapter 76

Falk made his way over the wet cobblestones, following the route taken by Herschel and his team. Once out of range of Koski's light, he faced nothing but thick, palpable blackness. The ever-present dust made breathing dangerous and difficult. He stopped for a moment, listening for any sound. Nothing. The silence was tomblike.

Falk snapped on his flashlight and let the beam creep over the wall until it discovered the rockslide blocking the gallery. Slowly he approached the unyielding pile of earth, stone and twisted iron. Dropping to his knees, he rested his head against the impassable barrier.

It was evident that any attempt to dig through the mass would cause the entire tunnel to collapse. He pounded a fist in frustration against the immovable blockade that separated him, Koski and Mifflin from the others—if there were others—and a trickle of stones ran down the pile into the water.

Koski had turned off her flashlight. Now she and Mifflin sat side by side in the inky blackness.

"It's ironic," she said. "So many times in Brno I thought I'd never get back to Vienna. Now I may never get out."

"Nonsense," Mifflin replied gruffly. "You'll get out. We all will."

Koski tensed at the sound of someone approaching. Then she

heard a familiar voice quietly call, "It's me, Joe."

"Emma?" Koski asked once Falk was beside her.

"I don't know. A landslide has sealed the gallery. It's blocked solid. We move one rock and the whole damn place could cave in."

Koski responded with a resounding, "We have to try something."

Falk squeezed her arm. "Don't worry. We'll get her."

Falk and Mifflin stared at the rushing water by the light of Mifflin's flashlight beam, gauging its speed and depth, considering the possibility of navigating it as a means to reach the others.

Falk finally decided. "I'm going to make an attempt to get through by swimming downstream."

"Let *me* go, Falk. I'm a strong swimmer and a damn sight more buoyant than you."

"No. I'll go."

Mifflin sighed. "Then we'll go together. Koski can stand watch. If a search party shows up she can fill them in."

Koski nodded emphatically. "Go, both of you. I'll be okay until you get back."

"We'll need some dry clothes when we return," Falk said. He and Mifflin stripped off their coveralls, shoes and shirts and slid over the edge into the cold Canal.

The water took Falk's breath away as he swam with the flow, forcefully stroking to maintain his direction. For a moment he was back in the river with Jan, swimming for his life.

The current swept them along faster than Falk expected and they stroked hard to keep themselves close to the gallery's edge. Ahead the passage curved then Falk saw the beam. It was in the center of the stream, coming toward them.

"Over there...see it!" Falk called out but soon his mouth filled with water and he spat to expel it. He swam toward the light, using every bit of energy in the process. As he drew closer, he realized it was a man swimming against the stream. He was near enough now to see his face from the downward glow of the light. "Eiker!"

The Englishman acknowledged him and Falk began pointing toward the gallery. Together they swam until they saw Mifflin waving and clinging to the side of the gallery floor.

"Over here..." Mifflin yelled. "Iron rungs in the wall..."

"Ladder rungs," Falk sputtered. "See them... There."

Both men kicked hard toward the recessed rungs in the wall, reaching them in tandem.

Once on solid ground the three men updated one another on their current situations.

"Emma is the only one left alive and she's trapped with a broken leg," Eiker reported, breathing laboriously. "We've got to get her out of there immediately."

Falk nodded. "Can you find your way back to that spot?"

Eiker seemed sure he could. "Shout when I tell you and she'll signal with the flashlight."

Once again the three men entered the nearly freezing water and headed downstream.

"Emmmaaa...Emmmaaa..." The sound of her name echoed eerily in the blackness. Still there was no return light in answer to their calls.

"It should be about here," Eiker yelled as they trod water, attempting to remain in place against the current.

"Let's get in closer and try again," Falk suggested. The cold was biting through him. He knew it would only be a matter of time before hypothermia would overtake them and they wouldn't be able to rescue anyone.

"Emma!" Falk yelled at the top of his lungs. "Emma!"

Suddenly there was a flash of light through the blackness.

"There it is." Mifflin gulped, pointing back upstream. "We passed her." He was right. They had overshot her position by several hundred yards. Falk moaned and doggedly headed back, keeping his eyes fixed on the weaving beam glinting from the darkness.

Falk's light finally traced the outline of the outcrop, exposing how totally the landslide had cut them off, leaving a ledge less than ten feet long and eight feet above the water.

Falk swam closer until he felt the rocks from the landslide underfoot. Then his foot hit something metallic. He cursed softly and turned his beam downward to reveal the scuba diver's tank, harness and flotation jacket tangled among twisted iron conduits. "Herschel's diver. Poor son of a bitch."

"Up here...I'm up here." Emma's voice sounded weak and distant.

"Don't move, Emma. We'll get you down," Falk called back. Then he gingerly climbed up on the ledge with Eiker behind him.

"We're going to get you down into the water. It'll be tough going and damned cold." Falk reached out and took Emma's hand. "Think you can make it?"

"Of course," she said bravely.

"Right, love," Eiker said with a gentleness Falk had never heard before. "Soon... get you down... now."

Falk also was surprised at Eiker's apparent breathing difficulty throughout their labors. Certainly the ordeal was punishing on all of them but Eiker always kept himself in top physical condition.

Falk had seen evidence of his extraordinary stamina in the past.

Why now as they suffered nearly identical physical challenges did Eiker's strength lag noticeably behind his own?

Mifflin tapped Falk's leg with a piece of iron pipe and passed it up to him. "You can fashion a crude splint, might help a bit."

Seeing Eiker's torn coveralls, Falk yanked off more strips and crudely attached the pipe to Emma's leg. She grunted with pain but didn't complain.

Eiker took the remains of the coveralls and tossed them to Mifflin. "Wrap those around your head to keep them dry. Emma will need them when we get back. Now for the difficult part." Eiker grated as he and Falk lowered her to the turbulent water.

"Wait," Falk said. "We can use the diver's vest." He went back and picked up the inflatable lifejacket, pulled the release cord operating the air valve and the device inflated. "You're going to travel first class," he told Emma. "This is how we'll get you out of here..." Emma never took her eyes off him as he spoke.

"Once in the water, lie on your back with your head facing the direction of the flow. I'll slip the flotation jacket under your shoulder and ease it down to your hips. Keep your legs slightly elevated to take the pressure off the broken one. Eiker and I will be on either side. We'll keep you balanced and float you back to the undamaged part of the tunnel. Mifflin will be behind you at your head."

They pushed off slowly, Mifflin moving quickly into position for a man of his girth. They were no more than ten feet from the landslide area when a crack split the air and the portion of the shelf that had supported Emma seconds before broke free and sank into the water. Silently the group exchanged glances and began to swim upstream.

Koski saw the bobbing light as the three men pulled Emma through icy waters. She quickly sent three short beams in their direction ready to assist in any way possible. A sinking feeling came over her at the sight of Emma lying on her back, not moving.

Chapter 77

"She'll be okay," Falk said as he clambered onto the gallery walkway and leaned down to receive Emma. "She has a broken leg and is nearly frozen, but she'll be fine."

"Welcome back," Koski whispered to Emma as they lifted her from the Canal and eased her to the floor.

Mifflin unwound the dry coveralls from his head and passed them to Koski, who got Emma settled. Falk turned to Mifflin and Eiker. "You two stay with her. Koski and I have to go. We'll be getting into some tight spaces and I don't mean that figuratively."

Mifflin rubbed his hand across his face. He was tired and knew it showed. "Yeah. I could do with a little rest," he admitted through chattering teeth.

"No doubt half of Vienna's finest are on their way down here by now," Falk said. "If they ask what you're doing here say you were abducted by terrorists. That should make the media happy and confuse everyone else."

"Then you'd better take this." Mifflin offered his automatic. Eiker reached for it but Koski beat him to it.

"Cool Hand Koski," Eiker quipped then coughed. Falk watched the mercenary's eyes that betrayed his matter-of-fact delivery.

"Look," Eiker said hoarsely, "I was assigned as backup, to be

327

there at the end of this caper." He made an effort to straighten to full height but didn't quite pull it off. "I'm going with you and Koski."

Falk shook his head. "No. The most dangerous part is over," he said, hoping it was true. "We won't need you from this point on." He turned again but Eiker put a restraining hand on his arm.

"I have a duty to Cerberus," Eiker announced firmly.

Falk scowled in disgust and jerked his arm away saying, "Duty? What duty? You were to be here if we needed you. We *don't* need you, Eiker. The only duty you have now is to yourself, to collect the money Cerberus owes you for services rendered."

Falk was aware that Mifflin and Emma were silent throughout this brief exchange. He figured that Mifflin, no doubt briefed on Eiker's background at the onset, would understand. Emma, on the other hand, would probably wonder what he meant. Falk took Koski's arm. "Come on. We're wasting time."

"Falk..." Eiker started but spluttered into his hand and made a fist around the spittle that ejected from his mouth. "You don't understand..." He wheezed then suddenly doubled over and collapsed.

Falk was at his side. "Eiker! What's..." Falk stopped when he saw the Brit's fist fall open, exposing blood mixed with the ejected mucus that clung to his palm and fingers. There was a trace of crusted blood at the corners of Eiker's mouth as he groaned and rolled to his right side.

"Internal injury," Koski said, echoing Falk's thoughts. She knelt beside him and saw the once powerful, intimidating man pull his knees into a fetal position, forcing a new trickle of blood to ooze from his lips.

Eiker turned his pale face toward them and whispered, "In the explosion a chunk of flying concrete...caught me and broke at least three ribs...punctured something, I'm afraid...." A paroxysm of coughing overtook him.

Falk shook his head. That explained the obvious fatigue he saw earlier. What exertion, he thought. What superhuman strength it must have taken to swim, to help guide Emma through the swift channel current. The man was phenomenal. "Why the hell didn't you tell us?"

"Listen," Eiker whispered urgently. He winced and his eyes closed. "Left leg pocket..."

Falk jabbed his hand into the man's pocket. His fingers extracted an oilskin package.

"Open it," Eiker wheezed. "Tear the top off..."

Falk inverted the waterproof pack. Two metal spools of thin wire slid into his palm. He looked quizzically at Eiker, about to ask what it was when suddenly he knew. He heard Koski gasp beside him.

"'The Judas List,'" Falk whispered. A cold chill prickled his spine, the hair on the back of his neck rising as if drawn by a magnet.

"Stewart gave it to me..." Eiker rasped.

Falk finished the sentence, "To plant with the loot."

Falk saw it all clearly now. Tom Stewart hadn't exactly lied but, in Clintonesque style, hadn't told the whole truth. He said that Eiker had come on board in case he was needed. Oh, Stewart needed him, all right. Needed him to do exactly what Falk had, in Stewart's office during their first meeting, hypothesized that some rogue faction might do.

Doubtless this recording contained a list of names that Cerberus wanted the world to believe aided and abetted the Third Reich so a Fourth Reich could be born along with a new world order. Individuals and organizations that Cerberus needed, for one reason or another, to discredit mightily and irrevocably.

Falk didn't need to study the recording. He had no doubt that it was expertly crafted to assimilate an authentic, vintage 1940s German-made wire recording. Stewart thought of everything. The bastard!

"We've been betrayed, Joe," Koski exclaimed. "When you suggested that some unscrupulous group might make and plant such a device, Stewart said he wouldn't do such a thing."

Falk shook his head. "That's just the half of it. He merely said it probably would be impossible to generate and plant that type of a recording. He never said he wouldn't do it."

"It's up to you now, Falk," Eiker said weakly. "I can't go. You'll have to…"

"No!" Falk said harshly. "I don't fucking think so. It would be unethical, immoral…illegal."

Eiker managed a snort. "Immoral—high and mighty Joseph Falk —you and Will Rogers. I prefer Mark Twain: 'An ethical man is a Christian holding four aces.'" He stopped and choked up more blood.

"No more talking," Koski said gently. "Just lie still and relax."

He waved her advice aside. "Just doing my job, Falk, and doing it well was always my goal." He clutched the front of Falk's shirt and his head suddenly slumped to the floor as a spasm heaved through his body, pumping out a final mouthful of life.

"He's gone," Koski whispered, touching two fingers to his carotid artery.

Falk was aware of a soft whimpering. He knew that Emma, seated on the concrete several yards away, saw and recognized the throes of death. Mifflin left her side and walked over to Eiker.

"He was a good man in a way not everyone could understand," Mifflin said and crossed himself.

Falk rose and walked away from the others. It was possible that corruption could sometimes be sanctioned but not without outrage and outrage was what Falk felt when he saw the recording spools. He readily admitted he was furious that Stewart had trusted Eiker with the device. It meant that when he got back home he would need to have an honest ideological discussion with Tom Stewart and reexamine his future role in the organization.

He jammed the recording deep into his pocket, looked over at Koski, who had covered Eiker's face with what was left of his coveralls, and said gruffly, "Come on, Koski. We've got things to do."

The Judas List

Chapter 78

Emma and Mifflin saw the flashlight beams bobbing crazily as the footsteps grew louder. "Here," Emma shouted. "We're over here." Three soldiers with automatic weapons at the ready hurried toward them.

"Don't move," the officer said in German.

Emma grimaced and replied in perfect German then switched to English. "My friend doesn't understand."

The officer lowered his weapon. "Who are you?"

Emma gave what she thought was an impressive account of how she and Mifflin had been walking innocently along the street and witnessed a group of masked men descending into a manhole. They had been spotted, taken prisoner and forced to go with them. After what seemed like miles, they heard gunfire then a terrific explosion in which she suffered a broken leg. The men retreated and left them here.

"Why are you wearing city coveralls?" the officer asked.

"They made us wear them." Emma's voice sounded reedy and she nervously cleared her throat. She knew they would find the yellow lifejacket next. "One of the men, a diver, went into the water over there." She stretched her slender neck upwards and aimed her blue, wide-eyed orbs directly at him. "Can you get me to a hospital? I need medical aid and I…I think I'm going to faint."

The story seemed a gross fabrication yet something caused the officer to postpone further questioning. "I will see that you get attention." He looked at Mifflin, leaning against the wall like a deflated whale. "Both of you."

Mifflin was thankful he'd had the time to slide Eiker's body over the edge into the Canal before the soldiers arrived. He also was sad at the unchristian way in which he had to clear the scene.

Captain Vlad was still at the Dorotheum when he received the call.

"See that they are well cared for. Notify their respective embassies immediately. When Herr Mifflin has changed into dry clothes tell him I'll be waiting here for him. Show him every courtesy." Vlad recradled the phone and looked thoughtfully across the main hall. Where else would he expect Mifflin to be when an explosion rocked the building but in the middle of the damned thing.

Chapter 79

"We turn left at the third slot," Falk said as they cautiously entered into a narrow, dimly lit entrance off the gallery.

"Slot?" Koski asked.

"Old inspection slots," Falk replied. "They once were used by inspectors checking the electrical conduits that are like a maze, zigzagging throughout the sewer system. Computer does it nowadays. I saw the slots on Herschel's maps, made notes and a rough sketch when he was out of the room. I also tore a page from one of the map books. Unfortunately," he stopped, reached into his back pocket and pulled out a handful of soggy pulp, "they weren't waterproof."

They were standing a few feet into the passage when Koski queried, "How far do we have to go?"

Falk grunted. "About a quarter of a mile but a tough quarter mile."

"Meaning what?"

"The passageways get narrow—very narrow—in places. The floor gets steeper the further we go. The brick roof will cause us to be belly crawling in spots."

Koski felt her stomach flip. She suffered from what she once called "discomfort in tight places." She hadn't revealed it to anyone, fearing it would compromise her chances of getting through the FBI

Academy. So far she had managed to tough it out in situations where it might have surfaced. Over the past few years, however, the condition had worsened. Despite attempts to ignore it, she recognized indications that it had solidified from mere discomfort to full-blown claustrophobia. Now she would be nearly flat on her belly, deep underground in another extremely confined space...

"I'll be okay," she said with dubious conviction. "I've been in tight places before."

They moved forward in silence then Falk suddenly hissed, "Quickly...to the left!" They slipped into a recess in the wall. "Don't move...listen." They heard voices that grew louder. Hardly daring to breathe, they looked back as a parade of Austrian soldiers filed past the end of the entrance.

The squad of men never so much as glanced in their direction. When they passed, Falk whispered, "No doubt trying to discover the reason for the explosion. They'll find Emma and Mifflin and take them out of this hellhole." Eiker, he silently added, already left it.

Air noticeably lessened as Falk and Koski went deeper into the narrow passage as if squeezed between the ancient stonewalls, its life-sustaining properties lost. The ground beneath their feet turned to hard-packed earth. Once they passed the last dim light, there was only a bulb cupped by a corroded enamel shade dangling from an old-fashioned flex cable. Darkness was ahead.

"You sure this is the right passage?" Koski asked.

"Yes. From here the ground steepens to nearly meet the ceiling."

Koski was already aware that she had begun to stoop slightly.

"This passage will get narrower," Falk said. "You have to imagine a wedge of pie on its side. We must almost reach the tip before we come to the third slot on the left."

The air had lost its buoyancy and was flat and oppressive. Sweat streamed down Koski's forehead and into her eyes. Venerable dust rose from the floor with every step then resettled. Soon they had to crawl forward on hands and knees.

"Just like the monks in the *Book of Hours*," Falk recalled. "We're on our knees. To me it makes more sense every minute."

Koski shivered despite her rising body heat and the discomfort of perspiration. She merely grunted in response and crawled mechanically behind Falk, trying to gain strength from his determination.

A few hundred feet farther and they were nearly flat on their stomachs, inching forward by elbow and toe movements. The passage had shrunk drastically. Koski could scarcely raise her head without it touching bare rock. Dust swirled in her face as Falk squirmed forward ahead of her.

"Hold on!" Falk's voice came back to her, muffled and distorted. "I see a metal door recessed into the wall on my left." There was silence for a second then his exuberance faded. "Shit! There's a fucking padlock and it's rusted to hell."

In that moment Koski judged the dimensions of the surrounding passage to be no more than thirty-six inches wide and less than twenty-four inches high. The full flare of panic rose within her. She tried to move but couldn't. The walls closed in. Dizziness and lightheadedness gave way to hot, oppressive heaviness of heart and mind. Her throat constricted. She was a candle burning at both ends, dual flames dueling… inescapably approaching each other… doomed to collide, to eat each other up in tongues of exploding fire.

Primal instincts made her thrust her arms before her and clasp her hands. She wrung them in writhing, tortured undulations. Some

337

synapse in her brain arced—or failed to—and blackness whorled inside her head.

"Koski," Falk said softly.

"Wha…"

"Koski!" Falk repeated. This time she consciously heard his voice.

"Yes."

"Are you okay?" The concern in his voice made her aware of how far she'd strayed.

"Yes." She said it stronger now, breathing deeply, having conquered nothing but undergone a lifetime in that black moment and survived. It had taken that moment to send her back to some semblance of control. She sighed again. "I'm fine."

She knew she wasn't, not entirely. She had no idea how much longer this slight revival would sustain her but she took a second to thank God for it. Her thoughts were clearer now.

"Try bashing the lock with the flashlight handle," she suggested, surprised she remembered his last words.

The sound of the attempt clanged resoundingly through the small passage. "Damn it. It won't budge." After trying everything in his tool pouch, Falk cursed again, his breath coming in high, heavy wheezes. "We have to get in!"

"The plastic automatic I gave you," Koski said impatiently. "It's a 9mm. That should do the job."

"In this small confine it'll be dangerous as hell…"

"You have a better idea?"

Falk propped the flashlight into a position that gave full beam on the padlock. "I'm going to make a side-on shot and pray that it penetrates and doesn't ricochet. Here goes."

The sound of the shot was shattering. There was a flash and the area filled with the smell of cordite. For several seconds a miniature dust squall obliterated everything.

The Judas List

Chapter 80

A fit of coughing came back to Koski then Falk's voice.

"It worked! Blew it to hell and gone."

Koski heard the sound of a metal door groaning on complaining hinges. Falk passed the automatic back to her. "Hang on to that. If my navigation is on track we should be at the hiding place within fifteen minutes."

They entered through the metal door and found themselves in a near duplicate of the passage they'd left. In some areas, this chamber's substratum had sagged from water seepage, leaving hollows and deep ruts. Small piles of rock and stone had fallen from the walls and they had to rake them aside with their hands. It was, however, deeper and wider, Falk noted with some relief, thinking of Koski.

"Fifteen feet to the right and we'll reach the shaft at the side of the cistern," Falk reported. He paused to catch his breath. "Then through the wall and we're inside."

"Through the wall? How?"

"There's a wooden service door ten feet from the end of the east wall. If it's rotten it won't take much to bust through."

"Did your homework, I see," she said, her voice less pinched due to the increased space between their bodies and the walls and ceiling.

"Yeah," he said, wondering if he would pass the test. Would the treasures be where he envisioned them?

Finally Falk halted. "There it is!" He steadied his flashlight on a small, wooden door set into the wall. A surge of excitement ran through him. He felt sure the cistern and Goering's plunder were behind that door.

Koski was able to position herself beside Falk now, the area allowing them to stand upright. He traced the outline of the door with his light. "Looks in pretty good condition, no sign of rot."

Koski snorted. "Sure. Where's rot when you need it?" She thumped her hand against the door and rattled the latch. "We're going to have to break it down to get in."

"Can't shoot this open. The hinges are on the inside." Falk bit his lip in concentration. There *had* to be a way. He sank to the floor, laid on his back with his feet braced against the door and kicked. Beyond a jolt to his knees, nothing was accomplished.

Koski hustled down beside him. "We'll do it together. On the count of three…" They kicked in unison. There was a creak but no visible sign of movement.

"Something could be jammed against it from the inside," Koski speculated. "Could there be another way in?"

Falk grunted. "Not that I know of. Let's try again." Their feet crashed against the door. "I think it moved. Did you feel it?"

Koski shook her head then cocked it slightly. "Listen…hear that?"

"What?"

"Sounds like water…" Koski turned on her flashlight and directed the beam back through the passage where they had come. "My God!"

Falk swung his light around and saw the earthen floor turning black—wet black. Water seeped slowly down the passage, curling and nudging into the dry earth. In the few seconds that introduced their horror, it had already started to puddle. Curving bays turned into circles and became pools as more water ran into the chamber.

They both jumped to their feet. "We have to get out," Koski screeched, the edge of panic in her voice. "We'll be trapped."

Falk trained his light on the small tunnel ahead. "I'm afraid it's not much use, Koski. Look…" A second snake of water wriggled into the area from the mouth of the escape passage.

Falk verbalized their fear. "Unless we get through the door and into the cistern, *now*…"

The Judas List

Chapter 81

Vlad's men drove Mifflin to the Dorotheum where he sipped a glass of cognac, sitting with Vlad in the head porter's cubicle.

Mifflin said, "There still are two members of the American team somewhere under the streets of Vienna."

"Do you have any idea where exactly?"

Mifflin took a long sip and eyed Vlad over the rim of his glass. "I'd guess somewhere between the Dorotheum and the two churches, Capuchin and Augustine."

Vlad frowned. "If memory serves that should be around the Neuer Markt near the Donner Fountain. We'll know soon if they're still down there. I have an expert from the Water and Power on the way." Vlad glanced up as someone passed the window. "In fact, I think that's her now."

The woman, escorted by one of Vlad's men, looked to be in her mid-forties with strands of gray hair visible beneath the brim of her yellow hard hat. "Captain Vlad?"

"Yes and this is Herr Mifflin, American security, working with us."

"I'm Gerda Dobbler, Vienna Water and Power."

"Have you been down to survey the damage?" Vlad asked.

"No. I understood we would go together."

They filed from the porter's office into the main hall and toward the front entrance. Three of Vlad's men followed a few feet behind.

Emma was transferred by car to the British Embassy following a trip to the hospital, where her leg was set and given a plaster cast. It began at her left knee and continued down to enclose her foot, except for her toes that were nearly the same off gray as the cast. Emma was now comfortably seated opposite Jack Blake, an assistant attaché.

Blake beamed across his desk at Emma. "It won't be too long. You'll have to wait until they take the curse off you."

"Curse?"

Blake nodded. "Our little joke. House arrest."

"They really can make me stay in here?"

"Step out the front door and you'll find out." He gave her a slightly lopsided grin. "You're safe here. Just sit tight. We'll have you on the next plane to Heathrow."

"I don't want to 'sit tight' or take a plane. I live in Vienna and I have permanent status rights. I own a business and I want to find my friends, who I believe are in danger."

"We're doing everything we can."

"Right. I'd like to know why the British Embassy sat on its backside while I was a fugitive in the Czech Republic."

The aide rubbed his chin. "I have a call out to one of our field people. When he checks in we'll see what we can do about finding your friends."

Emma glanced at the clock. "I'll give you one hour. If I don't have any news by then I'll defect to the American Embassy. *They'll* do something."

Blake raised his eyes, pushed an intercom button and asked for tea, lots of strong black tea.

Chapter 82

Falk and Koski lay on their backs. They pounded desperately with their feet against the door that Falk had trained his flashlight on. There was little time to concentrate on anything but getting into the cistern before the passage flooded.

Koski gasped.

"What?" Falk asked between tortured breaths.

"My arm. Felt like something…"

"Jesus!" Falk grunted. "There's something on my stomach!"

Two red agate eyes glowed at him and he felt the grip of quivering, rodent feet on his body. He brought the light down to reveal a rat the size of a rabbit. Its slick body glistened with moisture, its tail round and as thick as a man's forefinger. He shuddered and swung the flashlight at it but missed. It scurried into a corner, squealing with fear and desperation.

"Oh my God," Koski screamed. "It's been washed down the slots. AGGH!" She screeched again and grabbed the automatic. "Hold the light on him…" She fired and the rat's head burst and was gone, leaving a streak of vermilion gore on the wall and a twitching body floating on the water.

Falk felt the darkness closing in. Worse, as the water lapped in stinking little waves beneath his chin, he felt an awful aura of presence, a dreadful sense of countless living things sharing the shrinking chamber around him.

He turned and directed his light toward where he and Koski had entered. Dozens of terrified burgundy eyes and glossy black liquid bodies feverishly writhed over and under each other as they tumbled with water into the chamber.

Falk felt the tremor of terror that went through Koski's body. Without a word, they both resumed kicking furiously, grunting and groaning as their feet pounded the wood. Koski's screeches rose above that of their rodent companions. Finally, mercifully, there was a splintering crack and the door gave a few inches. Falk was on his knees, muscling against the stubborn old timber. It yielded with his final effort and they were through the opening like a shot.

They shoved the door back in place and Falk jammed against it. His foot touched something cold and solid as stone. Koski slumped against the wall beside him.

"That'll keep the bastards out," Falk exclaimed. However, a thin thread of water continued to inch slowly beneath the door and into the cistern.

An overpowering mustiness hit them. Falk had never breathed such air, thick as a wall and utterly still.

"Do you hear it?" Koski whispered.

"What?"

"The sleep of ages."

He did. He picked up his flashlight and its beam found three metal-shaded light bulbs hanging by cloth covered electrical flex, typical of Europe in the 1940s.

"Overhead lights," he said with relief. "Need to find the switch."

"Here." Koski was on her feet and snapped the toggles up. Two of the lights came on, casting a dim amber glow around the room and revealing the fact that Falk and Koski had indeed found what many sought.

As Falk's eyes grew accustomed to the gloom, he noticed the article he used to prop against the door was a piece of Classic Greek sculpture. It looked like it was from the east pediment of the Parthenon. His mouth fell open and he thought he said, "Jesus!" but it was Koski who spoke. Falk turned to see what she saw.

It was a scene from the caves of Ali Baba, the inner sanctum of a Pharaoh's tomb, a museum with an encyclopedic range of fine art. The long, low space seemed to flow with gold and silver.

Falk took several steps and assessed his surroundings in detail. Beside him, a deep, three-tiered metal shelf began and ran about thirty feet to the end of the room. A desk, lacquered with chinoiserie decoration in Queen Anne style, reflected the dim glimmer of the second light.

The shelf held silver and gold chalices, rows of urns and vases and ancient glazed pottery. There were Byzantine mosaics, sculpture and paintings from the Renaissance, Gothic, and Baroque—all periods it seemed. The floor space was jammed with sealed wooden crates. The black eagle and swastika on each appeared as clear as the day they were stenciled. The whole room seemed to shimmer eerily in the diffused light.

"How ironic," Koski said introspectively. "Here in the middle of all these beautiful things I only feel anger. I think of those who once owned and cherished these treasures and from whom they were stolen."

Falk nodded. "At least some may find their way back to their rightful owners." He looked around. "But now we've got to figure out how to get out of here."

Remembering the plans he had scanned with Herschel prior to leaving the tailor shop, he said, "This place was once part of a Roman water system, a bricked cistern that later became part of the Donner Fountain's original water supply." He concentrated his flashlight along the wall near ceiling level. "That's our best place to break through the ceiling. Water once flowed in there—you can see the slight difference in coloration—and exited out the other end as needed, water in, water out."

Koski made a move to follow a double row of gilt framed oil paintings stacked on a long, low bench when Falk stopped her.

"Don't move!" His voice was harsh and deliberate. "Don't touch anything. It's occurred to me that this place might be booby-trapped."

Koski remained motionless. A trickle of water continued to seep into the cistern behind them. They heard the squeal of the rats as they fought for their lives outside the wooden door. "If there *is* a booby-trap can you locate and disarm it?" she asked.

"I took a course in mines and booby-traps."

"Then we can use the explosives to blast our way out through the roof."

"Good God, Koski! I didn't say I'm a demolition expert."

"You have a better idea?"

Falk sighed. "Suppose I do find it? If I make the slightest error we'll be gone in a flash. Explosives are touchy any time, old explosives even worse."

"Better than drowning, Joe." Koski trained the beam into each corner of the room. "I've read about ancient diggings where traps were set to kill the intruder while leaving the treasures intact. Seems odd this place would be wired to destroy everything."

Falk's voice began low and rose as he spoke. "Of course. Good thinking, partner. An AHD—or anti-handling device—usually is a small, anti-personnel explosive that kills the intruder but protects the inventory." He began sweeping the floor with the light. "Remember, a small explosive trap can be a trigger for something more lethal so don't touch anything."

Falk cautiously made his way toward the other end of the room. Recalling his FBI training as a young man, he still heard the instructor, an old ex-sergeant from the Corps of Engineers, as he held up a detonating cap for the class to see. "This type of detonator is so sensitive that two flies copulating on its surface are enough to set it off." His students laughed at the time but later the sergeant's words proved to be only a mild exaggeration. Falk knew the search would be difficult and dangerous, a visual—touch and smell procedure. His instincts and training had saved his life in the past. He had to trust them now.

As Falk checked out the antique Queen Anne desk, Koski scanned the room for a possible alternate exit. She walked cautiously, stepping only where Falk had stepped, touching nothing.

Falk quickly concluded a search of the desk's exterior, carefully running his hands over the decorative lines. Once convinced it was not booby-trapped, he was prepared, grudgingly, to finish the task for Cerberus that Rod Eiker had started. Quickly he went through the desk drawers, pushing papers aside. Finally he tried the bottom right hand drawer. Locked.

Falk cursed and removed a penknife from his pocket. With a few expert moves, the drawer opened in seconds. Stewart's hunch was right. A compact wire recorder was the only thing inside. Thoughts of booby-traps again ran through Falk's mind as he reached in. His hand hovered over the piece of equipment as his eyes searched for hidden wires. All seemed clear. He lifted the lid slowly and carefully and saw the two spools of wire. Easing them from their spindles, he quickly put them in his pocket and replaced them with the ones Eiker had given him, being sure to wipe off any fingerprints.

He stared at the Cerberus replacement, knowing that he had dropped the stone into a pond of time whose ripples would reverberate for untold generations.

For a moment, he almost reached back into the drawer to remove the recoding then quickly shut it as Koski appeared at his side. They exchanged looks and immediately she knew what he had done.

"You made the switch." Not waiting for an answer, she added, "The water has eased off. Apparently the slots are filled. It's found its own level."

Falk nodded. "Yeah. I made the delivery." He patted his pocket. "I've also thought over the trigger idea and narrowed it down to one possibility based on the German love of chemical warfare, poison gas. We might have already unwittingly unleashed a silent booby-trap."

"Whoa!" Koski retorted. "An ideal way to get rid of an intruder and not harm the inventory. Could we survive by getting air from the slots until the gas dissipates?"

"Not if the gas was mustard or lewisite. Either of those old wartime chemicals can be released in mist form. It only has to touch the skin and it can enter the blood stream in seconds. You don't even have to inhale."

"We've got to break out of here now." She glanced around for something to use to batter a hole in the ceiling. Her vision fell on a ceremonial spear propped against a nearby wall. It was nine feet long with a thick, wooden shaft and a tip of hand-forged beaten iron. "I hope it's not wired to explode," she said, grabbing it.

With Koski behind him, Falk moved cautiously toward a stack of crates. He took no more than three steps when he froze in midstride. "Stop!" he hissed. "For God's sake, don't move a muscle. I've triggered a mine."

The Judas List

Chapter 83

The water cascading from the slots and across the gallery into the Danube Canal told Gerda all she needed to know. She stopped and called back to Mifflin and Vlad.

"We can't go any farther. Too dangerous. There's been extensive damage from the explosion and water from the inspection slots indicates breakage higher up, possibly in water and electrical lines."

The three stared at the gushing stream spewing vile-smelling water. Dobbler waved for them to follow. They returned to the surface by way of the iron ladder Mifflin and the others had descended a few hours earlier.

Mifflin felt his legs quivering as he stood in the cold air on the street level. He needed rest. He needed... Vlad passed him a hip flask.

"Thanks." Mifflin tipped it back and let the fiery liquid race down his throat. He needed brandy. He also needed to come to terms with the fact that he was definitely out of the running. It was Falk and Koski who were going down to the wire.

The Judas List

Chapter 84

"I felt the mine activate." Falk remained frozen on the mined flagstone. Koski was a statue behind him. Beads of sweat oozed to the surface of his skin. "A German Teller mine, I'd guess and it could be tied in to release gas when the mine explodes. It's safe as long as my weight remains on the firing pin...like holding in a hand grenade pin."

Falk grew utterly calm. A mine wasn't a rat or water creeping up and stalking you. It was a patient device that waited for you to find it. Falk would need to bring all his experience to this worthy adversary. He reasoned that somewhere in this space was a locked valve that would turn off the gas. He also knew the key to that valve wasn't in this room. It was "out there" somewhere having journeyed from Goering to Youmatoff to Lego to...who knew where?

"Koski, you'll have to gently pry the flagstone to my left. There could be a set of wires beneath it, an electrical connection to a hidden gas canister set to trigger when this device explodes. I want you to cut the wires so it won't set off the gas when I get off."

"Get off?"

"Yes. Now listen carefully. Cut the wires to immobilize the electrical circuit then we'll pull one of the crates onto this flagstone to simulate my weight and keep the firing pin in place. You'll have to work fast. I can't stay rigid like this for long."

Setting down the spear, she sank to her knees and started scraping at the edge of the two-foot slab of paving stone, trying to get a grip with her fingers. Using a screwdriver from the kit around her waist she soon had the slab loose. It was too heavy to lift. She needed something to wedge beneath it.

"Hurry, Koski," Falk urged. "Please."

She grabbed the spear again and dragged a small nearby box to her side. Using the box as a fulcrum for the spear's shaft, she pried down and the slab, at least two inches thick, lifted slightly. Grunting with effort, she angled the stone to allow her to slide it aside with her hands. She stared at the flat black earth, hard-packed and rock-smooth from years beneath the pavement. There weren't any wires.

"See anything?" Falk tried to conceal the strain in his voice.

"A small metal box sunk into the ground with a keyhole."

"Gas activating lock," Falk said grimly. "Move carefully and stay clear of it."

She gently scratched the earth's surface with the screwdriver, being careful not to dig too deep and disturb hidden wires. Her hand trembled as she traced the tip of the tool across the packed soil. Sweat trickled into her eyes. "The blade touched something!" she exclaimed suddenly.

Abandoning the tool, she let her fingers gently probe the damp earth. Neither of them dared breathe as she scraped around the object. "It feels oval, like a large egg and…there's another…" She stopped.

"What is it?" Falk demanded as he heard her swallow deeply. Her voice was small as she replied. "It's a skull. History is riddled with documented cases where the victors hid the spoils then killed those who aided them. The reason we're in this mess is because one man lived to tell tales." She paused. "I just uncovered the remains of two who didn't."

"Koski, quit the history lesson. You see any wires?" he demanded as much to refocus Koski's thoughts as to hurry the process that would relieve his cramping leg muscles and get them out of there.

"No."

"Okay...try the flagstone to my right."

She wiped the sweat from her eyes with the back of her hand, moved to the stone on Falk's dextral side and repeated the process. This time she saw copper wires when she lifted the slab. "Bingo!"

"Good." Falk fell into his groove now, his thoughts concise. "If the gas lock mechanism was keyed and gets triggered, we'll need something to cover our faces, to serve as crude gas masks. First I need a crate to counterbalance my weight. That one," he pointed.

She hesitated. "How can we be sure it's not booby-trapped?"

Falk winced from the pain in his aching limbs. "Pray and hurry."

Then the ballet began. Both were aware that the slightest jar or jolt could end their lives in a flash. Koski disturbed the six-foot tall wooden crate from its spot then pushed until it rested on the edge of Falk's stone slab. The dreadful silence of the room seemed to close in on them, broken only by the grating and rasping of the crate on stone and their harsh, urgent breathing.

Koski pressed with all her strength, willing the crate to move closer. It slid across the stone inch by agonizing inch until it touched Falk's feet.

"Okay," he said. "I'll take it from here." He tugged and pulled the heavy wooden crate into the center of the stone slab. He prayed he could get the box into the exact center to be certain the weight continued to hold the mine's firing pin in place.

Koski unzipped her coveralls and removed her shirt. She pressed it into a puddle of water to give temporary protection against the possibility of gas. Next she ripped it in half and handed a section to Falk, who stuffed the wet cloth into his pocket. Koski knelt beside the flagstone that had covered the wires.

"Which wire do I cut?"

"This will be by-guess-and-by-God," Falk rasped. "Try the one farthest from my right. A quick tap should do it. Then get up on the crates and start bashing a hole in the ceiling." He paused, looking down at her, hoping that all the words he had never said but meant to were in his eyes. "Good luck, partner."

An eerie sense came over Koski as she placed the screwdriver's blade on the wire with her left hand, an almost out-of-body experience. Her hand became remarkably steady as she delivered the first blow to the screwdriver handle with her right palm. The blade cut through the soft copper wire with ease.

For a second, a heartbeat, nothing happened. She stared up at Falk not daring to breathe. Then she heard a soft, sibilant hiss like a nest of disturbed vipers.

She broke from her spot, scrambled and clawed her way to the top of the crates. Furiously she jammed the spear's shaft into the crumbling mortar between the old brick ceiling. An acrid smell curled around her. She pressed the wet cloth against her mouth and nose with her left hand. She turned to look at Falk and what she saw unfolded in slow, agonizing motion.

Falk quickly edged around the crate that now covered the explosive flagstone and eased up the wooden side until he was standing on top. He ripped out the wet cloth and wrapped it around his nose and mouth at the same time pushing Goering's "Judas List" deeper into his pocket. Then he made a headlong dive from the top of the crate in Koski's direction. The mine exploded as his body arched through the air like a gymnast.

The blast ripped through the cistern with an erupting orange flash. The pungent smell of cordite came to Koski on a wave of piercing heat. The crate disintegrated and a discharge of dazzling color —gold coins, strings of rubies emeralds and diamonds—blew into the air and fell with Falk to the wet, stone floor.

The Judas List

Chapter 85

When Captain Vlad received the call about an explosion beneath the Donner Fountain he ordered his bomb squad to the scene, and his driver to take Mifflin and himself to the fountain.

The huge ornate fountain, dry and turned off for the winter, was a bustle of activity. Vlad handed his flask to Mifflin. "Stay here. Don't come any closer."

The bomb squad, already down in the dry basin of the fountain, was removing an iron grating used by maintenance crews.

As soon as Vlad neared the opening to the pumping room beneath the basin, he caught a whiff of dreadful, fetid air. Members of the bomb squad quickly put on their respirators. Vlad had one thrust at him as he called topside, demanding that exhaust fans be sent down on the double.

He slipped on the gas mask and crossed the basin. Next he descended the maintenance ladder to where two of his men worked frantically at the rusted bolt on an old iron door.

Falk lay in a fetal heap against a stack of splintered crates. A trickle of blood oozed from a gash on his forehead.

Koski kept the cloth pressed to her nose and mouth as she scrambled down to her companion. Expelling a gasp of relief, she realized that Falk, though unconscious, was still alive. She rewet both cloth masks, wrapped the torn, soggy shirt around his face again and tied it at the back of his head.

She felt her lungs searing but was thankful it wasn't the type of gas that entered through the skin or they'd both be dead.

Koski struggled back up the crates to the small, jagged hole she had managed in the ceiling. Feverishly, desperately, she worked to make the crumbling mortar wider, thrusting the spear upward with ever-weakening blows. Her head began to ring. Her eyesight blurred as dust and debris mixed with fading senses.

Soon each breath was an effort and she slumped forward onto the crate. Her eyes were closing. She thought she heard the sound of crumbling stone somewhere above her. She believed that a cool, damp, miraculous draft of fresh air flowed over her before she toppled on the edge of an almost welcome blackness. Suddenly the stone and plaster above her gapped into a three-foot wide opening and a pair of boots dangled for a second before the rest of one of the bomb squad dropped into the chamber.

Vlad beamed his powerful D6 into the darkness. Dust created by the explosion still swirled as other squad members inched forward. Vlad saw a dim, unmoving light and hurried toward it. Kneeling beside a jagged hole in the floor, he looked down into a dimly lit vault-like room that spewed the noxious air. No one could survive that, he thought.

The beam picked up the dull glint of the iron-tipped spear first then it found Falk and Koski, collapsed and still.

Mifflin stood on one of the three shallow steps surrounding the fountain. Nearby, Emma sat in a wheelchair wrapped in blankets.

Mifflin, ducking between members of the bomb squad, peered into the basin of the fountain. Utility lights were strung over the shoulder of one of the statues in the center of the fountain, past its wreathed head, over the oar on its shoulder and down into the basin.

Men scurried in and out of the manhole. Mifflin rounded his shoulders and jammed his hands deep into his coat pockets. The wind was cold and it occurred to him how very tired he was. He pushed over and joined Emma.

"Can't see much yet," he said.

"Why don't they hurry?" Emma moaned.

"Koski and Falk will be fine," Mifflin said with little certainty because he'd had a whiff of the air that boiled up from the manhole.

Emma turned to him. "What will happen if they've found the treasures?"

"I don't know. The United Nations most likely will take over. Each item will have to be inventoried and reported to the World Council down to the last nail. Everybody will be here…international organizations of every ilk, the media…" He shook his head. "I don't envy Franz Kutna being involved with the international problems that'll arise as a sidebar to all this." With his usual bulldozing tact, he added, "He lost Rosie Wimmer."

Emma nodded sadly. "I heard. So many lives have been destroyed." Yes, she thought. Rosie was gone. Steele was gone, too. For better or worse, they'd been her lifeline to Vienna. Her thoughts were suddenly interrupted by a flurry of activity at the hole.

"Hold on," Mifflin said and elbowed his way forward as Vlad emerged from the pump room. Vlad pulled off his respirator and stood aside as Koski and Falk emerged from the inner chamber. Carried by rescue workers, their faces were covered by gas masks.

Mifflin stood back as two stretchers pushed past then he peered into the basin again. Vlad raised his head and gave Mifflin a thumbs-up. Koski and Falk were alive.

Mifflin accompanied the unconscious forms of the agents in the ambulance to a military hospital in Vienna courtesy of Captain Vlad. That's when Mifflin surreptitiously removed the recording spools from Falk's pocket.

Chapter 86

It was less than twelve hours after their rescue. Koski and Falk, still somewhat pale, sat with Mifflin facing Tom Stewart in an American Embassy office.

"You did well," said Stewart calmly. "The United Nations Security Council already has the wire recording."

Falk gave an impatient nod. He still felt used. Koski quickly asked, "Did we learn anything from the German recording?"

He riffled the pages of a notebook on his desk. "Yes, although some of the information is old hat, such as the 1924 Dawes Plan that flooded Germany with an incredible amount of American capital and enabled Germany to build its war machine. The three largest loans went into developing industries, among them I. G. Farben Co. It became the largest corporation in Europe after a $30 million loan from the Rockefeller's National City Bank subsequent to the end of World War I." Stewart glanced up then back to his notebook.

"It goes on to mention that in 1939 Standard Oil of New Jersey sold I. G. Farben high quality aviation fuel. I. G. Farben's assets in the United States were controlled by a holding company called American I. G. Farben Chemical Corp."

Mifflin sighed. "What once was a dark secret has become known over time and the general public either doesn't know or care. I'd say probably a little of both."

"American funding was involved in helping the Nazis?" Koski sounded surprised.

Stewart nodded knowingly. "Not only America, Koski. England and many others, too many to mention. War is a profitable entity to its patrons."

"So other than locating Goering's ill-gotten gains it was a waste of time," Falk said bitterly.

"Far from it, Joe," Stewart replied quietly. "The recording gave us a look into the future planning for the Fourth Reich. There were items mentioned that already have been proven true. One name mentioned jogged the memory of some of the older members at the playback session. It was Hajj Amin al-Husseini, the viciously anti-Semitic grand mufti of Jerusalem, who lived in Berlin as a welcome guest and ally of the Nazis throughout the Holocaust. Hitler had a Muslim cleric broadcasting from Berlin, who called for the extermination of the Jews.

"The mufti was useful to Hitler on another front as well…Tito was stirring up some serious shit in Yugoslavia and in 1943 the Nazis were tied up on several fronts. He sent the mufti down to Sarajevo and raised 20,000 troops. Those troops served in the SS Hanzar (Hanjar) Legion and mostly dealt with local partisan actions. Hajj Amin al-Husseini avoided indictment as a war criminal at Nuremberg by escaping to Egypt. There he received political asylum and met the young Yasser Arafat, a distant cousin. Arafat became a devoted protégé to the point where they recruited former Nazis as terrorist instructors.

"Arafat continued to pay homage to the mufti as his hero and mentor until he died. This fact gave our government's intelligence agencies a lead that radical Islam could be a direct descendant of the

Nazis." Stewart paused. "Let me just say that what we found on the tape will be very useful in today's fight against Muslim terrorism."

Falk took interest. "You're saying that Youmantoff's information to Lego so many years ago will help us today?"

"Without a doubt," said Stewart softly. "The monies invested in the Nazi regime before and during World War II have gained billions in compounded interest over the years. They are now being used against the west in preparation for World War III. Remember, the Nazis first paraded themselves as only "removing" Jews from Germany then Europe."

"The Middle East, Jews and Arabs," Falk growled.

"No one ever said the Forth Reich was going to be a German entity," Stewart said. "Seems the Nazis that escaped after the war decided Europe had had enough of their organizational skills. So they hid out in various towns and cities around the world and finally agreed on an agenda to work the Muslim population. The Middle East at first then worldwide."

Falk picked up Stewart's line of reasoning. "The 'Odessa File' made that connection years ago."

"Yes, Joe, I read the book. However, Islamic fascism must be recognized for what it really is: rebirth of Nazism under a different name."

"Was there any mention of the book or the key?" Falk asked.

Stewart shook his head, rose from his chair and walked to the window. "Not a word." He moved the drapes to one side and continued staring out across Vienna before continuing. "Remember when I first briefed you on the assignment? I mentioned we'd learned via a letter from a soldier's widow who'd been ordered to give Goering a cyanide pill?"

"Yes."

"I omitted the fact that there'd been another confession, an ex-GI named Herbert Lee Stivers. He gave his story to the *Los Angeles Times* after being assured that any charges were time-barred. He went public. This was back in February 2005 and Cerberus was aware the story was a fabrication."

"Why would anyone make up such a story?" questioned Falk.

Stewart faced back into the room and shrugged. "Misinformation. It was decided to make an attempt to clear up questions about Goering's death. The growth of the Internet over the years and bloggers beginning to ask too many questions on the subject. We were concerned the true story would come out."

"Cerberus knows the true story, right?"

"Of course."

"Then I think it's time we did, too. I'm not certain we did the right thing in switching the tapes."

"Yes, Joe. I was fully aware of your feelings. That was the reason I called in Eiker." Stewart quickly raised his hand. "Hear me out, Joe."

"Herman Goering came from a wealthy family, born to power and privilege. His personal power increased during the years prior to World War II then multiplied during the actual war years despite his Luftwaffe's inability to win the Battle of Britain."

Stewart returned to his chair. "You see, Joe, Herman Goering had planned to blow the whistle on a secret international organization. The recording he stowed away in the vault was secretly made during an actual meeting of some of the most powerful industrialists in the world. It contained sensitive material, information on their ongoing plans for world domination.

"Hitler and Goering had become part of the total power of the

Rothschild organization during the 1930s and the Nazi party's rise to power; known to some as the *Illuminati*. World War III had already been blueprinted as World War II wound down.

"Goering, now a prisoner of the Allies, was bitter knowing those who had promised him everything had deserted him. Ironically he also knew many of those in power in the governments of freedom were also members of the same secret society."

"I never thought of you as someone who believed in conspiracy theories, Tom."

"I don't consider myself one either. Nonetheless, there's always a need to look closely at events of international intrigue. I'm aware that today's press would jump on what I've told you. There would be the usual denials, accusations of fake, forgery. Right-wing paranoia."

"The recording machine I saw wasn't a mini device like we have today," Falk blurted. "How could the recorder *not* have been discovered?"

"The briefcase under the table that almost killed Hitler made it into a secret meeting, Joe."

Koski and Falk exchanged glances and Mifflin spoke for the first time.

"The forces intent on killing you and Koski weren't out for the legendary war loot, Falk. They were out to locate the recordings and destroy them."

Stewart leaned forward. "You two need rest and relaxation. Tomorrow you'll both fly back home; two weeks leave, belated Christmas present."

"How about making that the day after tomorrow? Koski and I would like an extra day to recoup."

Stewart nodded. "Fine, I'll make the arrangements." He glanced at the paperwork on the desk. "Youmantoff was last seen in Ottawa. I've no doubt we'll discover a few more unanswered questions."

"Close the book on the past," rumbled Mifflin as he eased his bulk on the small office chair. "I'd like to suggest we all have dinner together tomorrow night. Emma, too, my treat, at the 'Bristol.'"

Koski glanced at Falk. "Sure, why not? Give us time to see what we learned from that old Russian fox, Youmantoff."

Chapter 87

Sgt. Pullbrook of the Royal Canadian Mounted Police stood motionless in the alley, less than two blocks from the Soviet Embassy in Ottawa, weapon poised as his lapel microphone crackled softly. He saw Youmatoff as a graying man, old and dying in a country not his own. Pullbrook lowered the gun to his side.

Had Youmatoff turned, he might have seen that Pullbrook's eyes contained a rheumy afterglow. He might have speculated why sometimes they break with tradition and don't get their man.

Youmatoff didn't turn. Years ago, a man he didn't know gave him papers that made it possible for him to avoid returning to Russia. Today another stranger was making his desired return possible. Youmatoff neither questioned nor required a look into the face of the compassionate providence responsible for delivering him into this human condition.

His chest rose then fell with a great exhalation as he continued toward the embassy. The crisp and cathartic wind off the Ottawa River whispered as it rushed by him.

He crossed Charlotte Street, slush crunching beneath his boots as he neared Number 287. He walked up to one of the guards outside the Soviet Embassy and straightened his shoulders. "I am a Russian," he said proudly. "My name is Nikolai Youmatoff. I wish to return home."

Three months had passed. Harold Mifflin was in his garden in Southern California, snipping away with his trusty Bahco pruners, working on his favorite floribundas. His cell phone chimed. "Yes," he said testily.

"Switching the tapes while in the ambulance was a work of genius," a soft voice whispered. "The society wishes to thank you for your past service and contributions to our worldwide endeavors. We feel, however, that it's time for you to retire full-time."

A dial tone droned in Mifflin's ear. Replacing the phone in his pocket, he swept away a fallen leaf. It was all over and he knew he only had a matter of seconds to live. He had no doubt he was in an assassin's crosshairs.

There was no pain as the poison dart entered his jugular. Mifflin sagged and crumpled beside his beloved roses.

The Christmas and New Year festivities had passed and Falk and Koski were back stateside. The jangle of his beside phone woke Falk. He reached across Koski's sleeping form and scooped it up.

It was Stewart. "Youmatoff's body was discovered last night in a snow bank beside the Ottawa river, a coil of barbed wire wrapped around his throat."

"So the Mounties didn't get their man," Falk grunted. Now Koski was awake.

"No. They got him only he was dead when they did. Cerberus also received word that Mikhail Brasinov was reportedly spotted in Beverly Hills."

"Brno getting too hot for him?"

"I doubt it, Joe. The Muslim Mafia paid that bastard millions to get 'The Judas List.'"

"And they got the wrong one."

"What concerns me is the sighting of Brasinov. This year's Easter Sunday service in the Hollywood Bowl is going to be a security nightmare. Religious leaders from around the world will be there as a sign of unity, including the Pope making his first official visit to the United States." Falk heard voices in the background and Stewart said, "I'll call you back."

Falk hung up as Koski asked, "What was that all about? I heard you say something about Mounties not getting their man and Brno getting too hot. What's happening?"

Falk leaned back and laced his fingers behind his head. "I'm not sure. Whatever it is could include a visit to the Hollywood Bowl."

If you enjoyed *The Judas List* consider this other Falk and Koski adventure, *Who's Killing All the Lawyers?* by A. G. Hayes:

Lawyers are being murdered by laser-driven arrows. The FBI believes that someone is training a Native American militia to take over the economic system in the U.S. Joe Falk and Susan Koski are assigned to find the hired killer and The Fox, the real force behind the killings.

About the Author

A. G. Hayes studied television writing at UCLA. He has published short fiction, including *Cover Up*, *Not a Penny Pincher*, *Home*, *Payment in Full*, *Small Wonder* and *Guided through a Mine Field*, and written scripts for CBS TV and other television production companies. He lives in the Sierra Nevada Foothills and spends his time writing and traveling to nearly every part of the world. He has used personal experiences gained during service with the British intelligence in Eastern Europe and the Middle East to enrich the characters of his protagonist teams. He is the author of *Who's Killing All the Lawyers* (Savant 2011).

The Judas List

If you enjoyed *The Judas List* consider these other fine books from Savant Books and Publications:

A Whale's Tale by Daniel S. Janik

Tropic of California by R. Page Kaufman

Tropic of California (the companion music CD) by R. Page Kaufman

The Village Curtain by Tony Tame

Dare to Love in Oz by William Maltese

The Interzone by Tatsuyuki Kobayashi

Today I Am a Man by Larry Rodness

The Bahrain Conspiracy by Bentley Gates

Called Home by Gloria Schumann

Kanaka Blues by Mike Farris

First Breath edited by Z. M. Oliver

Poor Rich by Jean Blasiar

The Jumper Chronicles—Quest for Merlin's Map by W. C. Peever

William Maltese's Flicker by William Maltese

My Unborn Child by Orest Stocco

Last Song of the Whales by Four Arrows

Perilous Panacea by Ronald Klueh

Falling but Fulfilled by Zachary M. Oliver

Mythical Voyage by Robin Ymer

Hello, Norma Jean by Sue Dolleris

Richer by Jean Blasiar

Manifest Intent by Mike Farris

Charlie No Face by David B. Seaburn

Number One Bestseller by Brian Morley

My Two Wives and Three Husbands by S. Stanley Gordon

In Dire Straits by Jim Currie

Wretched Land by Mila Komarnisky

Chan Kim by Ilan Herman

Who's Killing All the Lawyers? by A. G. Hayes

Ammon's Horn by G. Amati

Wavelengths edited by Zachary M. Oliver

Almost Paradise by Laurie Hanan

Communion by Jean Blasiar and Jonathan Marcantoni

The Oil Man by Leon Puissegur

Random Views of Asia from the Mid-Pacific by William E. Sharp

The Isla Vista Crucible by Reilly Ridgell

Blood Money by Scott Mastro
In the Himalayan Nights by Anoop Chandola
Rules of Privilege by Mike Farris
On My Behalf by Helen Doan
Fifty-Eight Stones edited by Daniel S. Janik
Traveler's Rest by Jonathan Marcantoni
Keys in the River by Tendai Mwanaka
Chimney Bluffs by David Seaburn
The Loons by Sue Dolleris
Light Surfer by David Allan Williams

Soon to be Released:
Path of the Templar—Book Two of The Jumper Chronicles by W. C. Peever
Shutterbug by Buz Sawyer
The Desperate Cycle by Tony Tame
Blessed are the Peacekeepers by Tom Donnelly and Mike Munger

http://www.savantbooksandpublications.com

www.ingramcontent.com/pod-product-compliance
Lightning Source LLC
Chambersburg PA
CBHW051443260626
47162CB00001B/230